THE INSANE GOD

JAY HARTLOVE

Published by Water Dragon Publishing
waterdragonpublishing.com

ISBN 978-1-957146-17-1 (Trade Paperback)

10 9 8 7 6 5

A NOTE ABOUT THE SONGS

Music is a huge inspiration to my writing. At the start of each chapter, you will see the title of a popular song. They stand in as if they were chapter titles. These are the songs I was listening to when I wrote these chapters. I hope to share with you the moods that drove the words. There are also a few references in the text to songs and artists the characters are listening to, in particular the songs Sarah plays on her phone.

These songs are all the intellectual property of the artists who wrote them and their producers who own the rights. I thank them for their genius. Please go buy them and listen to them.

"Brain Damage" by Pink Floyd
Lyrics © T.R.O. Inc.

"Frank Sinatra" by Cake
Lyrics © Wixen Music Publishing

"Close to You" by The Carpenters
Lyrics © BMG Rights Management

"River" by Bishop Briggs
Lyrics © Universal Music Publishing Group, Warner Chappell Music, Inc

"Close My Eyes Forever" by Lita Ford & Ozzy Osborne
Lyrics © Emi April Music Inc., Lisabella Music, Bmg Vm Music Ltd

"Enter Sandman" by Metallica
Lyrics © Creeping Death Music

"Dream Weaver" by Gary Wright
Lyrics © Universal Music Publishing Group

"Closer" by Nine Inch Nails
Lyrics © Leaving Hope Music Inc

"Dreams" by Fleetwood Mac
Lyrics © Welsh Witch Music

*This book is dedicated to transgender people everywhere.
Change is scary. Making changes to live as your authentic self is an
act of courage. Once you recognize how courageous you are, you can
face anything.*

1

"BRAIN DAMAGE"

PINK FLOYD

T ERROR GRIPPED SARAH when she opened her pale blue eyes and saw that the monsters were gone. The tall, black, insectoid wraiths that loomed over her and berated her every move were, for the first time she could remember, not in her room. Her heart raced as she clutched the scratchy polyester blanket to her chest and pushed herself back up against the wall. She looked furtively from empty beige corner to empty beige corner, sure they would leap out any second. As much as she hated them, as miserable as they made her feel, not having them here felt wrong and left her unsure whether she should even get out of bed.

She pulled the blanket over her head and listened. She could always hear them coming first. All was quiet. Not really quiet, what with the other patients and staff walking and talking in the hall. No voices. No ranting, doubting tirades which were the soundtrack of her life. She felt somehow deaf without them, but also awake.

Yes, she felt awake, able to see and hear. She cautiously pulled the covers down and looked around again. Only the nightstand and the one visitor chair.

Could this be a dream? No, she never dreamt about her room — or real life for that matter. *Could this be reality?* It was almost too intense in its simplicity. She had to see for herself.

She sat up and put her stockinged feet on the brown linoleum floor. It was cold and hard, just as it should be. She realized that she was making decisions and no one was questioning them. She got up and walked to the door, the door that was locked to the wall, always open for inspections. Other patients came and went from their rooms. They were all dressed in sweats and tee shirts, the same as Sarah. She knew them all, even though the monsters never let her talk to any of them.

She also knew they were all born female, which Sarah was not. Having not ever really engaged with any of the other patients, she realized she did not know how many of them knew she had a boy's body under her loose clothes. Her tormentors always argued with her about her gender dysphoria. They never failed to scream at her when she got her estrogen shots; they screamed until shecried. Initially the staff thought she was crying about getting them, but she made her wishes known over the voices. Now, with the monsters gone, she stood in her doorway with a blank introspective expression, revisiting her identity as transgender.

No one looked at her weird. No one yelled at her. She still felt like a girl. She had always felt like a girl, even when she was a child, before she lost touch and came here. All the other patients were girls, and no one was freaking out about a boy on the floor.

She marveled at how easy it was to just stand there and have no one reject her.

She made eye contact with a black teen with her hair all in cornrows. "Hi, Josie," she tried.

Josie stopped and blinked. "Hi, Sarah. How you doin'?"

Sarah kept waiting for the voices to cut her off, trying not to cringe. "I'm ... doing well, I think."

"Girl, is this the first time you've said 'Hi' to me in what, a year?"

"Yes, I think so. I'm really sorry. I've always had a hard time ... relating."

"Well, whatever cloud you've been under, welcome to the sunshine! You look like you're about to faint. You want a nurse?"

"I am a little unsteady. This is all coming at me awfully fast."

"You just lean against that wall. I'll go get Clambottom."

Josie hustled away and Sarah hung on that name. *Right, Clambrell. The night nurse was Jane Clambrell.* Had she been paying attention to details all along without knowing it?

Josie came back with a tall white woman wearing scrubs. Her brown hair was tied back and her face was jowly beyond her middle age. "Sarah, are you really talking to us?"

"Yes, ma'am. I'm scared, but the monsters and their voices are gone."

"Gone? How long has it been since you heard one?"

"Since I woke up. Ten minutes, maybe. But they aren't lurking either. No chatter. I've been listening. How can that be? What does it mean?"

"I'll be honest with you — I don't know. But we're going to figure it out together. Is Doctor Alpaca your therapist?"

"Yes."

"Okay, she'll be in at ten. Until then, how about you come down to the nurses' station and sit with me and I'll keep you safe."

Sarah looked from Josie's wide-eyed caution to Jane's maternal smile. "Thank you. I'd like that."

As they walked, Sarah took her hand, which the nurse held reassuringly. "Sarah, can you tell me what happened this morning that made the voices stop?"

"I have no idea. I woke up and just noticed they weren't there anymore. It really scared me."

"You've been with us a long time," she started carefully.

"Since I was nine."

"Right, and you're sixteen now. You've never responded very well to any of the treatments."

"Doctor Alpaca brings in new doctors every few months to try the latest drugs. They never help, even the ones that knock me out."

"Right, but now you're suddenly not having either auditory or visual hallucinations? At all? Not even positive, affirming voices?"

"Nothing that isn't really here. At least, I think I'm seeing what's real." She turned to the nurse. "Are you real?"

Jane smiled at her, squeezed her hand, and nodded.

They arrived at the nurses' station and Sarah took a seat behind the counter.

The nurse pulled up records on the computer. "I've got you taking all your meds on time. Bed checks are all done. No notes." She turned and looked her in the eye. "I dunno. Maybe the drugs all together finally took effect. I, for one, am thrilled to see you make a breakthrough." She turned back to the computer. "I'll put you in with Doctor Alpaca as her first appointment."

•   •   •

Nate Meyer's palm still smarted from smacking the steering wheel as he got out of his car.

"Goddamn traffic," he swore to himself as he jogged across the parking lot into the Sandstone Rehabilitation Center. "Come on!" he muttered louder when he had to wait for the receptionist to come back to the front desk and sign him in.

By the time he walked down the long hall to the floor nurses' station, he made a point of unclenching his fists.

The young, petite, blonde nurse's cheery smile did nothing to calm him. She looked to be in her early twenties, same as him. He didn't bother to remember her name. He assumed she smiled like this at everyone. "Hi, Nate. Sarah is just back to her room. You can go on in."

"Thanks," he grunted.

He stepped into the door and stopped. His sister was sitting on her bed chatting happily with a black girl in the chair. He hadn't seen her smiling and talking and connecting like this since she was a child. Curiosity struggled to confuse his joy, but joy won out.

"Brother!" she exclaimed. She jumped up and flung her arms around his shoulders.

He hugged her back. "I came as soon as I could. Sarah, I can't believe this. They said you had a breakthrough, but wow. Just look at you!" He held her at arm's length and looked in her eyes. "No more voices?"

She shook her head and swung her bobbed brown hair around. "No more voices."

"No more visions?"

She looked around furtively, as if not sure, before meeting his gaze and saying, "The monsters are gone. I spent the last four hours talking to all the doctors here, answering all their questions. They say my recovery is miraculous, like they have never seen before."

"Did they have any explanation?"

"They think it was the cumulative buildup of the drugs and the therapy and everything just finally letting all the pieces fall back together."

Nate lowered his head and looked up at her. "They have no idea."

She grimaced. "Probably not,"

Nate remembered the girl in the chair.

"Oh, sorry. This is Josie. She lives next door."

Josie got up. "I'll leave you two alone."

Nate asked her, "Did you see her make her breakthrough?"

"Well, I was the first one to see after she woke up from her daze. She was freaked out. I would be too. But sorry, no, I didn't see how it happened."

"All right. Thanks."

Josie started to the door but turned back to Sarah "Does this mean you're outta here?"

"It sure does," Nate said.

Sarah held up a finger. "The doctors need to run a couple of cognitive tests, and they want to keep me for observation to make sure this isn't temporary."

Nate felt his heart race and his face flush. "I'll be talking to them about how long that will take."

"You know they only have my best interests in mind."

"You said they already questioned you for four hours. How many more tests do they have to run? How long will this observation take?"

Out of the corner of his eye he saw Josie quietly leave. He let her go.

"Don't forget, your commitment here is voluntary," he continued unabated. "You can leave whenever you want to."

Sarah blinked a few times. "I know that. What if this is only a flash, and it all falls apart in a few hours? I need to know I'm going to be okay when I leave here. I don't want to be walking down the street in a few days and have the voices jump me out of nowhere."

"Did they say how long they want to keep you?" Even Nate could hear the anger boil up in his voice.

"They said it could be a few days. They said they want to bring in an expert."

"That's bullshit." He turned and stormed down the corridor.

He walked past the nurses' station and headed toward the administrative offices. He heard Sarah following, but did not turn around. He pushed open the door and confronted the secretary. "I need to see Director Casey."

A woman's voice from the next room responded. "He's not here. I'm in charge." An East Indian woman in an expensive-looking skirt suit walked out of the office.

"Doctor Stevens, my sister Sarah has had a breakthrough and I need to know exactly what her discharge plan is."

"Mister Meyer," she began with only the slightest lilt of an accent. "I heard about Sarah's apparent recovery, and, I must say, we are all very happy for her. Our doctors examined her this afternoon and, since they have not been able to quantify what happened, we have called in an authority on psychosis recovery. He will be here on Thursday."

He narrowed his dark brown eyes. "The day after tomorrow? So she just sits here waiting for this expert?"

"We will take that time to carefully observe her and document the extent of her recovery. What happens over the next 48 hours will make the difference for her treatment plan going forward."

"Treatment plan?" he spat with one eyebrow lifted menacingly. "You act like she will continue under your care indefinitely. You need to understand that as soon as she is deemed stable enough to no longer be a danger to herself, I will be taking her out of here."

"I do understand that," she said with a clearly practiced calm. "I know you want to take her home. We don't know what happened to her. It would not be ethical for us to release her without knowing she will stay safe. She has suffered with her illness for a very long time. The human brain is far too complex for us to assume her lack of symptoms means she is entirely healthy again. Her recovery may well be the cumulative effect of her medications. So until we know better, she should continue with them even after she is released. You know this. You got your degree in Psychology."

"Working on my Masters," he corrected.

Sarah stepped up beside her brother.

"Hello, Sarah," Doctor Stevens said, again with a professionally practiced smile.

He knew the doctor was right, but something about her smooth delivery stuck him as just too smug. She knew she had control over his sister, and she wasn't going to let it go.

Nate stepped up, closing the distance threateningly. "I want to be kept informed of every step."

Sarah surprised everyone by stepping in front of him and throwing her arms around his shoulders. He didn't know what to think. She held him tight, her head pressed against his shoulder, and didn't let him go.

He was about to object, to say he really wasn't going to attack anyone, when he suddenly felt the anger in him melt away. His shoulders relaxed, his heartbeat slowed to normal, and his breathing eased. The warmth of her grip penetrated him with a comfort he did not understand.

After several seconds, she let go and looked up at him with a compassion that matched the calm he felt.

He looked past her to the doctor and the secretary, who stood there unsure what to make of Sarah's display. Out of nowhere, he cared what they thought.

"I hear you. I understand and I agree. Better to be safe than sorry. It'll only be a couple more days. It'll be good to have a clean bill of health."

The two women relaxed a little, but were clearly still skeptical. "We will, of course, keep you fully informed," Stevens said.

Although he did not understand why, Nate felt compelled to reach out further. "There's one more thing. I know you were responsible for getting Sarah moved out of the boy's ward three years ago when you figured out she needed to live as a girl."

"Well, it was more complicated than that," the doctor said with a smile.

"Yeah, I know. But I don't think I ever thanked you for advocating for Sarah like that. Even with the psychosis, that made a huge difference for her quality of life. So thank you."

"You are very welcome. I don't recall who thanked whom, but I appreciate your saying so. Sarah, did that move let you feel better about yourself?"

"Oh yes, ma'am." She grinned at Nate and then back to the doctor. "Can I ask you a question? May I have a furlough tonight so I can go out to dinner with Nate?"

Nate saw her blink rapidly. "That's a big step." She met Nate's gaze and said, "Are you two sure you're up for that?"

Nate understood the question. "Yes. If anything goes south, I will bring her right back."

"All right then. Sarah, curfew is ten."

•   •   •

Watching his sister fidget with the laminated diner menu, her eyes never alighting on anything for more than a second, reminded him of the puppy his friend Chooly got from the pound back in middle school. The poor creature was so unsure of himself he hesitated and double checked every decision for a reprimand. The dog had spent his whole life in cages, and didn't know how to be at ease, to be at home. Sarah had explained her caution as a lingering fear the voices would attack her again. Her knowing why she felt this way didn't seem to be helping her cope.

She put aside the menu and busied herself doodling on a paper napkin with his borrowed pen.

"Is this place too public for you?" he asked.

She looked at the high walls of their booth. "Can't get much more private. I'm just going to have to get used to this. I mean, I'm loving not being berated for every thought. It's going to take me a while to feel like this freedom is normal."

"I understand. Hey, what happened with that hug?"

"How do you mean?"

"I was fighting mad, and the next second I was completely calm, even compassionate, to Dr. Stevens."

"I don't know, you just looked like you needed a hug. I've gotta say, it felt really good to make a decision and act on it without the voices criticizing me."

"I'll bet."

Sarah squinted at him. "You brought up how Dr. Stevens moved me to the girls' ward. What was all that about?"

Nate took a second to consider his answer. "It was remarkably open-minded of her to advocate for your transition given your other diagnosis. I remember the conversations like they were yesterday. Director Casey, and all of his advisory board, all thought you wanting to transition was a delusion of your condition. Dr. Stevens, and Dr. Alpaca, both agreed with me that you were always meant to be female, and they went to bat for you. You've always been a girl, even before we lost Mom and Dad. We put you on anti-androgens when we moved you off the boys' ward to slow down puberty, and put you on estrogen last year so you could finish as a girl."

"A delusion? I don't remember that."

"We kept the fight away from you. Technically, the profession allows it to be diagnosed as Gender Identity Disorder. Under that definition, helping you transition would be adding another layer of dysfunction. The system is not usually friendly to transitioning. That's why I got so worried about them releasing you. Hospitals need to show they've made a difference before they let you out. They hold all the definitions."

Sarah sat there looking at the tabletop lost in thought.

"Let's order. We need to get you mainstreamed as soon as possible. The more normal things you do, like eating in a restaurant, the better."

She picked up the menu and looked at it in earnest. "God, there are so many choices. Not used to that."

"How hungry are you?"

"Pretty hungry."

An elderly black waitress with an elaborate hairdo and long bejeweled fingernails was walking by and stopped. "You ready, Princess?"

She caught Sarah by surprise. "I don't know. What's good tonight?"

"I heard you say you were hungry, so lemme suggest the Special, which is meatloaf with mashed potatoes. You can get that with a salad or the tortilla soup, which I recommend."

Nate noticed the woman's fluid easy style visibly put his sister at ease. He also noticed her name tag had glitter and jewels around the name Pearl.

"That sounds great," Sarah said, handing her menu to the waitress.

"And to drink?"

"Um, Coke."

"And you, Professor?"

Nate had to smile. "I'll have the spaghetti, with the salad. Ranch dressing, please. And just water."

"Aw right. Bless the man who knows what he wants." She took his menu. "I'll be right back with those drinks."

Once she was out of earshot, Sarah leaned forward and said quietly, "She called me Princess."

"Yes, and she called me Professor. Oh, you mean she gendered you right."

Sarah chuckled weakly. "Yeah."

"And you didn't expect that? You pass perfectly."

Sarah looked down at her loose-fitting sweatshirt and jeans, then around at the other diners. "Well, no one ever cared at Sandstone. And my voices never let me accept who I am. Now I'm out, and I don't know what people will think."

"They think you're a girl. They have no reason to think otherwise."

"You're sure?"

"Positive."

"Good, 'cause I need to pee."

"Then use the Ladies' room. People would only object if they saw you go into the Men's. I know it's a big deal. I'm not trying to make light of it. But you have nothing to worry about."

She slid off her bench seat and stood up. "Okay, here goes."

He watched her walk straight to the restrooms, looking at the ground to avoid eye contact with anyone. Not surprisingly, she made it without incident. One step at a time, he thought.

The napkin she had been sketching on caught his eye. He spun it around and was alarmed at the image of an eyeball with tentacles being bitten by several bodiless, tooth-filled mouths. He had seen the disturbing drawings she did in therapy. This was new, and even more violent. He knew he should not read too much into a doodle. It reminded him how fragile she was.

Pearl breezed over with the drinks. "You all set for now?"

"Yes, thank you."

He was still looking at the drawing when Sarah came back. "Sorry to snoop. Is this one of the specters that followed you?"

"No, no. They were basically shadows. I could never see them clearly. They were tall, like people, but moved like insects. No, this is an image that popped into my head on the drive over here. I can't seem to shake it, so I scribbled it down."

"I'm sorry the first thing your imagination does with your new freedom is come up with something with so much pain."

"Well, that's what's so fascinating. The eye thing in the middle is not in pain. The mouths are biting it, but it's still serene. I feel like it's some kind of lesson about rising above."

"At least that's appropriate."

"What's more is, I've never liked to draw. I hated doing all those art therapy drawings. I had to force myself to come up with something. This came right out, like I knew exactly what I wanted. I mean, I just did this here to calm myself down. Art's never worked like that for me before."

"Drawing calmed you? When you drew this, were you still worried the voices would pop up and yell at you?"

She lit up at the thought. "Oh wow, you're right. It distracted me. When I was alone in the bathroom, I was a bundle of nerves the voices would come back. But before I went, when I was sketching, I stopped thinking about them."

Pearl arrived with plates of food on her arms and hands. "Here you go, Princess. Now, you let me know if that Special is not special enough. And Professor, I'll expect a complete analysis when you're done."

"Will do," he played along.

•   •   •

Sarah didn't want their evening to end. Her heart sank as Nate drove them back to Sandstone in time for her 10:00 pm curfew. She knew if she let Nate see how she felt, he would get angry all over again about taking her out right away. So, she smiled pleasantly the whole trip back. Surely it would only be a few more days, and the tests they would give her would put everyone at ease that she really was cured.

Assuming she was cured. How long should she continue to take the meds? How long would it be before she could trust the voices would never come back? They had been her constant tormentors for so many years. Every time she thought about them, she got anxious all over again at their possible return.

She watched the city of St. Louis roll by, not recognizing a single landmark. She had a hard time grasping how she'd lived most of her life in a town she'd never seen, that she knew nothing about.

"Is this a nice place to live?"

"St. Louis? Sure, I guess. It's got some big city charm and some Midwest country flavor too. It's been home since High School, and I've found everything I need here. Yeah, it's nice enough."

"Do you think I'll fit in?"

"Well, Missouri is pretty conservative, but they don't have the awful anti-gay laws they have in Kansas. Nobody knows you, so nobody could out you anyway. I'll have to figure out how to get you lined up to graduate. Tutors or home school or something. I've never made any of those plans, I'm sorry to say."

"You didn't expect me to suddenly rejoin normal life," she said.

"True. You know, now that I think of it, we should get you into regular school as soon as you're ready. You have no friends. What sixteen-year-old girl has no friends? One that has just moved to a new town."

"You're going to have an awful lot to figure out. Do you have room for me in your house? The hospitals are going to make a mountain of paperwork. We have to legally change my name from Timothy. I don't even know how to do that."

"I'm pretty sure it's something a judge can do. That, and change your legal gender."

"This is all going to be a huge burden on you."

"I'm completely down with all of that. Besides, I won't have to do it alone. The trust fund Uncle Ron set up to pay for your care will easily cover any lawyers and accountants I will need to sort everything out."

Sarah frowned as she digested the details. "Were Mom and Dad rich?"

"No, but they were well-insured. They made sure you and I would not lack for anything."

She didn't understand how that worked, but left it. She decided Nate could handle the money. They passed a billboard for "Deadpool 2", with the red-clad hero posing on a chair under a shower of falling bullets.

I've got a lot of catching up to do.

She was glad to have Nate as her guide. She smiled at him. "What? Did I say something?"

"No, I was just thinking how glad I am to have you helping me."

"Me too. Oh, we're here."

She looked at the long windowless walls of the center and thought of how those walls looked the same inside and out. She put her brave smile back on and got out.

As they walked to the front, the clear night sky caught her attention. "Oh my goodness!"

Nate frowned. "What is it? Yeah, it's a pretty sky tonight."

"No," she said breathlessly. "Don't you see it?" She pointed up in an arc. "The eye. And the mouths. It's all there. You didn't tell me it was a constellation."

Her brother stared intently where she pointed. "It's not. And I don't see what you're talking about."

She came around the car to him and pointed. "There. That circle is the eye in the middle. And those lines out are the tentacles. Those smaller blobs around it are the mouths."

He shook his head. "I'm familiar with Pareidolia, but that's usually seeing faces in random dots. I don't even see a face where you said the round eye should be."

"Do you have your phone?" she asked. "Take a picture and I can show you better."

He pulled it out and aimed it up. "The resolution isn't good enough. I'm not seeing any stars at all." He looked again with his bare eyes. "I'm not an astronomy fan, so I don't know constellations, but I'm just not seeing what you're seeing."

She sighed and looked at him. "That sounds familiar."

"No, no, I didn't mean I think you're seeing things. You don't have to be hallucinating to pick out patterns that aren't really there. The brain is wired to make sense of what you see."

"Patterns that aren't really there," she recited impatiently.

He flung his hand at the sky. "They're just stars. You can't get a more random distribution."

She looked up again and saw the design clearly. "Maybe I shouldn't mention this to my doctors?"

"This is not a sign of mental illness. In fact, it shows your brain is working normally, making the kinds of assumptions a healthy brain makes. But you're right. Why complicate the diagnostic work with irrelevant details? Yeah, keep this to yourself."

She looked at him skeptically, then took his arm and started walking to the entrance.

"If it will get me out of here sooner."

2

"FRANK SINATRA"
CAKE

SARAH FLUSTERED AS THE BLACK DRY-ERASE MARKER ran out of ink in the middle of her drawing a long, curling tentacle. She dropped it and grabbed the last one from the four-pack on the floor. She stepped back and surveyed her drawing, seven feet high and nine feet across, filling the end wall of the breakfast nook in Nate's kitchen. The bulging eye, prominently in the center, sat surrounded by its own tentacles, many of which were being bitten by a swarm of sharklike creatures that were mostly mouths filled with teeth.

She closed her eyes to see more details. The vision came to her as if recalling a memory. She felt weightless as she focused on the details, like floating underwater. She drifted and the sensation frightened her. She didn't want to let go of the images, but she feared she would fall too far in, that she wouldn't be able to open her eyes and return to the dining room.

Of course she could. All she had to do was open her eyes. There was nothing to fear. Maybe she could see more, around the sides, if she let herself drift.

As if responding to the thought, she moved around and saw the eye creature was elongated, deeper than it was wide, with tentacles reaching out from its entire length. There were dozens of the biting attackers, their teeth all tearing and yanking into flesh. She had never seen them in motion before. Then she noticed there was no sound and the surroundings were entirely black. Their sheer viciousness repulsed her and the silence frightened her further. Yet through it all, she remained convinced the eye creature was at peace, like it knew some great secret that made the pain of the attack meaningless. She didn't know why she knew; she just knew.

She realized she was all the way around, alongside the creature, and didn't know what that meant for her position in the kitchen. The possibility that she was somehow inside the wall terrified her. She clenched her teeth, held her breath, and jerked open her eyes.

She was standing right where she had been, facing her drawing, breathing raggedly, fists shaking.

The front door opened and Nate came in. The sound startled her further.

"Hello, I'm home!" he announced before walking into the dining room. "What in the world?"

"It's dry erase. It should come right off."

He stepped up and wiped a line with his hand. It did not budge. "Really?"

"Oh, sorry. I needed to see the whole thing in detail. I've been thinking about it for the last ten days, but didn't dare draw it out at Sandstone. They would have kept me inside for sure."

Nate blinked as he took it all in. "It is pretty worrisome. Where did all this detail come from? I thought this was just an impression, not a detailed battle scene."

"I realize this has become an obsession. I don't know where it comes from, but the more I think about it, the more I explore it, the more it feels like a memory."

He looked at the drawing and then back at her. "Where could you have possibly seen this before?"

"I don't know. It's like when you remember a piece of a song, like just a line of lyrics or a bit of the melody, and the more you play it in your head, the more of it comes back to you. The rest of the melody and words fill in after you've gone over it a few times. That's what this feels like. Obviously I've never seen this monstrosity in person. But I feel driven to recall the rest of the details, so I keep going back and remembering more."

Nate saw her sincerity, how much she believed it. The drawing was so disturbing, he made himself look away from it to focus on his sister. Was this a symptom of decline? He did not want to send her back inside. Had it been a mistake to hide this vision from her doctors?

"You haven't been in touch with the reality around you for a long time. Your brain could have made up stuff, or you could have caught glimpses of things, and we would have no way to tell which memories are real or not." He glanced back at the wall. "That is not to say I am dismissing what you are experiencing." He paused and met her gaze. "You've been home for two days. This is going to sound bad, but I have to ask."

"Yes, I am still taking my Clozapine every morning, just as prescribed. I had the same worry about my dopamine levels when this vision started filling itself in."

He looked back at the drawing. "Feels like a memory, eh?" He took out his phone and stepped back. "Move aside, okay?" He took a picture of the wall.

"I don't know if it's done," she interjected.

"That's all right. I'm sending the picture to myself, so I can pull it up on the computer. Come with me."

He led her to the living room desk and opened his laptop. "Got it. Okay, I can copy the image into the browser and let Google search the world for your picture."

"Geez. That's kind of amazing. I've seen people taking pictures with their phones, but I didn't know you could use the Internet like this. Oh, look at all the hits you got."

"Well, sort of. Now we have to go through them and find ... oh, hold on. This one looks promising. Let me click through. Well, it doesn't have the bitey things, but that looks like your same tentacled eyeball, yes?"

"Yeah," she said leaning in. "That's my eye."

"It's the icon of a religious cult in Arizona called the God Seekers. It was founded by a woman named Roxie McClenahan twenty years ago. Here, she's got a website."

"Whoa," Sarah let out as the page came up. "She got visions from a meteorite she saw fall in the desert. Meteorite?"

Nate shrugged. "Radiation? This says she thinks the eye thing is God and the meteorite was God's way of picking her as His prophet."

Sarah closed her eyes for a moment. "No. The eye isn't God. It's called the Dreamer. And the mouths are all part of something called the Devourer."

Nate did his best to not react to this rather disturbing revelation. *How does she know that?* "Roxie doesn't seem to have the whole story. She's only seen the eye thing." He looked away and laughed to himself.

"What's so funny?"

"At least you aren't piling up mashed potatoes and insisting they 'mean something',"

Sarah frowned and waited.

"CE3K?"

"Is that a movie?"

"Yes. Sorry, I thought maybe. No, I guess not. *Close Encounters of the Third Kind.* It's a Spielberg film. Richard Dreyfuss plays a phone line guy who is visited by aliens and he becomes obsessed with a shape that turns out to be an actual mountain in South Dakota or someplace, which is where the aliens are going to make first contact. This Roxie woman in the desert with her meteorite and you with this obsessive image just reminded me."

"Are you mocking me?"

"No, no, I'm sorry, I'm really not. The coincidence was just too much to ignore. I'm glad we found this cult in the desert. Her story might give us some clues about your vision."

"Or we should go talk to her."

He rolled his eyes. "That's what happened to Richard Dreyfuss."

"Well, did he find anything?"

"Well, yeah, he found the aliens. But you haven't found a meteorite. And I'm not sure having you, fresh out of therapy, talking to some tinfoil hat religious zealot is a good idea."

"Okay, you talk to her first."

He turned his chair to face her. "What?"

"You said Mom and Dad left us money. I'm not using that on hospitals anymore. We can go to Arizona. You go talk to Ms. McClenahan, and I'll stay in the hotel until you figure out her story."

Nate looked in his sister's eyes and saw clear, sane, determination. She wanted answers. He did too.

"All right. I'll make the arrangements."

•   •   •

Ten miles west of Winslow, Arizona on Interstate 40, Nate slowed the rented Jeep 4x4 when open range turned to fruit orchards. Off in the distance, he saw a group of buildings where his phone's GPS said should be the God Seekers' compound.

He turned onto the unmarked driveway and followed it to several metal Quonset huts that were surrounded by vegetable gardens. He had called ahead, but no one answered the phone. He left a message that he would come, but he did not know if anyone had listened to it. He was therefore pleased when a sixty-ish woman with long frizzy greying blonde hair walked up to him as he got out, and greeted him with an outstretched hand.

"You must be Nate. I'm Roxie."

"Very nice to meet you," he said shaking her sun-weathered hand. "I'm glad you got my message."

"Welcome to our village. Come inside out of the sun and have some lemonade. And welcome to Arizona," she said as she led him to the nearest small half-barrel shaped structure. "You said you came all the way from St. Louis. What about us did you find so interesting that you would come so far?"

The room was an office with several desks and bookshelves arranged to make the most rectangular space out of the curved walls/roof. The furniture was mismatched and second-hand, probably donated.

Roxie stepped to a side table set up like a coffee service, but with a pitcher of lemonade. "Please, have a seat," she said, pointing.

"I am a Psychology grad student and I've studied a few non-mainstream religions. A friend of mine told me of a vision she's been having of a giant eye with tentacles. I found the image very similar to the icon of your religion. I couldn't find any other source on your faith except your own website. I thought the coincidence was extraordinary, and worth the trip."

She joined him at the desk with two glasses. "Is your friend also from St. Louis?"

"Yes, but she couldn't make it today."

"How old is she?"

"Sixteen. I'm hoping to find similarities in her experience to yours that might explain how she got this same vision."

"When did her visions start?"

"Just a couple weeks ago. And she did not encounter a meteorite, as you did. I read you had your vision twenty years ago."

"That was when I first found the stone. It has sustained my visions ever since."

"Do you still have the meteorite?"

"Of course. It has brought the vision to all my followers too. There are thirty-two of us living here. They're all out working in the orchard today."

"Does exposure to this stone give everyone the same vision?"

"Oh yes, but the stone chooses who will get the sight. Most folks get nothing from it. In fact, the stone stopped choosing followers four years ago. Everyone who came to convert was rejected. After that, I locked it up."

"I noticed you don't invite people to join your church on your website."

"There's no point. If the stone doesn't choose you, and you don't get to see God, then you can't be one of us."

"Yet somehow my friend, hundreds of miles from here, got the vision. Can you please tell me about your initiation rite? Maybe there is something else you do that my friend might have done, besides seeing the stone."

"Oh, you don't just see the stone. You have to touch it. It's a laying of the hands. The initiate lays their hands on it, and it either chooses them or not."

"Surely there is a ceremony, maybe in a church setting?"

"Oh, of course. Would you like to see our sanctuary?"

He was a bit surprised at how forthcoming she was. "Yes, very much."

She led him across a courtyard planted with cacti and what he assumed were indigenous plants to a larger stone building. He noticed the other half dozen Quonset huts around the church. The church looked like it might have originally been a government building of some sort, like a post office. It had been remodeled, but it was clearly the original building at this site.

The back wall of the waiting room had been torn out. The ceiling of the work area behind it had been removed to create a high, wide congregation hall. He noticed Roxie watching him check out the building.

"Nice use of the space," he said.

"Thank you," she said quietly as she walked him to the altar.

As soon as he stepped forward, his gaze was drawn to the enormous sculpture of the tentacled eye suspended above a large table on a low riser. It was fashioned from carved and painted wood and was about the same size as the drawing Sarah had made on his dining room wall. It did not have the biting mouths that Sarah's had.

"The Insane God," Roxie said reverently.

"Why that name?"

"Once the stone has accepted you, this vision compels you to spend your life spreading peace and love, trying to end conflict - even to those who hate you, even if it means sacrificing your own life. Bringing such unconditional love into the real world is illogical, insane. Love must wipe away hate, no matter how insane it is to risk personal consequences."

"Ending conflict," he thought out loud. "Do you use hugging to calm angry people?"

"Yes, that's how we do it. That's the lesson God gave us. How did you know that?"

"My friend. Do you ever call your god The Dreamer?"

"No. Is that what your friend calls it?"

"Yes," he said, looking back up at the icon.

•   •   •

Sarah tossed the box of sour belts and the bag of crunchy Cheetos on her double bed before joining them in a belly flop. The trip to the motel snack machines hadn't been a complete bust. She thought about climbing out of her new jeans, but stopped herself. She was comfortable and didn't want to tuck in case her brother walked in. She hadn't talked to him about her genitals, so she didn't know if her showing in boxers would make him uncomfortable. The pants didn't bind lying down, so she left them on.

From her head down position, the twenty-something-inch TV looked bigger. That was good since it was going to be her only companion this afternoon. Half a dozen channels later, she happened upon a tall, smooth-talking black man who was explaining some kind of physics with beautiful graphics. She didn't know what he was talking about, but he was so pleasant to watch, and his manner was so confident and helpful, she was drawn in.

"It's easy to imagine history taking a different path if some important event played out differently than the way it actually happened. Let's say in our timeline, someone is hurt in a car accident. Their life is interrupted and they have to deal with all those consequences. Now if the accident somehow was avoided, then their life would go on without the interruption, and, instead of dealing with ambulances and hospitals, they got to their destination unimpeded. That would change the lives of everyone they interact with. We can imagine the effects of their not having the accident rippling out and changing a lot of things in the world."

"Yeah, if Mom and Dad had survived our car crash," Sarah grumbled to herself, "I wouldn't have lost my mind and everything would be different."

"Science fiction writers have fun spinning tales of time travelers who alter the past and affect the future. What would happen if someone stopped the *Titanic* from sinking, or assassinated Hitler before he started World War Two? These are nice intellectual exercises, but there are practical things we can learn about how our universe works by looking at how cause and effect ties everything together. Haiku master Paul Reps famously said, 'Drinking a bowl of green tea, I stopped the war.' What if every decision, every possible turning point, led to a world with a different outcome?

"The Greek philosopher Plato thought everything in our world was the physical manifestation of an idealized notion of the thing in a heavenly Ideal Plane. Every chair is one version of the ultimate notion of 'chair' in Heaven. He felt versions only made it to the Material Plane if they were worthy. I guess that would explain chairs that break easily." On screen was an old-timey, black and white clip of an acrobat in a chair collapse pratfall. "It also shows how easy it is to imagine different versions of reality."

Sarah pushed the MENU button on the remote and pulled up the title slide. "Parallel Universes with Dr. Neil DeGrasse Tyson." She switched back to the show. "Okay."

"If we imagine every event that has a consequence as a potential turning point leading to a different version of history, what we are left with is an infinite number of universes, all the same except for the one thing that changed. They are side by side, parallel if you will, separated only by the divergent paths their histories take, starting from that point of change. It is even possible that some future event will turn history back to the path it took in our universe."

Sarah liked the parallel lines on the screen, spreading but sometimes coming back together. She wondered if there was a parallel universe where she had been born a girl. She liked the idea that intervening events could set the world back on its proper path. She liked Dr. Tyson's soothing voice. She liked the way the bed held her body heat under her stomach. She laid her head down and her eyes drooped closed.

She caught herself napping and looked back at the screen. The TV was off. Had she turned it off? The remote was under her hand. The sound of surf outside distracted her.

Surf?

She got up and went to the open window. The breeze that met her smelled of the ocean. She looked out across a beach at crystal blue-green waves tumbling onto the white sand. She breathed deep and let the sound wash over her. She felt completely relaxed and refreshed at the same time. She started to walk out the door to go explore, but the sensation of peace took her by surprise and she just stood there reveling in it. She was so caught up in the moment, she didn't stop to question how the motel was at the beach when Nate and she had driven to the Arizona desert.

Nate opened the door and she startled. Only she startled while lying on the bed, face down, napping.

"Hiya. Whoa, sorry. I didn't mean to scare you awake."

She pushed herself up and blinked as she adjusted to the desert motel room. "That was vivid."

A rushing sound outside the window made her perk up. *The surf?*

Nate pointed outside. "Trucks on the highway. Was it a solid dream? You didn't used to dream hardly at all in the hospital."

She noted that the breeze blowing in the door was hot, but dry hot, not beach hot. She took a deep breath to reset.

"Yeah, I didn't dream much. I always assumed it was the meds. But I'm still on the meds. You know, I spent so many years trying to avoid the voices and to see what was real, I never thought about how dreams take you to a different reality. Just now, I dreamt we were at the ocean instead of the desert. I had a hard time telling the dream apart from the real room."

"That happens a lot with dreams. Your brain takes clues from your environment while you're sleeping. It works those details into the dream, probably so noises and such don't wake you up. The brain is really clever, even behind our backs."

"What if you woke up in the world you had dreamt?"

"Well, that would mean you never actually woke up."

"I guess." She rolled her eyes and thought about that. "What did you find out? Did you get to meet Roxie?"

"Yes. She's exactly as she appears on her web site: this old hippie, holed up in her commune with about thirty followers, all of whom saw the eyeball vision after being exposed to the meteorite."

"What does it look like?"

"Oh, she wouldn't let me see it. She said it stopped converting people four years ago. Now it's just their treasure. She gave me this pamphlet."

Sarah started looking at it and asked, "If she's not taking any more converts, then why does she have literature?"

"I don't know. Maybe it's left over from when the meteorite was active. Maybe she gets curious tourists and she just hands them the brochure."

"Have you read this?"

"No. I drove straight back here."

"This says they call it 'The Insane God'. That doesn't sound very reverent."

"She picked that name because they admit it is insane to love people in the face of hate. She said their god compels them to end conflicts, even if it puts themselves in harm's way. They use your same hugging thing to take the fight out of angry people. They don't call it The Dreamer."

"Oh, they have the same calming touch?"

"She said it was the gift of their god." He took a breath. "To be clear, I don't want you putting yourself in danger if you see someone angry. That's their interpretation, their cult."

"I get that you want to keep me safe. But you've got to admit, we're not talking about delusions anymore. Multiple people can't have the same hallucination, can they?"

She could see his jaw muscles tighten. "You're right. Not even with LSD. This looks disturbingly reproducible."

Sarah pursed her lips. "Does that mean we can move ahead assuming I've seen something real?"

"It means we can assume something has acted on all of you to create this common experience. Now we have to figure out what affected you in St. Louis, and also affected them here in Arizona up until four years ago."

"Wasn't there an article you found about Roxie from when she first started her church that said she suffered from schizophrenia before she found the meteorite? Whatever it is that gives us the vision, it also seems to cure mental illness."

Nate cocked an eyebrow at her. "That's some half-decent deduction there, Watson. Since it happened to her too, it looks like the vision and the cure are linked. This could be huge."

"Maybe we should have me go visit Roxie after all."

•　　　•　　　•

Nate pulled off the highway and parked in front of a roadside diner. "I saw this place on my way out this morning. The parking lot was full, so I assume it's good."

Two spaces down from them, a pickup truck pulled in and four men got out: two from the cab and two from the back. The men in back had rifles which they put down in the truck bed before hopping out. Nate noticed they all had the same blue cap with a red insignia even though they were not otherwise in uniform.

The driver, who sported a huge bushy beard that rested on his chest, wasted no time berating one of the men from the back. "I still say your stomping around like a horse spooked any wetbacks we might have seen today."

"Your driving like a maniac spooked them. They were gone before our boots hit the ground."

Nate noticed Sarah staring at them. He stepped in front of her to usher her into the diner. "Don't let them focus on you," he advised quietly.

She sidestepped him. "Are they hunters?"

"Not exactly."

The other man from the back of the truck spoke up, just as boisterously as the others. "You should let Pete drive next time. He knows how to flush 'em out. Last week Pete cornered three whole families coming across. What was the take?" he asked the ponytailed man who had been the cab passenger.

"Eleven of the bastards. We had a hell of a time keeping them under wraps until the Patrol could take 'em off our hands. I wanted to just shoot the fuckers, but Bobby here wouldn't let me."

"Hell no!" said the bearded driver. "That's my payday too."

"Fuckin' mercenary!" Pete accused. "You're in it for the money. I'm in it for my country!" To make his point clear, he pushed Bobby in the chest.

"The money's good. And the sport," Bobby fired back.

Sarah asked Nate, "Are they talking about catching Mexicans coming across the border?"

"Yes. Keep your voice down. They're private militia. It sounds like they get a bounty from the Border Patrol. We should not be here."

Pete was working himself up fast. "Do not question my patriotism!"

Bobby threw back his shoulders which made his beard bounce on this chest. "Nobody's questioning any fuckin' thing!"

Nate turned to push Sarah back toward the diner door, but she slipped his grasp and walked straight at the fighting men. Pete raised his fist at Bobby, and Sarah stepped right into his body, wrapping her arms tight around his beer belly.

"Wha-hoo!" one of the other men cheered. "Looks like you've got a fan, Petey!"

Pete tried to step back, but Sarah held firm. "What the hell? Who are you?"

She didn't answer, but just buried her cheek in his wide chest.

Nate hustled up and tried to explain. "Sorry, guys. My sister just does this sometimes. She's a little mental that way."

Pete put his hands on her back to ease her off. "You're a skinny little thing, aren't you?"

Bobby looked closer and spoke up. "Wait a minute. Is that even a girl?"

Nate clenched his fists, ready for a fight.

The other two stepped up, "What the fuck?"

Suddenly, Pete caught his breath in a sob. Nate and the other men stopped. Then Pete did it again, and started to cry in earnest.

"What the hell, man?" Bobby asked.

Pete put his hands over his eyes and broke down bawling.

Sarah let go and stepped back.

He sobbed, "I can't believe I've been so ..."

Bobby shook his head which made his enormous beard jiggle. "What?"

"Mean!" he barked between heaving breaths, tears streaming down his face. "Hateful! I've been obsessed. Lilly avoids me. I fly off the handle at nothin'. What's wrong with me?"

"Ain't nothin' wrong with you," Bobby said flatly. "What the hell did this freak do to you?"

Nate pulled Sarah back by her elbow.

One of the other men spun Nate around by his shoulder, trying to get to Sarah. "What the fuck did you do to him?"

Even though the man had two inches on him, Nate stood his ground and the man punched at his head. Nate ducked the swing and it only grazed him.

"No, don't attack her! She's shown me the truth. Those families!" Pete pleaded.

"Oh, fuck this!" Bobby grabbed Pete by the arm and walked him back to the truck. "You are not gonna make a total fool of yourself out here on the street. Come on, guys. Pete needs to soak his head in a bucket of ice."

Nate and Sarah watched as they all piled into their truck and drove off. The man who had swung on Nate leaned out the window and flipped the bird at them.

Nate noticed Sarah run her hands up the back of her neck and fluff her six-inch brown bob.

When they were gone, Nate said, "You could have gotten us killed."

"I had to. I'm sorry. He was so consumed by hate, I had to help. It didn't matter if I got hurt. I couldn't stop myself."

Nate chewed on this for a long moment. "That's what Roxie said. Insane God, indeed."

3

"CLOSE TO YOU"
THE CARPENTERS

"**W**HAT DO YOU FEEL when you calm someone down with a hug?"

Sitting next to Nate, Sarah rested her clutched hands on the front edge of Roxie McClenahan's weathered wooden desk. She was pretty excited. He still wasn't convinced this was a good idea.

The frizzy-haired hippie looked happy to discuss her passion with a fellow believer. "When the urge comes on, all I can see is their anger and hate, and I just need to smother that fire. It's all I can do. It's like I'm pushed from behind and I have no choice."

"Yes!" She turned to Nate. "That's what I've been having such a hard time trying to explain. When it comes on, it's bigger than me, and I can't stop it." She turned back to Roxie. "It feels like their hate and anger is a fire in them and you have to put it out before it kills them."

"That's what you saw in that militia guy?" Nate asked.

"Yes, and in you at the hospital."

Roxie raised her eyebrows. "She did it to you too?"

"Yeah, I was getting pretty irritated dealing with rigid-thinking doctors. I didn't think I was all that mad. Then Sarah hugged me down, and suddenly I could see things much clearer." He traded a smile with his sister. "I guess I was madder than I realized at the time."

"Have a bit of a temper?"

"Sometimes, when I'm frustrated," Nate admitted.

"I used to have a temper, before the meteorite." Roxie looked away with a frown. "For me, it was bullying. I had long red hair when I was young. All the Mexican boys thought it was great fun to try to yank on it. I could have grown up racist, but I just grew up angry." She turned back to Nate. "How 'bout you? You seem like the classic chip-on-the-shoulder type. Not too happy with the parents dying and the sister losing her mind. Got ya feeling like you got dealt a bad hand?"

Nate wasn't about to take that bait. He stared at her as blankly as he could manage. "That's really none of your business."

She waved her hands broadly. "I'm an empath. That's what I do. That was my gift from God."

Sarah spoke up. "Let's talk about your god. I think you and I might have slightly different visions of him." She shot Nate a sideways look as if to make sure he was okay with how much she was about to share. "See, my vision also includes sort of a Devil. My god-creature has the same big eye and tentacles, and he's just as serene as yours. But mine is being bitten, attacked by a swarm of smaller creatures that are mostly just mouths with lots of sharp teeth. All together they make up one thing, which I call the Devourer."

Roxie did not try to mask her reaction. "That's some disturbing shit."

"Yeah, well, the thing is, my god-creature doesn't seem bothered by the biting at all. He's just chillin', putting up with it like it was nothing. Now, I've spent a lot of time sitting with this vision, really exploring it, and the god-creature shared with me how he feels and what's he's thinking about. He is dreaming of better things, great things. He knows if he dreams of the right things, he can change the world around him for the better. That's why I call him the Dreamer. The Devourer is biting him trying to seize pieces of his dreams."

Roxie worked this for herself out loud. "It sounds like we're seeing the same God, but yours is actively in conflict with this Devourer devil thing. Maybe you're seeing something that happened before my vision, since the Devourer is gone when I see him."

"Or before the Devourer shows up," Sarah suggested. "I'm pretty sure something big came of their conflict. Like they were never the same after. So your vision of him alone might be before. You saw your vision what, twenty years ago?"

Nate cut in. "Hang on. Do you think you can attach a timeline to visions? Even if these are real creatures, meteorites brought these visions to Earth. That could mean all this happened ages ago, untold millions of years ago."

"Okay," Roxie said with a nod. "Still doesn't mean it didn't happen." Her antique wooden desk chair squeaked loudly as she leaned back. "Now darlin', you said the Dreamer is working on better things, and the Devourer wants to steal his dreams. Any idea what's so important the Devourer would divide himself up into all these pieces for a chance to grab the right dream bit?"

Sarah looked unprepared for that. "I've never thought of it that way. All this time I've spent in the vision, I never looked at the Devourer's motive." She thought for a moment. "You're right, it must be something pretty big." Her eyes lit up. "He's inviting the Devourer in. It's like when we can't stop ourselves from hugging an angry person. The Dreamer is so calm through the attack because he wants it."

"Like a masochist?" Nate asked, confused.

"No, it's a ploy to get the Devourer to give up his anger. Like the hugs." She turned to Roxie. "That's why you call him insane, right?"

"Well, yeah."

"I wanted to talk to you about that name. I guess it's no big secret that both you and I spent some time in mental hospitals before we got these visions. Isn't the word 'insane' kind of an insult?"

Roxie laughed. "You kids today with your sensitivity. We call him that not only because he drives us to do illogical things, but as an inside joke that we all used to be what society calls insane. He's our god. When I checked all the folks who he rejected, they were all mentally stable. He only accepts crazies like us. The visions bring the cure."

"Oh, okay. That makes sense."

"Let's focus on this devil you see. From what you say, this Devourer certainly seems to be the Dreamer's enemy. Which brings me back to my question. What do you think he's dreaming of to tempt his enemy like that?"

"The Earth."

Both Nate and Roxie recoiled.

"No wait, really. Think about it. These meteorites fell to Earth. These two beings, or gods or whatever they were, must not have been that far from here. I mean, at least on our side of the galaxy, right? The Dreamer as much as told me he could make his dreams into reality, that he had the power of creation." She looked at her brother. "How many planets have just the right conditions for life, and then are lucky enough to survive and blossom? I've heard that that's super rare, like almost never. If you had the power of creation, and you could make whole planets, like experiments, wouldn't you keep trying until you got it just right?"

"And you think this gem, this perfect attempt, was the Earth," Roxie said. "That would explain why he seems so benevolent. I thought I was seeing God, as in the one and only God Almighty."

Nate was impressed with how readily Roxie incorporated Sarah's additions into her cosmology. That wasn't usually the case with religious fanatics. "You think the Dreamer was cooking experimental planets, and he finally hit on the right formula, and maybe that was Earth. And this tempted the Devourer to attack, to steal the dream, but it was actually a ploy to get the enemy to give up his anger? That's a wonderful, almost romantic story, but I think you've filled in a lot of details with just conjecture." He got blank stares from both women. "It's really a stretch. I mean, the Earth?"

"The meteorites fell here," Roxie offered.

"Right, the meteorites. How do they fit in? How did they come to carry this message here?" Nate asked.

Sarah shrugged. "We don't know. The vision doesn't have them."

"Okay. Then let's stick to what we know, which is that you two have this vision and this ability and this mission to use it. We can fill in the cosmology later. I still don't want Sarah joining your group of followers. She has only just recovered from a long bout of illness and she needs time to get her feet back on the ground."

"She doesn't have to 'join up' with anything. That she has my same visions tells me we're already sisters under this Dreamer god that has found us. Somehow you got a more in-depth version of the vision. I'm happy to share my journals that I've written over twenty years of meditating on this vision. I want to be a resource to help you figure this out."

The sound of speeding tires sliding to a halt on gravel drew their attention outside.

"Somebody's in an awful big hurry," Roxie said getting up. "If you'll excuse me."

When she'd left, Sarah turned to her brother. "Don't push her away. You said yourself that most of what I've got is conjecture. She's been working on this for twenty years. She's bound to have insights that can help."

Raised voices outside made Nate raise his hand. A man was yelling at Roxie. Nate headed for the door with Sarah right behind him. A bearded man in a black, Jack Daniels tee shirt and jeans was brandishing a pistol and swearing at Roxie, who was slowly walking up to him closing the ten-yard distance. "Don't act like you don't know why I'm here, McClanahan. I'd shoot you right here if I thought it would stop your bullshit colony. Where's the rest of your clan?"

Roxie kept walking, her long floral dress flowing in the light breeze. "They're out in the fields working. There's no need for bloodshed. We're not harming anybody."

The man brought the gun up straight at her. "Stop! I know about your fucking touch! One more step and I will kill you where you stand!"

To Nate's and Sarah's amazement, she kept walking. Sarah started to step past Nate and out the door.

"Where the hell are you going?" he whispered.

"I can feel his hatred," Sarah pleaded. "I can help her."

He grabbed her shoulders. "If he sees you, he'll fire on you. He hasn't shot Roxie yet."

Roxie got about five feet away and the gun went off. The impact knocked her back a step, but she kept her footing. The man looked at once horrified at what he had done, and enraged that she remained standing and was still walking up to him.

She made no effort to dodge or plead. She just took the last steps and flung her arms around him. He let out a roar and bit her viciously on the shoulder. The gun went off again and her body lurched. But she held on.

Nate was so horrified he let his grip loose and Sarah ran out. He ran to catch up, still watching the armed man.

He flung his head back and screamed in agony. He pushed Roxie away and she crumpled to the ground at his feet. "No!" he screamed so loud his voice broke.

At Sarah's approach he looked up. Nate saw blood on the man's mouth, but his face was covered in tears. He looked from Sarah to Roxie to the gun in his hand.

Nate caught up to Sarah and pulled her back by her arm.

The man brought the gun up, but not at Sarah. With no hesitation, he shot himself in the temple and fell dead.

Sarah and Nate stood there for a moment, stunned. They both blinked a few times, trying to make sense of what happened, then looked at each other in disbelief.

Sarah walked very cautiously to Roxie. Nate stepped to the fallen man. Among the man's many tattoos were several designs that looked like the biting mouths Sarah had drawn on the kitchen wall.

"Sarah? Is she dead?"

Sarah was sobbing and touching Roxie very tenderly. Nate realized this was likely the first dead person his sister had ever seen. He also remembered how their parents' deaths had sent her into mental illness.

She shouldn't linger on the body.

"You need to see this. Seriously, please come here. Are these tattoos the Devourer in your vision?"

Unsteady, Sarah came over, then recoiled at the sight. "Oh, yes. That is definitely them."

"That means there is a rival cult that worships the other god." Nate examined his body and found he wore a ring with the large letters CSA, and a leather thong necklace with a smooth greenish-gray stone pendant around his neck. He looked over at the man's pickup truck and saw it had Florida plates. The front of the truck was spattered with bugs from a long highway trip.

Sarah was looking back at Roxie. "I could feel how his anger drew her to him. I felt the same urge to fling my arms around him. It was bigger than me. It was terrifying."

A police siren coming up the highway caught their attention.

"Who called them?" Nate looked back at the Quonset buildings and saw several faces at the windows. "Great."

"Don't we want the police involved?" Sarah asked.

"I guess, but we're going to be stuck here trying to explain what happened to the cops while not telling them why we're here."

She frowned at him.

He could hear the tension rise in his own voice. "We do not want them thinking we're cult members standing over a couple of dead bodies."

He held out his hand to her and backed them away as the gold and tan highway cruiser pulled in.

The Arizona State Trooper got out with his hand on his pistol but did not draw the weapon. "Did you call this in?"

An old man with very short white hair opened the front door of the nearest building and walked up. His skin was golden brown from long exposure to the sun; his jeans and t-shirt were tinged with desert dust. "I did. I saw the whole thing. These two were just standing here when it all went down."

"What's your name?"

"Jake Goldblatt. I live here at the ranch."

"What did you see?"

"This guy pulled up all full of piss and vinegar, starts waving a pistol around, screaming obscenities. Roxie McClenahan, our President, came out to talk to him, and he shot her, twice. Then he blew out his own brains."

"Any idea what they were fighting about?"

"No idea. I couldn't hear if they said anything."

The cop turned back to Nate and Sarah. "You were right here. What did you hear?"

"Like Mr. Goldblatt said," Nate began, "the guy was just screaming mad. I don't think Roxie said anything. She walked up to him to calm him down and he shot her. It was all so sudden and terrifying."

"And your names?"

"Nate Meyer. And this is my sister Sarah."

"Do you live here too?"

"No, we were interviewing Ms. McClenahan for a story Sarah is doing for her high school newspaper."

The officer walked to the bodies and looked them over. "And this guy just shot himself in the head after killing the woman?"

"Yes sir. Like I said, it all happened in a matter of seconds. I hardly knew what I was watching."

He turned to the old man. "This is a church compound, right?"

"We're a farm. We run an avocado orchard and grow vegetables for ourselves."

The officer looked from Goldblatt, to the bodies, to Nate and Sarah. "You all need to stay here, on these grounds, while I call in a team to investigate. Is that your car?" He said pointing to Nate's rented Jeep.

"Ah, yes sir. Why?" He did not like where this was going.

"Gimme the keys. You'll get them back when I'm done asking all my questions."

Nate felt himself turning nervousness into anger. Apparently it showed because Sarah stepped closer and put her hand on his shoulder.

He took a breath as he walked over and handed the keys to the policeman. He noted his nameplate. "Officer Morris, may we wait inside out of the sun?"

"Of course."

Jake Goldblatt waved them to join him in the building he had come from. Nate noticed Sarah looking around behind her as they walked, like she thought she saw something following them.

When they were out of earshot, Jake said, "I always wondered if there might be a Devil worshipping cult that would come to do us harm."

Sarah nearly blurted out, "Does your vision include a Devil?"

"Oh, no," he chuckled. "I don't have the vision. My wife had the vision, but she died three years ago of a stroke. I stayed on to help with the farm. But I know all the lore. It just made sense if your god gives you the ability to calm anger, that there would be a devil, an enemy, that breeds anger."

"You think that's who this guy was?" Nate asked.

"Drove like a bat out of hell all the way from Florida just to kill poor Roxie. Looks that way."

"You should tell the police. These guys might send another killer."

"Good idea." He turned to Sarah. "Doing a story on us, eh?"

"Yeah. I'm, uh, doing a segment on non-mainstream religions. I found you guys on the internet."

"Well, you've got a lot to write about now. I'm sorry you had to see this, though."

·　　　·　　　·

Sarah set her tray down and sat across the yellow Formica booth table from Nate. She smiled at her food and said, "I haven't had McDonalds since they took us out for a day trip last summer."

"Three fucking hours," he muttered.

She shrugged. "It's not like we had anywhere else to be this afternoon. Roxie told us all she was going to." She took a second to gauge whether her brother was going to climb out of his funk and talk to her. "The cops were nice enough about it. They could have been jerks."

He took a too-big bite of his hamburger.

"And Mr. Goldblatt answered all their questions about their group, so the cops didn't suspect my involvement, which is what you were worried about."

"You were chatting with him the whole time the cops questioned me. Did you find out anything interesting?"

"Not really. Well, I think he may have figured out I wasn't just some kid writing an article."

"What?"

"He picked up on how I asked him if their vision had a devil. He asked some follow up questions before I could change the subject."

"Great."

"I don't think he's going to tell anyone. He's been living with this vision in his life for decades. I think he knows not to go telling tales."

"Well, we're out of here first thing in the morning."

"Back to St. Louis?"

"Yes. The sooner we get off their radar, the better."

"You mean the rival cult from Florida?"

"If they send someone to check up on their killer, I'd rather we were halfway across the country."

"I thought we wanted to find out more about them."

"Oh, we do. The detective was very interested in the killer's tattoos, like he had seen them before. And I wrote down the guy's license plate. The internet is a wonderful thing."

Sarah drifted back to the crime scene. "He bit her," she said in disgust. Then her face lit up. "He bit her!"

"Yeah, like his god bites."

"No. Well, yes, that. But not just that. She let him bite her."

"She let him shoot her."

"She left her flesh wide open for him, like she knew he was going to bite her. Like she knew what biting her was going to do to him. Don't you see? She wasn't just compelled to bring him down from his anger. This was meant to destroy him. That's the missing piece. The Dreamer isn't just letting his enemy bite him — he's planning on it. They must have been at war for eons. They knew each other all too well. The Dreamer would need a deception so subtle, even his ages-old enemy wouldn't see it. He's so serene because that's the plan, to destroy the enemy. Whatever he's dreaming is poison to the Devourer."

"I'm guessing your gods ended the same as these two. Mutual destruction." He shook his head. "What a waste."

"And their destroyed bodies are the meteorites."

Nate stopped chewing. "Actual chunks?"

"I don't know. It's a theory."

"All I know is I'm sorry this has gotten complicated and dangerous. We came here to get you answers about your vision. I thought making sense of it would help get you to a stable place."

"Do you think I'm not stable? You've seen me for over a week now. I'm staying on my meds."

"No, you're stable. I see no indication of illness. I saw you looking around at shadows right after you saw Roxie killed."

"I was so freaked out, I was convinced the voices were going to yell at me again. I'm very glad they didn't."

"You went from deeply troubled straight into having this vision. You haven't landed on normal yet."

She stifled her reaction to that word. Being trans, was there a normal for her? She took a second to size up his meaning. "I know what you mean. It has been out of the fire and into the frying pan." She ran her hands up her neck and fluffed her bob. It was a touch point she found gave her comfort with her self-image.

"What's that around your neck?" Nate asked.

"You mean my necklace?" She fished it out of her shirt and held up the greenish-gray stone, tear-shaped amulet. It was about the size of a quarter, and hung on a thin metal chain.

"Where did you get it?"

"A nurse gave it to me at the center. She said it would give me protection. I'm always afraid the chain is going to break with it so thin. They wouldn't let us wear anything we could strangle ourselves with. I wear it cause the stone warms up and feels nice on my skin."

"How long ago did this nurse give it to you?"

"I dunno. A few weeks ago, I guess. You look upset. What is it?"

"Roxie's killer was wearing the same necklace."

"What? You didn't say he was wearing a necklace."

"I didn't think anything of it. I saw it when I examined his body before the cop came. Have you been wearing it the whole time since you've been released?"

"Not all the time. But a lot of the time. Like I said, it feels nice." She watched her brother's fixed gaze on it. "Oh, wait a minute. You think the Florida guy with the Devourer tattoos was wearing this same necklace, and now I'm getting visions of the Dreamer. And Roxie got the Dreamer visions from a meteorite. So maybe this is also a piece of a meteorite?"

"Sure looks that way."

She looked down at it in a whole new light and started to take it off.

"If that thing is giving you the vision, it might be what cured your schizophrenia."

"Do you think I should I leave it on?"

"It doesn't seem to do you any damage. Being in constant contact with it might explain why you got a more complete vision than Roxie and her followers."

She didn't know which was more frightening: being under this thing's power, or taking it off and losing her mind again. "I think I'll leave it on for now." She looked closely at the fine marbling of different shades of gray. "Is there some way to tell if it's from a meteorite?"

"We can find a rock shop and get it looked at tomorrow morning. Out here in this desert where prospectors used to find gold and uranium, we should be able to find an expert."

"You think it's radioactive?"

"I have no idea. Everything is to a tiny extent. We'll head home right after."

She looked at her half-finished burger and fries. "I'm not hungry anymore."

•   •   •

Hiram Cutler looked around the room and could hardly make sense of it. He saw he was tied with heavy leather bands to the rails of a bed. That seemed pretty normal. The bedroom he was in, all in floral wallpaper and wood furniture - that seemed completely wrong. He took a breath, getting ready to scream back at the voices that were certain to berate him, but they didn't come.

"Fuck you! You can't hide from me!" he yelled into the quiet room. His rage at the voices seemed normal too. He yelled even louder. "Can you not hear me? Where are you hiding?"

He yanked at the bindings, his strong arms and massive frame jolted the bed on the carpeted floor, but the rails held. His twisting flung his long blond hair across his face. He shook it off and looked around the room more carefully. This was somebody's bedroom, in somebody's house. How did he get here?

The door was open and he could see down a hallway. He was mad as hell, and that felt right, like he was always mad. Only he wasn't mad at his constant tormentors. Now he was mad because he didn't know what was going on.

"Hey! Can anybody hear me?"

A skinny redheaded teenaged boy with big ears and glasses ran down the hall to him. "Oh good, you're awake. How do you feel?"

"How do I feel? What kind of question is that? Who the fuck are you and where am I?"

"I'm Johnny Simons, and this is my bedroom. Colonel Davis brought you here for you to recover. He told me to ask you if you see anything weird or hear any voices that aren't there."

"The only thing weird I see is some gawky kid asking me stupid questions and not answering mine."

"You seem pretty lucid. Can you see that I'm the only person in the room with you?"

"Of course! Oh wait." Hiram craned his neck to look around. "Is there somebody else that I can't see?"

"No, we're alone. And Colonel Davis said that would be a good sign if you only saw what's really here."

"Who the hell is this Davis asshole you keep on about? If he cares so damn much about me, why isn't he here?"

"Jefferson Davis is the leader of our group. He busted you out of the mental hospital and brought you here to see if the cure worked."

"Cure?" he blurted out laughing. "He thinks he can cure me? I've been locked up for violent delusions my whole life. Ain't nothing' gonna cure me."

"He said it was called paranoid schizophrenia. I don't mean to upset you, but you're awfully clear-headed right now. Aren't you?"

He blinked and scowled. "How do I know you're real?"

Johnny smiled as if Hiram had gotten some answer right. "Colonel Davis told me that was the question I should wait for." He stepped up to the bed and slapped Hiram across the face. "Your delusions never did that, did they?"

Hiram raged and yanked on his restraints with all his might. The metal rails complained with a high-pitched creak and the wooden bed frame groaned. He bit at the air like a wild animal.

Johnny just stood there and watched until he calmed down. "I'll go get Colonel Davis now."

"Wait 'til I get out of these bindings and we'll see how real you are, you little shit!" he spat at Johnny's retreating figure.

Johnny didn't come back for a while. Hiram lifted his head and looked around the room. A desk in front of the window looked unused. The kid looked too old to be in high school. An ivy plant grew on the windowsill. A trophy with a bike on it sat on a far dresser. More than the stuff in the room, he noticed he was able to identify and think about these things without being interrupted. In fact, the room was freakishly quiet.

What had they done to him? He looked at his arms and didn't see any needle marks. They had a stone pendant necklace around his neck. Whatever the fuck that was for. Had they fed him drugs? None of the drugs the hospitals gave him ever did any good. He didn't feel drugged. What did the kid say? *Clear-headed.* He stopped moving and just listened. Nothing. Nothing but his own thoughts. It felt weird; it felt wrong.

He heard footsteps in the house and, a moment later two men entered with the boy following. The one who was obviously in charge stepped up to the bed. He was tall, though not as tall as Hiram, fit, with a neatly trimmed beard and mostly gray hair.

"Mister Cutler, I am Jefferson Davis," he said with a gentile Southern accent. "How are you feeling?"

"Mister Cutler was my asshole father. What did you do to my demons?"

Jefferson smiled a crooked, knowing smirk. "I sent them away. You're going to have to learn to live without them."

"What if I don't want them gone?"

"God has called on us to do his work. Your demons were getting in the way."

"Did you faith heal me? How the hell did you do that without me knowing?"

"I have my ways, Brother Hiram. My calling is to save souls like you from torment. God has His own plan for you."

"Ha! God turned his back on me a long time ago. I'm the meanest, most violent son of a bitch you'll ever meet. What the fuck would God want with me?"

"You are exactly the instrument He needs to bring His new message to mankind. Like the Roman soldier Saul was turned by God into the Apostle Paul to found Jesus's church, God will turn your talent for destruction into His hand on Earth."

Hiram knew a line of bullshit when he heard it. "You want me to kill for you."

"Actually, no. I have many men who can kill for me. I need you to be a teacher, and, in time, a leader, of the new gospel of violence God has set before us. Do you believe in the End Times as foretold in the Bible?"

"I guess so."

"Those times are upon us. And it is up to righteous men to hear the call and put his fellow man to the test. Up until now, you have lashed out at whoever got in your way, or whoever your demons told you to destroy. Your mind is free now, and I can give you direction to use your rage for a much greater good."

Hiram glared at him for a long moment. "This stinks. All you've done is replace my demons telling me what to do with your plantation-ass voice telling me what to do. What about what I want to do?" he spat.

"Well then, what do you want to do? I have freed your mind, and you are suddenly in a quandary for what to do with your new freedom of thought. I do not want to replace your demons. I am here to show you the truth. You will decide how you will use that truth."

He then utterly surprised Hiram by stepping up to the bed and undoing the bindings on his arms. The other man who had come with Jefferson, a dumpy-looking bald guy with a little black goatee, whom Hiram had not really noticed until now, raised a hand in disapproval and took a step back, but he held his tongue.

Jefferson noticed his reaction and told him, "It's all right Jackson. He'll behave himself. He has no reason to be mad at us. Isn't that right, Brother Hiram?"

Hiram sat up in the bed and massaged his wrists. He frowned deeply at the gray-haired man. "I guess not."

"Now I must advise you of something very important. The cure I have given you comes from that stone around your neck. It is in fact a holy relic from God himself, a piece of divine intervention. You must wear it at all times, or all of this will unwind and your demons will return. You are not the first I have cured in this fashion, and I assure you the consequences will not be pretty if you take that necklace off."

The chain was just long enough to pick it up and look at it. It was a smooth green-grey stone, and did not look like much of a gift from God. He decided to play along anyway.

"You should also know that in the coming days you will receive a vision that is part of your deliverance. You will see biting mouths full of sharp teeth. You will see them in the pattern of leaves in the trees. You will see them in the gravel beneath your feet. You will see them when you close your eyes. They will seem terrifying at first. Do not fear them. They are not here to bite you. They are here to inspire you. They are the teeth of the violence God wants us to bring to the unworthy. Your mission will be to seek out the unworthy and destroy them."

Hiram smiled up at him. "I like the sound of that."

"Take a shower. Jackson here will show you around the compound. Get something to eat. I will come check on you later."

As Jefferson turned and left, Hiram noticed he wore a sidearm in a holster on his hip.

Jefferson skipped down the front stairs, but that shifted his holster around and he had to pull it back straight. Jefferson felt confident Hiram would be worth the work to bring him around. The big man had so much anger, and was so used to being angry, there was no doubt he could transfer it when the time came.

The sky had finally cleared up after the last tropical storm. It would rain later, but just the usual light afternoon rain. This was Florida, after all. He looked around the lush green grounds of his family's plantation estate as he walked to the big white main house. Half a dozen men unloaded supplies from a truck into the barn. Further afield, he saw men at shooting practice. It was going to be a good day.

He strode through the foyer and into the grand salon, filled with computer desks manned by earnest-looking men he did not interrupt. He walked past the large table spread with maps and into his office at the far end. He picked up a letter in his inbox. From the IRS to Pierce Clayton. He sneered and dropped it back in the tray.

He sat down, picked up the phone and punched in a number. "Hey, Smithy, any more word on the meteor shower? Oh good. What!? Really? You're shitting me. Two months? Oh, only eight weeks?" He leaned back in his chair and blinked several times, trying to process the news. "You're sure? All right then. Thanks." He hung up.

"Eight weeks," he repeated to himself as he shook his head. "Woo boy."

•　　•　　•

"I'm not convinced this is a meteorite. There are no chondrules. The minerals are fused together to form a grainy pattern, but it's not the pebbles you typically find in meteorites. This is from the middle of whatever the source rock was, so we can't tell if it had the usual dark melted crust from Earthfall. It could be an achondric meteorite, but those are extremely rare. I have never seen one myself."

Sarah watched Ted the rock guy examine the necklace with a jeweler's loupe while he talked. The lens looked small in his meaty hands held up to his broad face, made bigger by his thick blond beard.

"What's a chondrule?"

"They're grains of pure hard minerals, like a millimeter or two, that are buried throughout meteoroids. They were formed billions of years ago when the solar system was first formed. They were liquified and purified by the first high energy collisions, and then splashed out into space where they cooled immediately into these droplets. When everything accreted with gravity, these droplets were melted again and reformed into planetary material. But the stuff that didn't get pulled down into planets, the stuff that stayed in space, still have the original droplets. Your stone doesn't have any. It is mildly magnetic, so there is some iron in here. I could acid test it to see its nickel content. But it's not a classic iron-nickel, and it definitely doesn't have any aluminum alloy lines, which is something else we see in meteorites."

Sarah asked, "Could it be a fossil?"

Ted held it up to the loupe again. "This does not look like fossilized bone. You know, this pattern does look more organic than meteoric." Surprisingly, he then licked it.

"What are you doing?" Nate fired.

"Checking porosity. Fossilized bone is hydrophilic, and sticks to your tongue. This isn't a fossil either."

Sarah asked further. "You said it looked organic. Can we tell if it has organic material in it? Or if it used to before it was fossilized?"

"We'd have to use chemicals to test that. You said you only want my non-invasive opinion. Did you also say you want it checked for radiation?"

"Yes," Nate said. "We want to make sure it's safe to wear."

Ted shrugged his bushy eyebrows. "Fair enough." He walked into the back of the shop and retrieved a box with an attached wand from a cabinet. "Ol' Mr. Geiger," he said as he flipped on the switch and held the wand over the stone. The box made a rapid clicking sound. Ted checked a gauge on the box and nodded. "Nothing to worry about."

Sarah didn't think so. "Isn't that a lot of reaction."

"I've got it set for maximum sensitivity. This is about the same level as quartz people bring in here off the desert. It's quite safe."

"Is that level of radiation typical for a fossil?" Nate asked.

"That's a function of what minerals supplanted the original organic material. If they were radioactive minerals, then you get a radioactive fossil. I would not call this object 'radioactive.' It has a normal background decay. And like I said, I do not think this is a fossil."

He checked the needle again and paused. Then he frowned.

"What do you see?" Nate asked.

He tapped the side of the gauge box. "Something's not right." He looked around the room. "Something is interfering with the read. Like's it's also picking up another signal." He turned the gauge around to show them. "Every half second or so, there is a spike. Still not dangerous. But it's bouncing in a pattern. I've never seen anything like it. See that? Just a little jump, but really regular."

Sarah thought it looked like a heartbeat. She did not say so.

Ted looked out the front windows. "Somebody must have a shortwave broadcasting on an illegal frequency."

Then why did the tick only show up when he tested the stone?

Nate shot her a glance that told her he was thinking the same thing.

Nate scooped up the stone. "Well, thank you for putting our fears to rest. Fascinating stuff, really."

"Geologists at a university might be able to identify any organic material. Again, the only way to really tell is if you get out the chemicals."

"All right then," he said as Sarah joined him heading out. "Thank you very much!"

"My pleasure. Come on back if you find any other interesting rocks."

Once outside, Nate handed her the necklace and she put it on. "Your stone has a heartbeat."

"Sure looks that way. Which I find somehow comforting. Further proof this isn't just all in my imagination."

"Oh, I stopped thinking this was about hallucinations when Florida man showed up. Whatever people are seeing, gun-wielding crazies are all too real."

4

"RIVER"
BISHOP BRIGGS

"ARE YOU SURE YOU'RE OKAY going back in there?" Sitting in the car seat next to her brother, Sarah looked out the windshield at the front entrance to the Sandstone Rehabilitation Center. She had been thinking about this ever since they got back to St. Louis.

"I think I'll be okay. It will be nice to see familiar faces." She looked at Nate and he looked worried. "If I start to freak out, just get me out of there, okay?"

"Okay," he said as they got out. "Do you want to do the talking, or shall I?"

"I might be busy coping. Maybe you do the talking."

He reached over and squeezed her shoulder. "Deal."

The short, round, middle-aged blonde woman at the counter looked more like someone's grandmother than an intake nurse.

"Hi, Mrs. Cleary!" Sarah greeted her.

"My goodness!" she cooed back. "Little Sarah. What in the world are you doing back here?"

"We've got an appointment with Dr. Alpaca."

"Oh, all right. Both of you sign in, and I'll call ahead for you."

Sarah signed the clipboard and handed it to Nate.

He looked at Sarah earnestly. "How are you doin'?" he asked her quietly.

She flashed her brother a brave smile. "So far, so good."

Mrs. Cleary buzzed the door open and they walked into the suite of administrative offices. The hallway was empty, so they headed straight to the door marked, 'Dr. Mary Alpaca, MD, PhD'. Sarah knocked.

The very thin redhead in a dark blue suit answered the door with a big smile. "Sarah Meyer, come on in! Hello, Nate." She held her hand out and shook both of theirs before stepping behind her desk. "Have a seat. How have you been doing? What brings you to see me today?"

"Well, I only kind of wanted to see you. To let you know I'm doing really well."

"Are you taking the Clozapine every day?"

"Yes, ma'am."

"Are you having mood swings, like we thought you might? Have you needed the Lexipro?"

"No, my mood has been fine. I haven't had any of the depression you told me to look out for. I'm not taking anything else. And the voices are gone, not just positive like we talked about — actually gone. It took me a while to get used to the quiet."

"That is extraordinary. The best we ever see is eliminating the negative voices and then managing the positive ones. I am so happy for you."

Sarah smiled and looked away, not sure what to do with this attention. "I actually wanted to, well ... it's a bit awkward."

Nate hopped in. "We need to talk to one of your orderlies, a Native American woman named Judy."

"Judy Cloudfeather? May I ask why?"

Nate glanced over to get Sarah's permission to continue. "She gave Sarah a necklace some time before Sarah left here, and we'd like to know where she got it. It turns out to be a really rare kind of stone. The rock guy we had check it out said he would love to know where it was found."

"May I see it?"

Sarah took it off and handed it to her. Sarah noticed the suit jacket was really loose over the doctor's petite frame and it crumpled when she reached across the desk. In all the hours she had spent in this office talking to her, Sarah had never noticed Dr. Alpaca was so thin before. Odd the things she had missed.

"It doesn't look special."

"We didn't think so either, but the gemologist was pretty excited."

"Okay," she said handing it back. "I think I saw Judy here today. Let's go find her."

As they walked the long straight corridor down the middle of the building, Sarah remembered it was so long to give the staff time to catch a running patient. She didn't like that memory.

"So, Sarah, you said you are hearing no voices anymore," Alpaca resumed. "Do you have any fear they might come back?"

Nate shot her an angry frown.

Alpaca caught it. "Just making sure."

Sarah found her voice. "To be honest, the first couple of weeks, yeah, I was afraid they would come back. But I've gotten used to being the only occupant in my head, and I really like it."

"That's wonderful. Let's give the meds another month and then we can talk about weaning you off. I know how tempting it must be to stop taking them now that you feel better. Nate, I need you to be my eyes on the ground."

"No problem."

They stepped up to the nurses' station, but Alpaca spotted Judy down a side hall. "Judy? Look who stopped by for a visit."

The stout dark-skinned woman looked up from her cleaning cart and her face lit up at seeing Sarah. "Ah, Mariposa!" she exclaimed as she hustled over to envelop the girl in a bear hug. She held Sarah back by her shoulders and smiled. "Let me look at you. Are you really all better?"

"Yes, Judy. I'm completely recovered."

"Praise be!"

"Sarah came today to see you, in fact," Dr. Alpaca said.

"Oh, how nice."

"Yes, I wanted to ask you about the necklace you gave me." Sarah lifted it out of her shirt and held up the pendant. "Do you remember this?"

"Yes, of course. That was one of my blessings."

"One of them. Were there others?"

She looked at the doctor a little apprehensively. "I sometimes try to help the patients with little offerings, or gifts, or doing them favors. I was the first one to see you are two-spirit. Do you remember me saying you should grow out your hair?"

"That's right, I do remember that." Sarah turned to Dr. Alpaca. "You worked with me on my transition, but Judy encouraged me first. I'd forgotten." Turning back to the orderly, she said, "Thank you. About the necklace, you said it's a blessing. Every time I've ever seen you, you are wearing that gold cross. Does this necklace have something to do with Jesus?"

"Of course it does. And look at the miracle Jesus gave you!"

Nate jumped in. "You meant for it to help her?"

"It's for protection." She turned back to Sarah. "From the voices. Now the voices are gone."

"How long ago did you give it to me?"

"About two months ago. It was right after Easter."

"May I ask, where did you get it?"

"At the Easter bazaar, at my church. Alonzo the charm maker had a booth. I've bought charms from him before. He told me it could help you to see things clearly. I thought, that's what Sarah needs, to see those dang screaming shadows aren't real." Judy nodded to Dr. Alpaca. "I figured it couldn't do any harm. It's just a trinket. And maybe it might help. Looks like it did."

"Does that mean you put it around Sarah's neck without telling her what you were doing?" the doctor asked.

She averted her gaze. "Well ... um, yes ma'am. I told her it was for protection. Am I in trouble?"

"No, not really. You shouldn't bring your folk magic into the workplace. I appreciate your thoughtfulness, but I'm here to treat my patients. Is that clear?"

Not looking up, she said, "Yes, ma'am."

"To be even more clear, Sarah's recovery was due to years of drugs and therapy. I don't want you thinking the necklace cured her, and then go off and put more necklaces on other patients."

"I understand."

Nate jumped in. "We are still curious about the necklace. You said a fellow named Alonzo sold it to you?"

"Yes, he always comes to our bazaars. I expect to see him again next Easter."

"Do you know how I might reach him before then?"

"No, I don't."

"What about your pastor?" Sarah asked.

"I'm confused," she said holding up her hands. "Did the necklace help or is it just a necklace?"

"A gemologist told us the stone might be something rare," Nate explained. "We're here because he said he would like to know where the stone came from."

"Oh, okay. Alonzo talks about his home in the hills of West Virginia, if that helps."

"That's a start. Maybe I could talk to your pastor and get Alonzo's number. Where is your church?"

"It's the Sunrise Pentecostal Church on Southland Avenue. You should ask for Reverend Michael Smooly."

Sarah stepped up and gave her hands a squeeze. "Thank you, Judy. I know you've always looked out for me."

She lit up and clasped Sarah's hands as well. "Jesus has smiled on you, sweetie. I will thank the Lord every day for his gift to you."

•   •   •

Sarah tidied up after dinner in the kitchen while Nate worked on his computer at the desk in the living room.

"Judy turns out to be kind of deep waters, huh?" she asked.

"How do you mean?" he said not looking up.

"She is Native American, goes to a fundamentalist church, uses charms from some hillbilly magician, and believes Jesus is responsible for every good thing. Those don't add up."

He looked up. "Sure they do. Lots of fundamentalist Christians believe in faith healers and talismans. Have you ever heard of Holy Rollers? They go into religious ecstasy and start jerking around uncontrollably. Some churches use snakes. They do it to let Jesus' spirit in. Folk magic is easily incorporated. The fact that she has Indian ancestry is interesting, but irrelevant. Charismatic preachers convert anyone who wants to listen."

"You sound like you know about this."

"I had a professor who was fascinated by the psychology of charismatic leaders. We did a whole section on fundamentalist preachers."

"It was interesting watching Dr. Alpaca try to talk Judy out of the magic. That whole line about years of drugs and therapy. Which struck me as more accurate than she realized. I think of this necklace as a drug."

At that, Nate sat up and looked straight at her. "Really?"

"Yeah. If this radiation cured my schizophrenia, then the visions are side effects. And like a drug side effect, I'm learning to live with it so I can keep the cure." She noted Nate took a few seconds to digest that. "Make sense?"

"Sure. I had been thinking about it the other way around. The stone gave you the visions and the visions woke you out of the psychosis."

"Oh, you see, with this happening to me, seeing it from the inside, I'm focused on finally seeing who I am, seeing how I fit into the world for the first time. The visions are just something I have to deal with on the side. I'm finally getting to know Sarah. And Judy Cloudfeather was part of that. When she first told me I was a girl, years ago, and told my doctors I needed to be moved into the girl's wing and start living as a girl, that was the first crack in the walls that held me prisoner. In fact, I'm thinking I need to move along with my transition.

"You mean surgery? We started you on estrogen a year ago."

"I don't know what comes next. I'll have to talk to somebody, maybe Dr. Alpaca."

Nate got up and came over to her. "That's wonderful. I'm sorry I missed that, with everything that's been going on. I'm so happy you've gained a hold on who you are."

"Well, I wouldn't say how solid that hold is. I'm kind of hanging on by my fingernails. But yeah, it feels pretty good."

He looked her square in the eye. "That's awesome."

She was a bit uncomfortable with the sudden attention. "What were you working on so intently?"

"Oh, meteorite strikes. Come, take a look." He spun the laptop around to show her. "It looks like twenty years ago, a fairly large meteor struck the atmosphere and broke up over the United States, with two pieces big enough to survive landfall and to recover them."

She traced the lines and markings on the map. "Arizona and West Virginia. Well, that sounds like our guy." She paged through the research Nate had open and shook her head. "I had no idea so many hit the Earth. This shows landings every few years, all over the place. What about Florida man?"

"Let's see. Florida has had impacts every couple of years going all the way back."

"What about twenty years ago?"

"No, at least none that were reported. There was a rock that was recovered eight years ago. Your theory is Florida got a piece of the other god. That would have come here in a separate fall than the fragments you and Roxie found."

Sarah pointed at the screen. "Hold on. Click on that path from eight years ago. Look, it broke into two pieces also, and the other piece fell in Kansas."

Nate leaned back in his chair. "I may need to go check that out."

•　　　•　　　•

Cecilia Bledsoe spotted something green flapping in the gutter as she crossed the rain-slick street.

"Leave it! It's filthy!"

"Ooh, check it out, it could be money!"

"I'm just going to keep walking, and, if I see something good, maybe I'll stop and look closer," she tried to negotiate.

A young couple on the sidewalk she approached did a double take at her talking out loud to no one, and then walked on.

"Yeah, yeah," she muttered to herself. "Crazy old black woman. Nothing to see. Move along."

She stepped up onto the curb while purposefully looking straight ahead. She waited to hear if her angry voice would yell at her, and it didn't. She quickly reached down and snatched up the ten-dollar bill from the dirty rainwater.

"I told you it was gross! You're going to catch a disease! And homeless people like you die from the slightest little thing, you know that!"

She stood there and weathered the tirade, trying to keep her breath from racing away in fright. After a minute, the voice gave up. She looked down at the bill. This could feed her well for two days. Her stomach grumbled at the possibility.

"What if that money could make a bigger difference in your life than just a full stomach?" tempted her sweet voice.

"Like what?"

"Don't listen to her! She's always dreaming and scheming and she would starve you given half a chance!"

Cecilia set her back teeth and waited on her other voice.

"I know where there's magic. Real magic, that can change your life for the better."

"Magic is bullshit! That's why it's called magic, 'cause it isn't real!"

Cecilia sighed. "I'm afraid I'm gonna have to agree with him on that one."

"You'll find money again. The hipsters down at Starbucks are always good for change. You haven't starved yet. Don't you want to improve your life?"

"Of course I do. What damn fool thing do you want me to do with this prize?"

"Don't you trust me?"

"I don't trust either one of you. I may be crazy but I'm not stupid."

"May I at least make my suggestion?" the sweet voice asked.

"This is gonna be worse than jumping into the river last summer!"

Cecilia saw this was going nowhere if she didn't at least listen. "All right. What?"

"You see Grover's Smoke Shop down the street?"

"You mean the head shop? Ha! You want to get her stoned? That'll help. Not!"

Again she waited for the sweet voice to take the floor back.

"They sell jewelry."

"Yes, they do. I know the manager there, Todd. He's a nice man."

"Todd's a child molester."

Cecilia swallowed. "What about their jewelry?"

"They got a special talisman in the case. You saw it yesterday, but you didn't see what I saw. It's actual magic. You need to go ask about it."

"We saw it yesterday?"

"Yeah, I saw it too. Hunk of junk. Go get a burger!"

Cecilia started walking down the street.

"Where the fuck are you going?" demanded the angry voice.

"I don't remember seeing it. What is it again?"

"A necklace. Made from a magical star straight out of heaven."

"Bullshit!"

Cecilia gritted her teeth and opened the door.

"Ah, CeCe! How are you today?" The short, broad man with a goatee and long blond hair seemed genuinely glad to see her, which was unusual enough that she hesitated.

"Hi, Todd. Okay, I guess. I heard you have a new necklace in the case."

"Yeah, the vendor came in with some new pieces yesterday. I think I saw you looking in the window when he had everything spread out in here. Did you see something that caught your eye?"

"You need to leave immediately!" the angry voice berated her. "This guy is going to kidnap and kill you in the back!"

She had to take a breath and hold her face in her hands under the barrage.

"Are you all right?" Todd asked.

"Yes. I'm sorry. Sometimes I just need to take a moment to collect my thoughts."

"Yeah, I see you fighting with the voices. I know it's rough."

"How does he know?" the angry voice screamed. "He doesn't know shit!"

A tear welled up in her eye. "I'm sorry. I think I need to go."

"No, no, wait," pleaded her sweet voice. "Don't let him win. You're already here. I'll tell you a secret. You have to promise not to tell him."

"Okay, I promise."

Todd looked confused.

"The necklace will make him go away."

"What did she say?" demanded the angry voice. "What did she say!?"

Cecilia stepped into the store. She noticed Todd pushed the door open and left it there while she was inside. She knew it was because of her smell. She quickly looked in the case.

"It's that green stone there in front," came her sweet voice.

Cecilia looked back at Todd. "How much for the green necklace?"

"Ten dollars."

•   •   •

The raised arch façade of the Sunrise Pentecostal Church reminded Nate of a sporting goods chain store he couldn't recall. He thought this was a good repurpose for a building with a lot of open footage. He flashed back to how Roxie had turned a post office into her church. It was dusk and the sign on the front wall did not say they held evening services, so he was glad to find the door open.

He expected to step onto the previous open sales floor, but found himself in a vestibule lobby. Ahead double doors led into the church, to the left were bathrooms, and to the right was a hallway with offices.

He started down the hall, looking for Reverend Smooly, when he heard a familiar voice coming up a stairwell. He couldn't place it at first, so he stopped and listened. It was Judy Cloudfeather, having a rather heated exchange with an older man who had a peculiar drawl.

"She was completely cured," Judy insisted. "I've never seen one react so well."

"But she was asking about the necklace. They aren't supposed to question the charm."

"She's not stupid."

"But you are. You told her where you got it. You gave her Alonzo's name and where he lives. And you believed that cock-and-bull story about some gemologist."

"What was I supposed to say? I was shocked and amazed and joyful, and I couldn't hide that. Maybe I shouldn't have said anything."

"That's right. We are doing God's work, casting out demons. You never know when some dark spirit is listening to you. Discretion is paramount."

"Aren't we supposed to spread the Good News?" she ventured.

"Yes, when we testify! Did you tell her to come testify?"

"I told her to come talk to Reverend Smooly if she wanted to know more about the charm."

Nate didn't care about their demon casting, but he did need to know more about this charm that his sister now wore constantly. He walked down the stairs and rounded the corner to face them. The downstairs was storage rooms off a corridor, still looking like inventory space from the sporting goods days.

"Sarah won't be testifying."

The man wasn't tall, but his shock of long gray hair and his square shoulders gave him an air of authority. As did his forceful voice.

"Who the hell are you?"

Judy recognized Nate, but did not speak up.

"I'm Sarah's brother, Nate. Who are you?"

"Harold Fraily," he said coldly. "How much of our conversation did you hear?"

"Enough to confirm what I already knew. Your necklace has indeed cured my sister when nothing else could. For that I am very thankful. I am also obviously curious to know more about it. If you've found a cure for schizophrenia, shouldn't you share it with the world? What better way to 'testify' about your cure?"

"That's not how it works. Every charm is different, every poor victim is different, every exorcism is different." Fraily squinted ever so slightly each time he emphasized a word, making the bags under his eyes quiver. "When a spell works, we testify to praise Jesus for saving a soul. The power comes from Him, not from some rock."

Nate recognized the pattern Harold used of raising and lowering his voice for emphasis — very much the charismatic. "That means you've been putting these charms on patients at the center for a while." He pointed at Judy. "You said Sarah had the best reaction you've seen. Have other patients improved?"

"Are you some kind of psychologist?" Harold fired back.

"Yes, actually. Post grad. Even if this is Jesus curing people, you're on to something huge. You could really narrow things down if you tested it right."

"You want us to use your Scientific Method," he scoffed. "Set up double-blind testing. Oh, yeah, I know all about your methods. All they do is give drug companies a way to make money off people's suffering. We'll stick with the ways we know work from generations of tried-and-true experience."

"If you're so sure of your methods, why do you want Sarah to come testify?"

Judy couldn't contain herself and spoke up. "When Jesus drives out demons, the cured often are left with healing powers. Some of our greatest healers were originally possessed."

Nate shook his head. "Sarah doesn't have healing powers. We've had a couple of ugly experiences recently and we would have seen it if she could heal anyone. All that aside, I still need to know where the stone came from. You talked about an artist named Alonzo, from West Virginia. Do you have his number?"

"Maybe you weren't listening. Each charm is unique, and each is charged with different prayers. It's not the rock."

Nate studied his face for any crack in his resistance and found none. "So, no number for Alonzo?"

"No. Are you going to bring Sarah here to see if she can heal?"

"No."

"Then we've got nothing else to talk about," the old man said flatly.

Nate let that hang for a moment, looked from Harold to Judy, then turned and walked up the stairs.

5

"CLOSE MY EYES FOREVER"
LITA FORD & OZZY OSBORNE

I F NOT FOR THE GRAY coming in at the temples of his wavy black hair, Nate would have thought Matthew Franco to be too young and too fit to be a college Astronomy professor. His blue polo shirt and khakis didn't fit with Nate's tweedy assumption either. More Italian athlete than stodgy stargazer.

As Nate walked into the lecture hall, he took note there were only about a hundred seats. Apparently Washburn University had smaller class sizes than he was used to at UMSL.

"Professor Franco, I'm Nate Meyer. We traded emails about your meteorite."

Franco shook his outstretched hand. "Nice to meet you in person. I applaud your research. We don't publicize it, yet you seem to know quite a bit about it."

"I'm a Psych grad student, so I know my way around scientific journals."

"I am still a bit unclear on your interest in our find. You said you were interested in achondric meteorites, especially ones with unusual internal structures."

"That's right, and mildly radioactive. I am chasing down a hunch about their origins. You said yours meets all those rare criteria."

"Not that I don't appreciate cross-disciplinary study, but, if I might ask, why would a Psychologist be working on planetary formation theory?"

Nate hadn't expected to get down to this so quickly, but he did have an explanation ready. "I have met some people who say their mental illness was cured by folk magic charms."

Professor Franco took an involuntary step back at the mention of mental illness.

"I know, I know, rather tabloid. I've seen two of the charms, and they both had dramatic effects on the wearer's mind. I checked one of these charms and it had a unique radiation pattern. They don't look like typical meteorites. They look like metamorphic fused minerals, with no chondric particles or crystal splinters. I did my homework. Yet they appear to be recovered meteorites."

Franco walked around behind the table at the front of the classroom while looking thoughtfully at the ground.

He sat down on the high stool and met Nate's gaze. "So, you want to see if our rock matches the ones in the charms."

"Yes. Those have been carved and polished. I'm hoping to see one in its original state."

"Do you think these charms actually affected their mental health?"

"I don't know. There are too many variables in the samples I've seen, with rituals and beliefs tied up with any physical effects. I'm trying to sort out the science."

"Do you have a theory for how radiation could affect mental function?"

"I do. I still need to run this by my Advisor. This kind of mental illness stems from the metabolism of a neurotransmitter called dopamine, both its production and its absorption. Too much or too little can lead to visions and voices. It comes from poor regulation of a set of brain centers that make up what we call the Default Mode

Network, which contributes to our imagination. Schizophrenics can't shut down the DMN when they need to concentrate on external tasks, and so the imagination creeps into their perception of reality. All this radiation needs to do is coax the brain into changing how it uses dopamine."

"Do you have a mechanism in mind?"

"I admit it's a guess that will have to be tested. So far, we can only see the macro effects. We are finally starting to sort out the subtler, deeper rhythms of brain activity, and somewhere behind the big, easily measured electrical activity, there are the patterns of how the brain regulates itself. We have seen that drugs, religious ecstasy, and mediation can change those rhythms, change the way different systems in the brain interplay. Our sense of self, our consciousness, our perception of what is part of us versus what is outside of ourselves, are all products of this dynamic balance.

"There is a treatment that has had some success in dampening schizophrenic hallucinations called Transcranial Magnetic Stimulation. It exposes the brain to oscillating magnetic fields over repeated exposures.

"If this radiation does what TMS does, and alters one of these deep rhythms, increases or decreases some brain function, even one not related to thinking, and even only by a tiny amount, it could rebalance the whole construct."

"If I might comment as a fellow scientist. You're throwing a lot of partial explanations together, trying to get to your conclusion."

"If the change includes how the brain uses dopamine, it could tighten or loosen control of that Default Mode Network, and introduce or eliminate hallucinations, either making a person feel invaded, or possibly giving an unbalanced person clarity and sanity."

His explanation was making Franco look increasingly uncomfortable the more he talked. He decided to stop.

Franco blinked when he realized it was his turn. "I have to admit, this is exactly what I was hoping you would not say." He paused, took a breath, and looked around the room collecting his thoughts. "When we first got the meteorite, about eight years ago, a grad student who was working on it came down ill. We knew it emits a very low level of radiation, but his symptoms were not typical of radiation poisoning. Over the next few weeks, he started acting erratically, and then violently. He had horrible visions and he seemed to lose touch with reality. He was eventually diagnosed with schizophrenia. His parents sued the school."

"I didn't read anything about that in the press I saw."

"We settled to keep it out of the papers. We locked up the stone and haven't done much work on it since. I never heard of this interplay theory. No one mentioned it at the time."

"It's pretty new, and unproven. You said there was a lawsuit, so you probably can't talk about details. May I ask, did the student have a history of mental treatment before the incident?"

Franco blinked and stared. "Yes. That was a big piece of the school's defense, that he was mentally ill to start with. How did you know?"

"The people I have found who were affected by these charms all had histories of mental problems. The radiation does not seem to affect stable, mentally healthy people."

"You said these charms cured mental illness. This meteorite drove our student to insanity."

Nate considered how much he should share. "Actually, half the time it cures people, and half the time it pushes them over the edge." Nate paused in the middle of his explanation, struck with a thought. He had assumed there were two meteorite materials because of Sarah's two god explanation. What if there was one material and it affected different people differently? "Does your stone emit radiation in an odd pattern?"

The professor looked surprised again. "Yes. It pulses, very slowly. Do the charms also do that?"

"I only tested one of the charms, but yes. Wait a minute. You said very slowly. Can you describe that more precisely?"

"The intensity of radiation grows and diminishes sinusoidally over a one second cycle."

"So, no short burst spikes?"

"No. Did the charm emit with a different pattern?"

"Yes." Nate frowned. "So it might not be the same meteorite after all."

"Hold on. You're saying there are TWO meteorites, one that cures mental illness and one that drives people mad? Either one would be absolutely unique. For there to be two is preposterous."

"Unless they share one origin. What if there was a collision between two similar but opposing masses? They shattered and bits of both fell to Earth."

"Did yours and mine arrive at the same time?"

"No. The charm one I've seen arrived twenty years ago. Yours was eight."

"That's actually not a problem. In a collision, pieces would be thrown into different orbital arcs around the sun, and could arrive on Earth years apart. The whole notion is still pretty far-fetched."

"What if I told you the charm doesn't really cure, and your stone didn't really drive that student mad, but the stones give people two different kinds of visions? One vision is of peace and tolerance, while the other vision is of violence and hate. The peaceful vision centers unstable people and they end up more 'sane,'" he emphasized with finger quotes. "The violent vision drives its victims to lash out and appear unhinged from the world. Isn't that how you described that student?"

"That's true. He did have dark visions, and he became obsessed with them. They changed his personality completely."

"That part, the crazy visions, that's what I need to understand. Even the cured ones aren't actually cured; they're just focused on something constructive. They're still possessed by these visions."

Professor Franco shook his head. "This is not going to sound very scientific. What horrific twist of fate had these two vision-inducing materials collide, shatter, and fall to Earth where poor mentally ill humans would find them and be overcome? This is like some science fiction space virus. This is the stuff of nightmares."

"May I see your meteorite?"

Franco blinked rapidly. "Ah, no. We locked it away after the lawsuit."

"No one has been able to study it at all? Not even you?"

"Well, there was a waiver."

"A waiver? You mean a legal waiver?"

"When we realized I would have to handle it, even just to seal it in lead, our lawyers made me agree to accept the risk, that I wouldn't sue if it drove me mad."

"I would be willing to sign that if it meant I could see it. If I'm right, this radiation could be a key to unlocking all kinds of mental illness. Besides, I have no history, so I should be safe. And the charm I handled didn't give me the vision that it gave the schizophrenia patient who owns it."

He rolled his eyes. "This is way above my pay grade." He reached for the phone next to the lectern. "Let me ask my boss. She's the Chair of the Physics and Astronomy Department." He dialed, listened and hung up. Then he dialed again. "Hey, Judy, this is Matt Franco. Is Professor Camarda in? Her number goes straight to voicemail. Okay, sure, I'll hold.

"Hi, Karen? I need your help on the meteorite lawsuit. Yeah, agreed. Look, I've got a Psych grad student here who has an intriguing theory about why it influences people. Yeah, I was skeptical too. He wants to see it, but we have that legal prohibition from the settlement. Can I have him sign the same waiver I signed? Uh huh. All right. Really? Okay, hang on a minute."

He stepped to his open laptop on the other side of the lectern and started typing.

"All right," he continued into the phone he cradled with his neck. "I'm in the legal archive. Oh, sure. All right. Hey, look at that. Yeah, I've got it. Sure. Thank you very much."

He looked up at Nate. "I sent it to print in my office. Come with me." While they walked, he explained further. "Professor Camarda says the original lawsuit gave us the legal help to improve our general research liability waiver."

"You said you locked it away in lead. That means you decided it was radiation that gave that student visions. Did anyone check it for chemical toxins?"

"Yes, our Chemistry Department did a thorough analysis and found nothing."

"Did they find organic material?"

Franco stopped walking and turned to face Nate. "You know more about this than you're telling me."

He held up his hands. "Just theory. I don't know anything for sure. My thought was for it be so interactive with the human psyche, there might be an organic component. I take it there is."

"Lipids. The only extraterrestrial lipids ever found. Our chemists excused it away as heavy chain hydrocarbons, but our biologists were never happy with that explanation."

"So, you've had a lot of scientists examine it."

"Absolutely. Especially once we had a student injured."

"I haven't seen any papers published about it."

"No one's been able to prove anything. You're the first with a hypothesis about how it interacts with the mind." He interrupted himself. "Hold on. A report was posted out of a Harvard lab — it wasn't peer reviewed — but they said they found an actual protein in an asteroid."

"An entire protein? Not just amino acids?"

"That's what they said."

"Do you remember where they found that meteorite?"

"Yeah, Algeria, in 1990, I think. You're wondering if that might be another one that affects people with mental illness?"

"I actually hope not. The fewer of these the better. I mean, how many meteorites hit the Earth each year?"

"Ah, tens of thousands, actually. Granted, most of them are under a hundred grams. Most of them hit around the equator and are lost. The ones dragged down by gravity to the poles are easier to find. A lot are recovered from Antarctica. And the larger ones, like ours, are thankfully less frequent. But we still get one every few years."

"With organic molecules?"

"No, those are indeed rare." Franco stopped them in the hallway. "Your theory isn't just about radiation and brain chemistry, is it? You think there were organisms involved."

Again, Nate had to choose his words carefully lest he scare off this audience. "I strongly suspect there were organic molecules involved at some point, just because the impact is so pronounced and specific. I mean, how can this radiation affect people with a specific affliction, and in such a predictable fashion, if it isn't derived from something organic?"

Franco frowned at him and blinked. He then turned to the next door, opened it, grabbed a sheet off the printer and handed it to Nate.

"Got a pen?"

•   •   •

The heavy fireproof metal filing cabinet looked much like the half dozen others in the storage room — except for the radiation hazard sticker. Professor Franco unlocked it, pulled out the bottom drawer, and indicated one end of a large metal box inside. "If you could grab the handle on that end?"

"Sure," Nate said stepping around for a better angle.

"It's about 80 pounds because of the lead shielding. Let's put it up on that table."

They hefted it out of the drawer, then up onto a solid wooden table. Franco unlocked the box and pulled off the solid metal lid. The stone was about the size and shape of a loaf of French bread, lumpy, melted, and dark grey as expected.

"It's quite dense. It weighs about 35 pounds." He took a step back.

"May I take it out?"

He took another step back. "Sure."

Nate got a good grip and set it on the table. One end had been cut off, clearly for samples, exposing the familiar finely mottled green stone interior. "Interesting. The stone inside looks the same as the charms."

"Have you had any chemical analysis done on the charm?"

"No, the owner doesn't want to alter it in any way for fear that its positive effects might be changed."

Franco blinked as he processed that. "You said the owner was mentally ill before the charm."

Nate continued to examine the stone while he talked. "Oh yes. Floridly schizophrenic in full-time care for the last nine years."

"And a necklace cured that?"

He looked up and raised his eyebrows. "Seemingly. Now you can see why I'm determined to get to the bottom of this." He gripped the stone and frowned at it. "Normally I have a hair-trigger temper. If my two-meteorite theory is right, this should be the one that fills people with murderous angry visions. I'm feeling nothing."

"But you said your theory is it only affects people whose brains are out of balance."

"True. Good thing my brain is healthy." He startled, but couldn't tell at what. "Whoa, did you feel that?"

"I didn't feel anything," Franco said.

"It's like the ground moved under my feet. That was ... kind of disconcerting."

"You're still touching the stone."

Nate took a breath and wavered whether to take his hand off or not. The sensation frightened him, but his curiosity demanded that he not lift his hand. He spread his feet shoulder width to steady himself in case it happened again. They both waited a long tense moment. Thinking it might help him sense some minor effect, Nate tried closing his eyes.

He felt the ground vanish from beneath his feet as if he were floating in the air. He popped his eyes open and was relieved, but not surprised, to see and feel the concrete floor solidly under his feet. He ignored the professor and focused on what he was feeling. He closed his eyes again and again gravity ceased, leaving him feeling like he was floating. He caught a glimpse of movement, like a light had flashed across his closed eyelids. He opened them and found only the dull glare of the fluorescent tubes overhead, and one confused-looking astrophysicist.

"When I close my eyes, I get a sensation of floating, and I thought I just saw some movement. This is all very subjective and kind of hard to describe. Did you ever feel woozy when you handled it?"

"No, I never felt anything. Then again, I don't think I ever touched it with my bare hands."

"What about the person who found it and brought it here?"

"One of our scientists tracked it down when it fell. They wouldn't have touched it barehanded either, to preserve the stone."

Nate thought about how Sarah's necklace rested stone to skin. He realized these sensations he was feeling must be a glimmer of what she saw in her visions. She had talked about floating in space when she saw the monster gods. He closed his eyes again, but this time he got the clear sensation of movement forward, even though he could not focus on anything.

"It's pitch dark. No wait. I see faint pinpoints of light. Oh, hold on, they're all around me. My eyes are getting used to the dark. There are millions of them. I'm out in space. I feel like I'm moving, but I can't tell how fast. Wait. There's something up ahead. It looks like a mist. It's coming toward me, really slowly. No, it's just really far away. It looks like it's speeding up, but I guess that's just perspective as it gets closer. Oh man, it's a huge cloud. It's pressing down on me really fast. Shit, it's rocks! Thousands of rocks! One's coming straight at me!"

He jerked his eyes open and pulled his hand back while taking a staggering step to steady himself. "Damn, that was scary." He looked up at Franco. "It was a swarm of stones, some maybe big as a car, flying at me at high speed. I had to break it off."

"Were they coming at you, or were you falling into them?"

"I don't know. Does that matter?"

"If what you saw was an astronomic event, chances are you were the one moving. Meteors don't move in swarms. They exist in clouds. The clouds move around with planetary and solar gravity, but they don't rush through space like you're describing."

"Don't we get meteor showers?"

"Those are due to the Earth moving into a cloud. Most of the meteorites that reach Earth are fragments from collisions between large bodies in the Asteroid Belt. One large asteroid called Vesta lost about half its mass in a collision which sent millions of fragments into an orbit that intercepts Earth frequently. About half the meteorites that hit Earth are from Vesta. We also get broken off pieces of comets."

"So what is this rock trying to show me? That there's a swarm of thousands of these mind-altering stones out there, waiting for the Earth to slam into them? This one landed eight years ago, and the other one landed twenty years ago. Could these two be from the same cloud?"

"Sure. Like I said, collisions send bodies into different paths. It makes sense they took different times to find their way to Earth."

"What about the cloud itself? Could the Earth pass through the whole cloud?"

"If we knew the cloud had produced a meteor shower, that would mean the cloud's path around the sun intercepts the Earth. Space is enormous. Lots of things orbit right past one another and never collide."

"What if these fell because they were just on the edge of the cloud. How could we find out if there is a cloud of these things coming around to deposit more of them?"

"You could check orbits and timing. You have impacts at eight and twenty years ago."

Nate reeled at the thought. "Jesus, if enough of them fall, we're looking at a pandemic of mind-altering effects, with at least half of the victims becoming violently obsessed. That would be horrific. Is there any way to comb the solar system to find this cloud?"

Franco thought for a moment. "The radiation patterns. If you can get the charm stone here, I can record its radiation pattern. I have a friend who works at the NROA Very Large Array radio telescope in New Mexico. I can have him search near space for those two patterns."

6

"ENTER SANDMAN"
METALLICA

SARAH HAD A HARD TIME FALLING ASLEEP without Nate in the house. She was so used to having people around her at night in the hospital that the house felt too quiet. The constant badgering of her schizophrenic voices had created a background soundtrack in her life. Silence still did not sound right.

She also didn't trust her dreams to not take her someplace weird and frightening. Lately she would fall asleep and still think she was awake, but with disturbing changes. She could hear Nate trying to assure her:

"The brain incorporates outside stimuli into the fabric of your dreams to keep you from being awakened by every little noise."

His Psych degree was turning into a pain in the ass. Still, she wished he hadn't decided to stay the night in Topeka.

Once she finally fell asleep, it was easy to convince herself the tinkling sound of breaking glass was just part of a dream. But she didn't see what had broken. Had she really heard it? The thought woke her up. She looked around and was relieved to find her bedroom as she had left it. So what made that sound?

She made it to the door when it flung open and two men rushed her with open, grasping hands. She screamed and tried to jump out of the way, but they were too fast. One pinned her arms to her sides and the other pulled a bag over her head. She managed to yank a hand free and punched where she thought one man stood, only to miss and throw herself off balance. Someone grabbed up her wrists and handcuffed them behind her back. She tried to kick and suddenly felt her feet up off the ground. One of them held her legs tightly together as they lifted her up and out of the room. She screamed and yelled and writhed as hard as she could, but the men were too strong.

A moment later, she felt the chill night air and heard car doors opening. She yelled for help, "I'm being kidnapped!" hoping a neighbor would hear.

A pair of strong hands bound something over the bag around her mouth and muffled her. They rolled her into what she guessed was a car trunk, and she felt the air compress as the lid slammed shut. She bit at the bag and the gag and it didn't budge.

"Fuck fuck fuck!" she yelled into the fabric.

•   •   •

Nate had a miserable time falling asleep. At first he thought the hotel's pillows were lumpy, then the blanket was too warm, and the air conditioner was too noisy. He got up and drank a glass of water to reset. It didn't help. He usually had no problem falling asleep in hotel rooms. Was he feverish? Or anxious? The meteorite vision was disturbing, but not the kind of worry that should keep him up. By 1:00 am he was exhausted and finally fell away.

His phone rang and he snatched it up off the nightstand. Area code 636. That was St. Louis, but not Sarah's or their home number. The clock said 2:52. "Hello?"

"Is this Nathaniel Meyer?"

"Yes, who is this?"

"I am Detective Mark Johansson of the St. Louis Police. Your sister Sarah was kidnapped about three hours ago from your home. Where are you now, sir?"

"No! Shit! I'm in Topeka. I can be home in two hours. What the hell happened?"

"Our patrol responded to a neighbor's call about a commotion, but the perpetrators had already left the site when we arrived. We found a broken window and signs of a struggle. Have you not heard from the kidnappers?"

"No, I haven't heard anything until you called."

"Do you have any idea who might want to kidnap your sister?"

Nate reeled at the thought. Could this really be happening?

"Yes, actually I do. Sarah recently got caught up with some religious fanatics. God, gimme a second. Kidnapped?

"Yes, sir. Who are these people?"

"At the Sunrise Pentecostal church there in St. Louis. There's a preacher named Harold Fraily, and there's an orderly named Judy Cloudfeather. My sister just recovered from a mental illness, and they think she has some kind of healing powers. They wanted me to bring Sarah to them and I refused. That was day before yesterday."

"Can you describe them for me?"

"Sure. Um, wow. Fraily is about five six, gaunt, maybe one hundred-forty pounds, probably sixty-five, piercing blue eyes, big shock of gray hair. Cloudfeather is about five four, maybe one hundred-sixty pounds, Native American, long straight black hair. I've only ever seen her in a uniform."

"All right, Mr. Meyer, you said your sister had recently recovered from an illness. Was Ms. Cloudfeather treating her?"

"No, Judy is an orderly at the hospital Sarah was at. That's the Sandstone Rehabilitation Center. Sarah was released about two weeks ago."

"You said you spoke with Frially and Cloudfeather two days ago. Where was that?"

"At the Sunrise church. I went there to ask the pastor about another matter, and Fraily and Cloudfeather were there and confronted me."

"Oh, so Fraily isn't the pastor there?"

"No, he's a preacher of some kind, but I don't know his actual relation with that church. The pastor is Reverend Michael Smooly. I never saw him."

"Can you see my number on your phone?"

"Yes."

"Take note of it and call me right away if the kidnappers contact you."

Nate took up the note pad and pen on the nightstand. Someone had already written a phone number on the pad, an 812 number. He thought that was odd. He quickly jotted down Johansson's number.

"I will check out this church and these suspects you gave me. Can you be back here in St. Louis in the morning?"

"I can be there in two hours."

"There's no need. My evidence team is still working on your house. They'll be done around dawn. Go home in the morning and call me when you get there. If Fraily did kidnap her for the reason you said, then he probably won't harm her. I know it will be difficult, but try to get some sleep. We're going to have a long day tomorrow."

•　　　•　　　•

The sunrise was throwing long shadows across the parking lot of the Sunrise Pentecostal church. Detective Mark Johansson smirked at the coincidence and checked his watch: 6:32. Headlights in his rearview mirror refocused his thoughts. The car that pulled up next to his wasn't the priest he was waiting to meet, it was Nate Meyer. He rolled his eyes. At least he was easy to recognize. He liked how young people still looked like their driver's license pictures.

"Mr. Meyer," he said stepping around his car.

"Detective Johansson," Meyer greeted him with an outstretched hand which he shook. "You said you were going to meet with Reverend Smooly first thing. I hope you don't mind if I tag along."

"Do not ask any him any questions directly. You can take me aside if you need to, but he needs to only hear from me. Otherwise you can wait in the car."

"That's fair. What did you find at Fraily's house?"

"He's not home, and it looks like he packed. Same with Ms. Cloudfeather."

"So they did take her."

"That's my current theory."

Meyer's gaze shifted like he was struggling with something. Johansson waited. "You know, there's more to this I haven't told you. And I'm thinking you should know before questioning the preacher."

"I'm listening."

"You know how I mentioned Fraily thinks Sarah has healing powers. Well, I don't think she does, but there is a connection. Judy Cloudfeather gave Sarah a necklace, a healing charm, and it may have something to do with my sister recovering from her long bout of mental illness. It was frankly miraculous. The doctors didn't know what to make of it. When I confronted Fraily the other night, he confirmed what Cloudfeather had told Sarah, that she has been trying these necklaces out on mental patients for some time. They said Sarah had the best reaction of anyone so far."

Johansson quietly took a deep breath as he digested this news. Necklaces that healed mental illness? He knew about such charms, from very personal experience. He purposefully held his expressive bushy eyebrows still and did not let on.

"The charm was made by a jeweler named Alonzo who lives in West Virginia. This Alonzo guy sells his jewelry here at this church at fairs. I'm thinking there is a whole cult around these necklaces."

Johansson nodded. "You said last night that Fraily wanted your sister to come meet him."

"Yes, to testify about her being healed, and to see if she can also heal."

"Looks like they think they found someone who proves their folk magic works. That means we probably won't hear from them for ransom."

Meyer wrapped his arms around his chest and looked despondent.

"Still, that's good information. It gives me more to work with."

Another car pulled into the lot.

The detective glanced at his watch: 6:36. He met the man as he got out of his car.

"Reverend Smooly? I am Detective Mark Johansson from the St. Louis Police. Thank you for agreeing to meet with me so early this morning."

Smooly was six one, lean, probably 220, with a pampered looking fluff of graying blond hair.

"Yes, Detective. I understand you're in the middle of an active kidnapping." He gestured to Nate. "And this is?"

"This is Nathaniel Smith, a citizen ride along observer. Shall we go inside?"

"Of course," he began as they walked. "You said you want to know more about Harold Fraily. Is Harold a suspect?"

"Mr. Fraily is a Person of Interest at this point. I'm still gathering information. What is his relationship with your church?"

"He's a longtime member. Last year he sat on our Vestry — the parishioner advisory board. He's always been outspoken, but I've never known him to get in trouble with the law."

The priest unlocked the front door and led them in.

"Does your religious practice include the use of icons or talismans?"

Smooly stopped and turned around in the lobby. "That's kind of an odd question for a kidnapping investigation."

"I have my reasons for asking."

The blond priest frowned at him as if trying to read his face, which he held implacable. "I don't use them in my preaching, but I have seen some of our flock using them, particularly for healing. We have an aging congregation, and lots of folks have chronic diseases. I preach the transformative power of our Lord and Savior. Some folks want something they can take home to remind them."

Johansson looked over and was pleased to see Meyer was staying back and not interrupting. "I understand you sometimes hold a craft fair here, where jewelers sell their wares?"

"Yes, at Easter."

"Is there a jeweler named Alonzo who sells there?"

Smooly was looking more suspicious with each question. "Yes, he sometimes sells here."

"Do you know if Mr. Fraily and this Alonzo have any relationship? Are they in business together?"

"They seem to be friends. I don't know if they are in business. Is Alonzo tied up somehow in this kidnapping?"

"We don't know yet. What is Alonzo's full name?"

"Alonzo Giaminni, with two 'n's."

"Does he live in West Virginia?"

"No, he used to. He moved to Indiana a couple of years ago."

Smooly didn't see it, but the detective saw Nate react like he stepped on a tack.

"Can you please excuse me for just a moment, Reverend?" He walked Nate outside. "Why is Indiana important?"

He was blinking fast, like he was trying to figure out where to start. He fumbled in his pockets and handed over a page from a note pad. "When you woke me up this morning, the note pad next to my bed already had a number written on it. At first I thought maybe the maid had missed it from the last occupant. But it's an 812 number. That's Indiana. I was in Kansas. I know it's totally random, but it kind of freaked me out. I wondered if I wrote it during a nightmare or something."

Johansson cocked a thick eyebrow and looked from Meyer to the note and back again. "This is where you wrote down my number. The Indiana number is in different handwriting."

"Look, a bunch of freaky things have happened in the last couple of weeks. It would take me all night to walk you through them. Humor me, okay? When you look up this Alonzo guy, see if that number helps at all."

"It is a stretch. But I'm ready to chase down any lead at this point."

Meyer was breathing hard and looking pretty shaken.

"Tell you what. Let me look up this Giaminni in Indiana, and see if your number takes us anywhere. I'm going to wrap up questioning Smooly. How about you wait in your car?"

"Sure."

·   ·   ·

Someone untied the gag from around Sarah's head and pulled the bag off. Her hands were still tied to the chair arms. She glared at the skinny old man in a ski mask that stood before her. His long frizzy gray hair stuck out from under the knit cap. Three other men stood behind him, also in masks, all looking useless despite their considerable size.

"What the fuck do you want with me?"

The glare of the old man's bright blue eyes was intense, clearly trying to be intimidating.

Nice try, loser.

"You, my dear, have been given a gift from God. With it, you leapt out of the Devil's grasp and opened your eyes to the wonder of God's creation."

Oh great, a sing-song preacher who believes his own bullshit.

"With so much of God's love running through your veins, you no doubt have the gift of healing."

"I don't. One of your goons gunned down a friend of mine right in front of me and there wasn't a damn thing I could do about it."

The old man's overconfident delivery cracked for an instant. He looked to the other men, who shrugged. "We haven't killed anyone. We are doing God's work, spreading God's good news."

"That never stopped priests from raping children and killing innocent natives."

At that he raised hands and nodded. "We too share your loathing of organized religion. We believe in letting God directly into our lives, letting him work right through our hands. You are proof. The talisman Judy gave you cured your madness with God's grace."

"You know Judy?"

"Judy is one of my flock. I apologize for the rough handling. I wish we didn't have to abduct you like this. I asked your brother to bring you of your own free will. He said no, but our work is too important."

"If I show you that I can't heal your sick, will you let me go?"

"Yes. But if you can heal, then we will try to convince you to stay and join us. I have no hidden agenda."

Sarah sized up her options. She was surprised to notice they had not harmed her at all. Pretty gentle for a home invasion kidnapping. She also sized up the house. Shabby, older bungalow. Worn furniture, threadbare rug. Probably his house. Nitwit brought a kidnapped girl to his own house.

"Who's sick and with what?"

The old man clapped his hands. "Smart choice. Boys, untie her and bring her in."

One of the three large goons pulled out a knife and cut the zip ties while the other two held her arms still so she didn't bolt once freed. They led her into the next room where a man was tied up in a chair even more securely than she had been. He was also gagged and his legs were bound together.

"Brother Daniel here had a bad encounter with one of the healing charms. It drove him out of his mind, into violent outbursts."

"Does he complain of waking nightmares and dark visions."

"Why, yes."

"Did the charm come from the same batch as mine?"

The old man took too long to answer.

"That's a no. Did it come from Florida?"

"We're not sure where it came from originally. Yours was made by one of our own flock. This is his house. We thought Daniel's was the same, but clearly his was possessed by a demon and not by Christ."

Sarah looked at the guards holding her arms. "You can let go now."

When she stepped up to the man, he screamed against his gag and lurched against his bindings. His hair was slick with sweat like he had been fighting his bindings for some time. His anger grabbed her unexpectedly and her heart began to race. She stepped back, but it didn't help. She felt he was on fire and all she wanted to do was douse that flame. She started to walk from the room, but the guards blocked her way. She turned to look at the man, trying to see him objectively and not let her emotions, her Dreamer emotions, take over her actions.

She ignored the old man watching her intently. She had a bigger fish to fry. Very deliberately, she walked up to him and put her hand on his writhing shoulder. He froze and glared at her wild-eyed. She felt his anger try to seize her flesh like scalding water, but she held on. In a moment, she felt her hand, and his shoulder cool down. He stopped straining against his bonds and his expression took on more awareness. She put her other hand on his other shoulder and looked into his eyes. His breathing slowed, and she noticed hers also slowed from a ragged pace.

"Hallelujah!" the old man blurted out, surprising Sarah. "I knew you could do it! Praise Jesus!"

The three guards repeated in awe. "Praise Jesus."

The old man pulled off his gag. "Daniel, are you back? Do you feel like yourself again?"

He smiled and shook his head enthusiastically.

"Brother Harold, it's a miracle! I thought I was done for. You, girl. You are a miracle worker. Truly the touch of an angel."

Sarah decided she did not need to explain what just happened. There was no way these bible thumpers would believe an alien invasion via meteorite.

"Harold?"

He did not look happy that she knew his name.

"Daniel here was very lucky," she explained. "His affliction, from the wrong kind of charm, is in fact the only kind of healing I can do. The charm you gave me cured my schizophrenia, and it gave me the weird ability to cure the effects of the other kind of charm, the one that leads to more madness. Other than that, I can't even cure a head cold. Find out where you got Daniel's charm, and make sure you never use one from there again. It's poison for the mind. Where is it now?"

One of the guards spoke up. "I put it in the freezer."

"Wrap it up in multiple layers of tin foil, and never let it touch your skin. Then go bury it someplace deep where no one will ever find it." She turned back to Harold. "That was exhausting. It's what, three in the morning? While you figure out if and how you're going to release me, I need sleep."

"That's fair. You can sleep in the guest room off the hall."

As she turned to follow Harold out, she smiled at Daniel who was being freed by a guard. He nodded deeply.

•　　　•　　　•

Sarah woke with a start in the too soft bed that smelled of not enough fresh air. *Shit. Not just a nightmare.* She got up and tiptoed to the door, hoping to overhear her captive's plans. But the voices she heard were muffled and didn't sound right. She pushed the door open, peeked around the hallway, and found it empty. She followed the voices into the dark living room. The three guards were asleep on the couches with the TV playing. No sign of Harold. *Probably in another bedroom.*

She walked back through the kitchen until she found the yellow wall-mounted telephone with a long, tangled receiver cord. She picked up the receiver and suddenly realized she did not know her brother's phone number. She had never placed a call to him on her own from Sandstone. She didn't dare talk so long getting the number from directory assistance. *Dammit.* She did note the number on the base.

Escape. She walked slowly and silently to what she assumed was the front of the house, but she was wrong. She found the door into the garage. That could still work.

But the garage wasn't a garage, it was a hotel room. She stopped and blinked.

Hotel room? This must be a dream. Shit, not again.

There was someone asleep in one of the two beds. She walked in and saw it was her brother Nate. Should she wake him? How does that work? He's in Kansas asleep. She had no idea where she was, but in her dream she was right next to him. The notepad on the nightstand caught her eye. Oh, the phone number from the kitchen phone. She grabbed the pen and wrote it down. Would that make any difference? *This is just a dream, right?*

She turned to go back into the house when she caught her reflection in the bathroom mirror. It was dark in the room, but it looked like her hair was longer and redder. She stopped and gave it a better look through the bathroom door. *Kind of nice.*

She crept back into the house and felt overcome with sleepiness. She really was too tired to go wandering on some unknown streets in the middle of the night looking for help. She made it to the bed and fell fast into oblivion.

She was awakened by what she thought was a crashing sound. Sunlight poured in through the window. How late had she slept? More crashing was followed by yelling. She looked around the room for a place to hide if this violence came looking for her. The closet floor was piled with boxes, but she managed to squeeze in and close the door.

A man came into the bedroom and yelled her name. "Sarah Meyer! Are you in here? This is the Evanston Police!"

She pushed the door open and was very happy to see the blue uniform. "I'm here! You found me!"

"Yes, you're safe now." He talked as he escorted her out. "We apprehended your kidnappers and secured the house."

Sarah noticed she was still a little woozy from waking so suddenly. Then she had a chilling thought. *What if I'm still dreaming?*

A tall dark-haired man in a dark blue suit stepped up to her with an outstretched hand. "I am Detective Mark Johansson of the St. Louis Police Department."

"Are you the one who found me?"

"Yes. Your brother had a hunch that turned out to be remarkably accurate."

"Nate guessed where I was?"

"Here, let's get you out of this house and let the Evanston PD collect evidence."

"Did you catch Harold?"

"Do you mean Harold Fraily? No, he wasn't here when we arrived. We got four other men who were here. We found chairs with duct tape and zip ties in the living room, so we knew we had the right house." His thick eyebrows danced on his high forehead as he spoke. He spoke with confidence and had kind, blue-grey eyes that Sarah found assuring.

When they got to the cars outside, he stopped and shook his head. "Still, that's got to be the longest shot hunch I've ever taken. Real Dashiell Hammett stuff."

"You mean Nate's guess?"

"Yes. He found a phone number written on a pad in his hotel room that turned out to belong to Alonzo Giaminni, the jeweler who made your necklace, and who owns this house where you were being held."

Sarah's legs gave out and she clung to the side of the car.

"Are you all right?" he asked as he grabbed her under the arm.

Her head spun with the connections. *That's not possible. I must still be asleep.* She was glad for his firm grip, but still pulled herself up by the car door handle when she saw her reflection in the glass. Her hair was two inches longer and two shades redder than it was supposed to be. She stood there staring in disbelief. She reached up and touched it, bringing a lock around to look at it.

"Miss Meyer, do you need to sit down? Here, let me get the door for you."

He opened the car and she sat down, still looking at the end of her hair in a trance of doubt, confusion, and fear. She spent the entire ride back to St. Louis barely responding to the detective's questions, replaying the previous night in her head, over and over, especially the dream where she left Nate that phone number.

7

"DREAM WEAVER"

GARY WRIGHT

"Y OU DYED YOUR HAIR while you were being held captive?" Nate was only half joking as they walked to his car after spending the day answering the police's questions.

She turned to him and grabbed the edges of his jacket with both hands. "No. I dreamed that it was longer and redder, and when I woke up, it fucking was."

"What?"

"I also dreamed, in the same dream, that I wrote that phone number down in your hotel room while you slept."

"Oh, wait. The phone number? No. that's …"

"Do not say impossible. It fucking happened — possible or not."

"That would explain why you were so wound up all through the police questioning."

She finally let go of his jacket. "No shit."

He opened the car and they got in. He did not start the car. "You're saying you fell asleep in the kidnappers' house, and dreamed you had entered my hotel room?"

"Yes."

"And somehow the number you wrote down on that pad, in your dream, ended up on the real pad in my actual hotel room."

"Yes. It was the number I saw on their old-timey kitchen wall phone."

"And then your hair changed in reality to match what you saw in the dream."

"Yes."

"Has this ever happened before?"

"No. It feels like a schizophrenic split from reality, but it's totally real. I have no explanation. Worse, I can't get comfortable with any of it. I keep thinking it will all make more sense if I replay it a few more times. But it doesn't get any better. It's like I'm turning into the damn Dreamer god, cooking up shit for real."

Nate felt powerless. "I wish I could think of something to say that would make you feel better about this. Frankly, this is way over my head too. It's just so far outside of ..."

"It's terrifying. I can change reality with my dreams? Are you kidding? Can I ever fall asleep again knowing that might happen?"

"Wow. It's like *Forbidden Planet* all over again."

"What?"

"Sorry, never mind. Just me grasping for something familiar to make sense of it."

"Nate, there is no making sense of it. All your theories about the meteorite radiation affecting Dopamine production, all the guessing about how the stones replacing psychotic visions with visions of creatures that lived billions of years ago — all of it is bullshit. I'm doing things that are just not possible. How can a brain, in any forced chemistry, change the physical world like this?"

"I don't know. We can only assume the stone did something, unlocked some ability that we just can't grasp. You told the police Harold Fraily wanted you to cure one of their cult members. From the way you described it, without really saying what happened, I assume he had been exposed to another meteorite?"

"Yes, one of the Devourer cult. He was consumed by anger and I quieted that for him while he was taped to a chair. I hope he's cured."

"Being able to affect people's moods makes some sense. I mean *Chi*, or pheromones, or something biological, right? But altering reality?"

"Frankly, I'm more concerned about how to control it, to stop it, than to explain it."

"I'm thinking maybe this Dreamer power kicked in after treating one of the other side's victims. Maybe your dreams aren't world changing unless you have fired up the empathetic Dreamer powers."

"You're guessing."

"It is testable. If you do nothing with your abilities all day, then we can see if you change anything while you sleep that night."

"I wish I had more control over my dreams. For years I could barely remember my dreams at all, with all those drugs. And the ones I could recall where never about reality or about people I actually know in real life."

"You're still taking those same drugs."

"That may be true, but since I got out, I've been dreaming about things and places I am actually living. In that hotel room we stayed at in Arizona, I had a hard time believing I had woken up because I dreamed about that same room. And last night, I dreamed about being in that house and seeing that phone number."

"Before you dreamed about being in my hotel room."

"Yes. The problem is, if I'm dreaming about real-life things, and my dreams change something, I can't guide the dream, I'm just along for the ride. I could dream someone was dead, and then wake up to find they died. Wouldn't that make me a murderer?"

"Not legally. I don't know what to say. We can get you information about lucid dreaming. There are people who have figured out how to control what happens in their dreams. I can't do it, but they say it's very restful. If you felt you had a bit more of a handle, you might trust yourself to dream and not kill anybody."

"I took the necklace off."

"Okay. That's fair. We'll just monitor you closely. Maybe you only needed it to break free and now the meds will keep you there."

"That's what I'm hoping. It gives me powers I do not want."

"I understand how you feel. Even if I don't understand how the powers work."

"By the way, thanks for bringing me some day clothes. And my pills. I hadn't realized getting kidnapped in the middle of the night would mean walking around in public the whole next day in my pajamas."

She turned to him in the car seat as he backed them out of the parking space. "Something occurred to me while I was in there trying to get the cops to believe the crazy shit I was telling them. You've believed me all along."

"Of course. Wait, what do you mean?"

"Ever since I first saw the Dreamer in the stars in the parking lot that first night after I woke up, you've taken me seriously, that my visions, and my hunches about what they mean, are all facts to be considered, not the delusions of a recovering mental patient."

"Oh, I don't know. I think I've been challenging a lot of what you've said."

"Yes, but challenging them to be proven, not discounting them as ravings. I was in there worried that the cops were going to ignore my version of what happened as untrustworthy because of my mental history. You haven't done that."

"I realized from the start that everything you see is subjective. I take it all through that lens, that you're telling me what you see and how it all seems to you. Your version is all we have to work with. I have no reason to think you're lying or making things up or hiding anything. A lot of it has sounded pretty unrealistic at first, but strangely enough, everything you've said has checked out."

She smiled at him. "Well, thank you for not writing me off as crazy."

"There's a story about a man who parked his car outside a mental asylum fence to go run an errand. When he came back, someone had stolen one of his wheels. He goes to pull out his spare tire when he sees the thief also took the lug nuts. So he's standing there cursing and carrying on, and one of the patients in the yard comes over and asks him what's the matter. The man says, 'They took the lug nuts too! Who the hell takes the lug nuts? Now I can't put on the spare.'

The mental patient says, 'Why don't you take one lug nut off the other three tires and use them to put on the spare. Each wheel then has three nuts, which is enough to get you to a parts store to buy four more.'

The man is stunned at the patient's deduction. 'Why, that's brilliant,' he says. 'If you're so smart, why are you in a mental asylum?'

The patient raises an eyebrow and tells him, 'I'm crazy, not stupid.'"

•   •   •

"Oh look, you've got a package," Nate said as he bent over to pick up the small box from their front porch. "Ah, it's heavy."

Sarah looked at the label. "Jake Goldblatt?"

"From Arizona," Nate confirmed.

They stared at each other for a second as that sank in. She opened the door and he placed it on the dining room table. Goldblatt had wrapped the box with a lot of packing tape, so Nate grabbed a knife from the kitchen. Sarah's face read curious and scared at the same time as he sliced it open. He pulled out and read the letter on top.

Dear Sarah.

I hope this finds you well. I also hope this package isn't too big a shock for you. The police are going to step up their patrols, but cannot guarantee they will get here in time to intercept another shooter. Our whole farm agreed it is important that our stone not fall into the enemies' hands. Personally, I think you will be able to put it to much greater purpose than we are, just sitting on it in the desert. You were so polite when we spoke, I'm sure you would have just declined if I asked first. So I am sending it without your permission. I apologize if that's rude. I don't know if it has any power left after being silent for years. I hope you find it useful. Good health and good fortune to you and your brother.

Sincerely, Jake Goldblatt.

Sarah looked at the box full of wadded up newspaper. "You've got to be kidding."

"Let's take a look," Nate said reaching into the box.

"Oh, don't get that thing near me. I took the necklace off 'cause I don't want the power this stuff gives me. That's a whole fucking meteorite of it."

"Fair enough. You don't have to touch it."

"What about you?"

"Oh, no problem. I handled one of the devourer stones in Kansas and it had no effect on me. Well, no negative effect."

He pulled it out, unwrapped it, and set it down on the nest of paper. It was the size of a grapefruit, lumpy, but spherical, brown and black, with smooth melted patches over most of its surface.

"Yep, it's a meteorite."

"Great. Now I own one of an ancient god's balls."

He grinned, but did not comment. "I'll get it tested to verify it emits the same radiation pattern as your necklace. Oh, that reminds me, I need to talk to Professor Franco about his sky search."

"Why didn't Roxie tell us her dreams could change reality?"

Nate had to stop and think about that. "Probably because she couldn't do that."

"This stone didn't show her the Devourer either."

"Maybe this one is less potent than your necklace. It only showed her the Dreamer and nothing more."

"You know, you say 'maybe' a lot lately," she commented.

"For good reason."

"So, maybe," she quipped, "my necklace is from the Dreamer's brain, and this chunk is from his bladder."

"Well, god anatomy aside, if this one doesn't give the user reality-altering dreams, but it does still cure schizophrenia, then it could give you the balance you need. Remember, Roxie had a history of mental illness before she found this."

Her face slowly contorted into a sneer looking at it. "We're guessing in the dark, about things that defeat physics."

"You're not wrong. But we can learn if we stick to logic and scientific rigor. If we talk about every new finding, and share every new theory, I think we can use this to your advantage."

"I wish I shared your devotion to the Scientific Method."

•   •   •

Sarah combed her red hair in the bathroom mirror, holding it out with each stroke, examining the new length. She was impressed with her subconscious's hairstyling talent. It wasn't just longer, it was recut from little girl bangs and bob to side-swept long model bangs. Although she was still trying to cope with how her hair had gotten this way, it did make her feel a lot more feminine.

She looked at her baggy jeans and loose tee shirt. *Hmm.*

She took fifty dollars from Nate's dresser and walked to the shopping center four blocks from the house. She stood on the corner and was pleased with her choices. Walgreens and Dress Barn were a good start. She hoped she brought enough money.

Two hours later, she was back in front of the mirror assessing her handiwork. A couple of magazines opened on the toilet back had been her guide for the foundation, eyeliner, mascara, and lipstick. She was grateful Sandstone had started her on estrogen before she started growing a beard. She couldn't imagine the trouble of shaving and covering up five o'clock shadow with makeup every day. The old-lady support briefs were a passable substitute gaff to keep her penis tucked back where it belonged. She was very pleased with how the tight jeans fit. She had run out of money to get a better padded bra.

The front door opened and she heard Nate's usual noisy entrance with coat flopping and keys landing. Comforting sounds. She joined him in the dining room. He was setting the meteorite back on the table.

His face broke into a broad grin. "Very nice! That's gotta feel good."

She nodded shyly. "It really does."

"It looks great."

She was amused at how he fumbled to change the subject and not let his reaction get weird.

"So I got this tested, and it radiates with the exact same pattern as your necklace. And I've got a recording of it to send to Kansas."

"What exactly is this professor of yours going to do with it?"

"He has a friend who works at a radio telescope. He's going to search nearby space to see if these radiation patterns are present in the Earth's pathway. Remember I told you the Kansas meteorite showed me a vision of a cloud of these fragments. We want to make sure this cloud is nowhere near us."

"You mean like a shower of these things?"

"Yeah. Probably both kinds if your mutual kill model holds up. Try not to think too hard about the possibilities."

His words did nothing to stop her from thinking exactly about how bad that would be.

She took a deep breath and let it out slowly. "We could be facing a possible worldwide spread of the Devourer's violence."

He didn't respond.

"With the stakes that high, shouldn't I continue learning as much as I can about these gods?"

"Do you mean handling this stone? Have you had any weird dreams since you took off the necklace?"

"No, they stopped. You've been scouring the Internet for the last week and you've found nothing. It's like no one has ever heard of this."

"Actually, I did find a story in France that sounded like someone may have come across a similar meteorite. I kind of had to read between the lines to see the similarities."

"I am ready to assume you're right about Roxie not getting the magical dreams. If all this stone does is keep me sane and let me see the Dreamer, then I might learn something new that can help. Her vision was different than what I got from the necklace. I think it's worth the risk."

Nate raised his eyebrows and let his gaze drift around the table. "All right. It seems to have cured Roxie's mental illness, but it stopped giving her and her followers any visions four years ago. She locked it up, meaning no one had regular contact with it. Yet her schizophrenia did not come back. Nor did any of her followers relapse."

"So, once cured, then cured permanently?" Sarah ventured.

"Well, after sixteen years of contact, yeah. You've had the necklace off for what, six days? And you haven't had any magical dreams. Have you heard any voices or seen any shadows?"

"No, I'm still taking my meds. It's been a perfectly boring week. All I've done is get caught up on movie musicals. Oh, and I taught myself how to make French fries.

"There is something else," she continued. "I'm having a hard time getting used to quiet. I find I'm leaving the TV going all day, even when I'm not watching it, just to provide background noise."

"Were the voices constant?" he asked cautiously.

"Pretty much. Quiet feels somehow wrong. I thought you should know."

"We should get you a phone. If you're going out shopping, you should be able to call for help. And a phone will let you play music anytime you want it."

"Music?"

"There are streaming services that let you download songs off the Internet and build playlists. You didn't know that?"

"We only listened to the music the staff played through the speakers."

"That was probably through somebody's phone."

"Okay, great. I'd love a phone." She got up and went into the living room to sit down in the armchair. "Bring me the stone."

"You mean now?"

"Why wait?"

She situated herself cross-legged and reached up with take it with both hands. She felt nothing. She closed her eyes and saw nothing.

"It took the Kansas stone a minute before I felt anything. The first thing I felt was ..."

"Weightlessness," she gasped. "The room just fell away and I'm floating. It's gotten really dark, like actual pitch black. Oh wait, my eyes are adjusting. There are pinpoint stars of light getting brighter. They're brilliant against the black sky beyond. There's a sun just off to one side. It's far away, but I can feel its warmth. Let me turn and look around. Oh shit! There you are behind me. The Dreamer is huge and I'm really close. I feel how peaceful it is, like it's swept over me. It's thinking hard about something, but it's taking its time and staying completely calm. It's staring at one spot. Let me turn around to see it.

"Oh my god. There's a cloud of dust gathering. No wait, it's not dust, it's huge chunks of rock, there's millions of them and far away. Oh, the Dreamer is imagining them coming together. They're forming a ball, and it's getting big fast. Oh my, the sun is spinning around us like crazy. What am I seeing? The stars are too."

"You might be seeing the passage of time. It might have taken the Dreamer a long time to pull these rocks together."

"That makes sense. Oh, the ball of rock is heating up from all the collisions. It's melting. This is astounding!" Still pressing her eyes closed, she called out. "Nate, I wish you could see this. It's so violent and beautiful! The Dreamer is forming a planet."

"Is the Devourer there?" Nate asked.

"No, it's just the Dreamer and me floating in open space. I can feel its concentration. This is so focused and intentional. It's kind of overwhelming." She felt tears run out of her closed eyes. "The planet is so beautiful, I just can't stand it."

"So, you were right. It experimented forming planets," he said.

"I feel it is sad, disappointed somehow. Oh, it must not like the way the planet is coming together. I think it's gorgeous. The more it forms, the sadder the Dreamer is. Oh, how sad, it's decided this one isn't going to work out.

"I'm going to move closer."

"Are you sure that's safe? It has god-like powers."

"Yes, but I'm only seeing what it left for me to see now that it's dead. I'm right up to it now." She started breathing fast, and could only manage words between short tight breaths. "It's done this … many, many times … it's been eons … I can't even … tell how long … it's so sad … another one failed. Oh, I can't even. It's too much."

She let go of the stone in her lap and grasped her head with her hands. She was weeping uncontrollably. She opened her eyes to see Nate kneeling in front of her, consumed in worry.

"It's okay. I'm all right." She sniffed and wiped her tears with her hands. "My god, that was intense."

"That's some kind of powerful if just a piece of its dead body can deliver that kind of memory."

"It was so … intelligent. And loving. It loved that planet. It wanted so badly for it to survive. I can barely grasp all the emotions I felt. I wonder if childbirth is like that."

"Probably. This certainly supports your theory about trying to dream up the perfect planet."

"Right! That's what I felt! It was remembering all the other planets that had not worked out before. So much sadness, going back forever in time. Yet it still had so much hope for getting it right."

"It sounds like a tough formula to get right."

"Well, what fraction of planets can support life and thrive?"

"I've heard it's a really low percentage. They call it Goldilocks. Not too close to its star, and not too far away. Just the right amount of carbon, water, and iron. It's really rare. If that's how the Dreamer spent eons of time, it makes sense that getting it right would be worth stealing."

"And worth defending. I could feel how much it cared for its creation, even a failed one. Based on what we saw of Roxie letting Florida Man bite her, and how that destroyed him, it looks like the Dreamer laid the same trap."

"You're saying, after God created the Earth, he died defending it from the Devil."

"Yes, but it's not God. And it doesn't call itself the 'Dreamer.' I felt it thought of itself as a sound. It was a hum, like a vibration. It was Oohhuumm."

Nate squinted on this one. "Eastern mystics say the background vibration of the universe is the word 'Oum.' They chant it to get in tune with the world.

Sarah blinked. "I think that's its name. Oum."

Nate's computer in the dining room pinged. He got up to check his mail.

"Oh shit."

Sarah left the stone on the chair and followed him.

"It's Matthew Franco. His friend at the radio telescope found a cloud of debris that is emitting two patterns of radiation. One of them is a spike every half second; that's your necklace. And the other matches the one-second cycle of the Kansas stone."

"They found the shattered bodies? They're actually out in space? That's fantastic," she said.

"Not fantastic at all. The Earth will pass through the cloud in six weeks."

8

"CLOSER"

NINE INCH NAILS

SARAH LOOKED AT HER BROTHER'S SANDWICH as the waitress set it down, and wasn't sure what she was seeing. "Is that powdered sugar?"

"Yes," he said, smiling broadly as if proud of it. "It's called a Monte Cristo. It's a grilled ham and cheese, but it's dipped in eggs first, like French toast, and sprinkled with powdered sugar."

"And served with jam?"

"Yeah, it's terrific. I rarely find a place that serves them. You want a bite?"

"No, thanks. Looks like dessert, or breakfast, not lunch. I'll stick to this steak sandwich."

"That's a French dip. You dunk the sandwich in the au jus gravy there as you eat it."

Sarah was pondering the mechanics of their meals when she felt a nagging tug at her attention from behind her. She turned around in her booth seat and saw a man most of the way across the diner staring at her. She made eye contact and he did not turn away. She felt he was angrier than he looked, and he was angry with her.

"What's up?" Nate asked.

She turned back and tried to appear unaffected. "That guy back there is staring at me with some serious anger issues."

Nate scanned the patrons.

"Don't engage him. Just some random hater," she said.

"Oh, I see him. He is rather bold, isn't he? Just staring at you. He isn't even phased by my staring back at him."

"No idea what his trip is. I'm gonna ignore him."

"Well, I'll keep an eye on him in case he tries to pull some shit. What tipped you off? Did he say something to you earlier?"

"No, I've never seen him before. I just felt him being mad at me."

Nate thought about that for a moment. "Like when your Dreamer sense forces you to quell someone's anger?"

She hadn't seen that. "Yeah, I guess so."

"That guy is at least thirty feet from you, and he is not outwardly looking mad. That's quite a sensitivity you've developed. Are you wearing the necklace?"

"No, no, I don't wear it anymore. Those dreams are too dangerous."

"I thought you loved the new hair."

"Sure, the hair is great. But seriously, who knows what limits those dreams have. I could dream someone is dead, and then poof! No thanks. Why would some random dude go off on me like that?"

Nate sighed. "I've been careful to always be with you when you go out in public. I kind of freaked out when you went out on your own last week to get the makeup. The truth is, there are a lot of assholes who just have it in for trans people."

"But you said I pass."

"You do, you totally do. But these transphobes can spot a trans person out of a crowd. It's like they're always looking for you. It's uncanny. And they're dangerously invested in their obsession."

Sarah took note of his words. Nate didn't use terms like 'uncanny' and 'obsession' unless he was talking about his Psych degree. "I never saw that at Sandstone. The other girls and the staff were all down with it."

"That was a purposefully nurturing environment. The staff was there to be supportive. And your fellow patients might have been glad to see someone making a positive change. You were frankly lucky to have no transphobes in there."

"Is it really that common? Why would my actions make some stranger so mad? Is it religion?"

"Not entirely. People just have very narrow views of what's acceptable. It's like racism. Anything different is seen as a threat. They're usually a little easier to avoid. This guy is unfortunately an exception with his daring."

"A threat?" Sarah could feel herself getting more and more upset. "What a perv to see anything a sixteen-year-old girl does as attacking his sexuality. Is he afraid I'm going to make a pass at him and endanger his manliness?"

She saw Nate glance over her shoulder at the man. "Keep your voice down, please. You're right. It is fucked up, but it's the way of the world. That's why they call it a hate crime when someone attacks a gay or a trans person just for being gay or trans. There are extra penalties for those crimes, to try to rein in the hate. I'm really sorry we haven't talked about this before. I'm really sorry we need to talk about it at all."

Nate's explanations always gave her an odd combination of annoyance and comfort. Even when he came across as a know-it-all, he was her know-it-all. She took a breath and regained her calm. "At least my Dreamer senses can help me find these haters before they can do me harm."

•   •   •

Jackson Pruitt stood with the nine men he had gathered in the old meat locker under the main planation mansion. The large room smelled acridly of musty aluminum cooling coils, stagnant from long disuse. The men fidgeting quietly added to the whole depressing atmosphere of the place. Pruitt rubbed his balding pate, and was about to check his watch when Pierce Clayton walked in. Jackson made a mental note to try harder to put that name out of his head now that Pierce had adopted his new moniker. He had worked with Clayton for two years before he became Jefferson Davis last year.

"Colonel Davis, here are the names of the volunteers," he said, handing a clipboard to their leader.

Jefferson brushed it aside and sized up the three men who stood to one side, the ones wearing stone necklaces. "Okay, then you three, Tom, Dick, and Harry, you're going to do something a little crazy here today. Y'all were in the loony bin not too long ago, before I gave you those necklaces to bring your minds back. While you were inside, I bet one of the rules was no biting anybody. Am I right?"

The three looked confused, but nodded.

"Right. Well, today you are going to bite these fine gentlemen, first this group here, Manny, Moe, and Jack, then this three, Huey, Louie, and Dewey. Ol' Jackson here is gonna record your reactions," he said to the six victims. "I need you to be mensches today. The bites are gonna hurt some. Tough it out. Do not get upset. Do not get mad at Tom, Dick, and Harry for biting you. Brush it off like men. We've got first aid over here on the bench. Nobody's gonna get infected with any diseases." He turned back to the first three. "I need you to break the skin, that's all. No tearing out a chunk. Just sink your teeth in till you feel a puncture."

Dick raised his hand. "I heard the human mouth is full of bacteria and a human bite can get really messed up. Is that what you're testing today?"

"No, this has nothing to do with disease. Like I said, we've got that part under control. Naw, we're testing a side effect of your necklaces. Just like they cured your insanity, we think they also give you the ability to change people's minds if you bite them."

Harry spoke up. "I had a nightmare night before last about sharks biting everything in sight. Scared shit outta me."

"That's right!" Jefferson said pointing to him. "These necklaces gain their power from God, and God created predators, like sharks. The power they bring you is the primal power of the predator. Your bite has all kinds of power. That's what we're testing today."

He turned to the test subjects. "You men okay with all that? Your reactions will help us move ahead with our war on the Lookers. Your pain will be for a very high cause indeed."

"Ain't no big deal," Huey dismissed to his fellows. He pulled down his tee shirt collar to show them a scar made of two circular marks. "A hooker bit me once so hard I thought she was trying to rip out a mouthful. It hurt, but not as much as her face after I broke it."

Everyone laughed, except for Jackson. He made a notation: *'All six starting in good spirits.'*

He turned to Davis while pointing to a table full of leather straps and chains. "Sir, are we still going to need these?"

"Woo yeah! Okay you six, I have reason to believe these bites might make you kind of crazy at first. I need you to come over here and buckle these cuffs around your wrists."

The men obliged, but then noticed the cuffs were attached to long chains. The guy Davis had called Manny spoke up. "What are the chains for?"

Davis grabbed up the chain ends and locked them onto iron rings set into concrete pillars in the middle of the room, three men to a pillar.

The six chained up men stopped joking around when they realized their situation.

"Like I said, things might get a little crazy and we don't want anyone gettin' hurt."

Davis stepped back and Jackson lead the three biting men to their first victims, standing behind them lined up to bite them on the shoulder. There wasn't enough room for all three biters to fit around one pillar, so Dick picked a chained man in the other set.

Davis continued. "I know this looks rather barbaric, but these are the gifts God gave us. It's our job to figure out how to use them best in the upcoming war on our true enemies."

Jackson noticed the pep talk wasn't helping either group of men feel better about what was about to happen. Jackson put his hands on the nearest pair, one on each man's back to assure them. "All right. Make your bite, then pick a man on the other pillar. Levitt, your other man is on the other pillar, so walk over there when you're done here."

He heard the biters all quietly apologize to their victims, and then bite down. The victims sucked in tight breaths but then seemed to take it in stride. "Not so bad," a couple of them said.

Jackson watched them carefully.

"Please make every effort to remain calm," Jackson reminded them.

The three biting men all looked at each other and smiled. "That felt really good," one of them commented.

In the three seconds it took for Dick to walk to the other pillar to bite his second man, the three men who had been bitten all turned wild-eyed at Jackson and Davis. They started breathing heavily and clenching their fists. The two bitten men on one pillar turned on the one unbitten man and began punching and clawing at him. Dick stepped in to hold them off while Jackson fumbled with the key to unlock his chain to free him. The two enraged chained up men landed several punches on the unbitten man and on Jackson before the three could get away. The one bitten man on the other pillar also went berserk, but the two unbitten men in that set managed to restrain him. Jackson then unlocked them as well.

Jackson, Davis, and the three unbitten men stood back in shock at how savagely the three restrained men yanked on their chains and clawed at the air towards them, growling like wild animals. They did not attack one another, and they had not attacked Dick or the other biters, all who wore necklaces.

"You three wearing necklaces, did you feel something when you bit them?"

"Yeah, it was a rush," one said, and the others nodded.

"The blood tasted fantastic," another said.

Jackson instructed. "Step towards them and see if they are mad at you."

They exchanged glances, then cautiously did so. The angry men ignored them and focused their rage at Davis, Jackson and the unbitten man.

Davis turned to Jackson. "We'll need to wear necklaces to mark ourselves as friendlies."

Jackson did not hide his concern. "Three seconds is all it took to strip away their humanity and reduce them to seething animals. They couldn't save themselves. Is that what you expected? 'Cause that's not what we talked about."

"Watch them to see how long it takes for them to come down."

"Clearly," Jackson said, shaking his head.

"Think about it. When they go up against Lookers, and have to face down the trance hugging, we need soldiers who are 110% committed and ready to face anything. If they were any less fearsome, they might hesitate, and we both know all it takes is an instant of hesitation and those bastards will suck the fight right out of you. And if there's a gun in the mix, both end up dead almost every time."

Jackson rocked back and thought about that.

"We need fast and uncompromising. We need animals. Hell, we need monsters."

"I'll keep an eye on them."

Davis started to leave but then turned back. "We need to start breaking more mental patients out too. Our timeline just got cut in half. We've got six weeks to get ready. We need to put all the necklaces we've got into play as soon as we can."

"We've got another eleven necklaces. Six weeks?"

"Yeah, the fucking meteor storm will be here in six weeks. Those eleven necklaces will not be enough. We need them to bite a lot more soldiers to cover the field. We need to be ready to indoctrinate anyone who finds a Biter stone, and to kill anyone who finds a Looker one."

"So, we're not worried about the authorities ..."

"Fuck the police. By the time they figure out we're springing mental patients, the war will be upon us."

"I'll call our network. I hadn't picked candidates for all of them."

"Well, get to it. And be sure to set aside a couple for us," Davis said, pointing at the seething chained men.

9

"DREAMS"

FLEETWOOD MAC

LISETTE ANDREWS PULLED HER STRAIGHT, shoulder-length brown hair back into a ponytail and glanced at her watch. She had gotten the watch from the pawn shop to make sure she wasn't late to work. It wasn't helping. "CeCe, are you sure you've got Clark under control?" she yelled as she walked fast to the front door. "He was really fussy when he woke up. I couldn't get him to calm down. I'm sorry to just run out like this, but I cain't be late."

Cecilia Bledsoe stepped out of the kitchenette holding the three-year old boy in one arm, while holding up Lisette's purse in her other hand. "I know, they don't brook tardy at the Wendy's."

Lisette looked at her son calmly resting his head on the middle-aged black woman's shoulder. "I don't know how you do it. You've got the touch. Thank you so much. I won't be back until almost dark."

"That's fine. I'll keep busy today with Mr. Clark here and his little friend Tyson across the hall."

Lisette scoffed. "Good luck with that one. He kept me up half the night crying."

"Well, the walls at this shelter are pretty thin. Now you run along."

Cecilia closed the door behind her and busied herself gathering up Clark's things. "Let's see. You want to take Mr. Fish with us down the hall today, or Mr. Duck?"

"He played with the duck all afternoon yesterday," her sweet voice reminded her.

"Okay, then Mr. Fish it is. Let me get your sippy into the bag, and some spare clothes," she said stuffing a fabric grocery bag, "'cause we know there's gonna be some kind of accident, right?" She poked at the boy's tummy and he giggled. "It ain't playtime if there's no accidents at all."

The boy pawed at her green stone necklace. "Oh, we need to leave that alone. That's my magic amulet. An angel told me it's a piece of a star fallen from heaven. And you know what? I think she was right."

"I'm not the angel," her sweet voice chided. "You've seen the angel, with the giant eye. And I told you it was nothing to fear. It got rid of the horrible angry voice, and it brought you your ability to calm children."

"Yes, that is a blessing."

She stepped to the front door and looked back over the three rooms that were Lisette's apartment. She was lucky to get a unit with its own bathroom. Cecilia shared a bathroom with four other women in her wing out back.

"That's still a big move up from the street where you were a month ago," the sweet voice added.

"You're right. More blessings to count. And Lisette earned this place, being in the return to work program. Good for her."

She walked downstairs and to the front of the repurposed apartment building. The tiny playroom was cheery in the way only children's crayon murals can make a room. She set Clark down and started looking through the handful of children's books on a shelf.

"Hi CeCe!" The young Hispanic man in a Portland Rescue Mission tee shirt greeted her from the door. "Is Lisette still here?"

"No, she's off to work already."

"Right, and she gets back late. Well, I've got great news for her, and you can pass it along when you see her tonight. Her placement came through."

"You mean her application to that family place across the river?"

"Yes, she's been on the PHFS wait list for a couple of months now. They just had a space open up, and she can move in as soon as tomorrow." The man looked around the makeshift playroom with a raised eyebrow. "We really aren't set up for families here. They've got much nicer spaces for kids."

"Oh, I've heard about it. She and Clark will be much happier, I'm sure."

"So, what about you? Are you ready to start looking for work? No rush. I know you've only been with us a month, but you've made terrific progress."

"Be careful how you answer him," her sweet voice advised.

"I've been making myself useful here. Lisette and Sharleen couldn't work if they didn't have me to watch their little ones."

"That's true, and we all appreciate how good you are with the kids."

"But?"

"But, as I said, we aren't set up for families. As soon as we find a family shelter for Sharleen, we will move her out too."

"I guess I should make a plan."

"You really do have a skill with kids. Have you considered working in day care?"

"I have a medical history that would likely stop that."

"We could write you a recommendation. Job placement is most of what we do here."

Cecilia waited for her voice to object, but it stayed silent.

"What was your name again?"

"Roberto, but you can call me Bobby."

She reached out and shook his hand. "Thank you, Bobby."

·　　·　　·

Sarah was busy sampling songs on her phone when Nate came home with a bag of groceries. She pulled an earphone out and smiled up at him.

"This phone is incredible! I've been sampling and saving, and the apps keep giving me recommendations. It's like the whole world of music in my hand."

He set the bag down on the table next to her. "It is pretty powerful."

"I had no idea you could pull down songs and save them on your phone like this."

"The Internet really has exploded in the last nine years. It isn't just music, it's the entirety of human knowledge. You saw how easy it was to find Roxie's church. I'd like to be your guide when you go exploring. There are no guardrails. It's everything all at once. It's a lot to take in."

She smirked. "Yes, big brother."

"What kind of music do you like?"

"They played a lot of slow, relaxing stuff at the center that I never really paid any attention to. So I'm starting from scratch with what's popular now. I like the angry young women singing about how unfair life is. Halsey and Billie Eilish kind of sing to me."

Nate started unpacking the groceries. "Makes sense. You've been through a lot."

Sarah was suddenly distracted by a sense of danger. She couldn't place what or why so she frowned at the table and tried to pinpoint it.

"What are you listening to?"

She held up her hand to quiet him while pulling the other earphone out. "Something's wrong. Something's coming. I can't pin it down, it's just a feeling, but it's really strong."

"Like the hate you sensed in that guy in the diner?"

"Yes, just like that, but worse."

"Get under the table," Nate said calmly as he reached into the kitchen broom closet. Sarah was shocked to see him pull out a shotgun.

"When did you get that?"

"After you were abducted," he said as he went to the front windows and closed the curtains.

"I don't think he's out front. I get the feeling he's coming up the back of the house."

Nate hustled to the kitchen windows and crouched down to peek out. He raised his eyebrows at Sarah and waved for her to stay down. He slunk to the back door, quietly unlocked the knob, and stood back out of the way with the gun held up with the butt facing the door.

The knob turned and the door creaked open. The man who stepped in was holding a pistol, but he did not look behind the door. Nate smashed the wooden butt of the gun into his crewcut blond head and sent him crumbling to the floor. He scrambled to get up, but Nate swung the barrel around to point at his face.

"Drop the pistol or I pull the trigger."

Lying on his back looking past the gun, he sneered up at Nate, "You're not a killer."

"I know who you are and I know why you're here. I have no reason to keep you alive. Your choice — pistol or shotgun."

Sarah was impressed with how composed Nate was, since she could feel his boiling anger. She also felt the hatred in the man — the same hatred she felt in the man who killed Roxie.

The man dropped the gun. Nate kicked it across the floor.

"Sarah, get our guest a chair."

She pushed one across the floor to him. The man sat down.

"Now get the roll of duct tape out of the kitchen junk drawer and secure him. Start by binding his hands together, then tape him to the chair."

Sarah stepped up to him with a length of tape pulled out. He started to raise his hands for her, but then jumped up to grab her.

Nate swung the gun around and bashed him in the temple with the gun butt. He fell over limply, all the way to the floor, smacking his head on the linoleum.

When the man did not move further, Nate asked Sarah, while pointing the gun down at him, "Is he dead?"

Sarah felt his face for his breath. "No, but he's out. Where'd you learn to fight like that?"

"Schoolyards. You know about my temper, but I don't think you knew about my history of fighting at school. Let's get him tied into the chair. I want to question him before we hand him over to the police."

•   •   •

The man moaned quite a lot before he opened his eyes to look around. "My head!"

"Be glad you still have a head," Nate said dryly. "Your ID says you're Burt Cowell from Dothan, Alabama. So, Burt Cowell, you wouldn't happen to have come here by way of sunny Florida, would you?"

Burt blinked a lot before saying anything. "Damn right I did. Jefferson Davis sent me."

"You do know Jefferson Davis has been dead for over a hundred years."

"Not that one, jackass." He looked past Nate at Sarah standing behind her brother, and he jerked to focus.

She could feel his anger ignite as he stared at her, and she felt herself drawn to it. It was the same as Daniel, the man Fraily kidnapped her to heal. Her Dreamer self wanted desperately to quench that fire. She resisted and stayed back to let Nate question him.

"Somebody calling himself Jefferson Davis sent you here. Did he give you the address?"

"No, I figured out where you live. He just told me you were probably in St. Louis. But if I can figure it out, then he can too. And he'll come with his army."

"How many are in this army?"

"Oh, he's got hundreds scattered all across the South. He's usually got at least twenty men at his mansion at any one time. You really are up shit's creek."

Nate stepped up and pulled open Burt's shirt. He grabbed the stone necklace there and snapped the chain.

"Hey, you can't take that!"

"How long have you been lucid with this necklace?"

Burt suddenly didn't look so confident. "Three months."

"Let me get this straight. This Davis character breaks you out of a mental hospital, gets you lucid for the first time in forever, and after following him for three months, you are willing to come hunt us down and kill us, possibly sacrificing yourself to get the job done. What kind of hold does he have over you?"

"It ain't him. It's the vision. The Biters have shown me this is the only way. Colonel Davis says the Biters are God's way of showing us what we must do. We must find people who have been poisoned by the Looker, and then eat the monster out of them, to save their souls." He yanked against his bindings, to no avail. "It's a higher calling."

Nate turned around and matched gazes with Sarah. "Biting them saves them?"

"It's like sucking out a poison. If we have to kill them, then that's better than letting them be damned. These people, like your sister, have been poisoned by the evil Looker. It's a demon from Hell. The fury and hate we feel comes over us like God's own hand. We can't help ourselves. We've been given this mission from God."

Sarah could not stand by and watch him be burned alive by his anger. She stepped around her brother and up to one step from Burt. "You see me possessed by a demon. But I am calm and rational. I have compassion for your distress. My god gave me one power, the ability to cool your anger. I want to relieve you, not harm you, and my powers cannot hurt you. Yet you are filled with hatred and want to harm me. Your god drives you to violence and destruction. Now you tell me, which of us is possessed by a demon?"

"All I know is what I feel. And I feel like tearing you apart!"

"Am I the first Looker you've met, face to face?"

"Yes."

"So, this Colonel you follow, he's told you what your visions mean, right? I'm the only Looker you've seen in the flesh. Judge for yourself. Ignore what he told you. Which is more godlike, a vision that drives followers to peace and calm, or one that drives folks to violence and hate?"

"I ... I don't know."

Standing only a foot away, Sarah felt like she was draining something away from him. It was like she was next to a boiling kettle and she could draw the steam out of it to cool it down. She sensed his anger was waning. Did she not need to touch him? This was new. Was this from handling Roxie's stone?

"You've probably been told to not let me touch you."

"That's right. I'm supposed to shoot you before you have a chance to hug me."

"Okay, I won't touch you. If your god really wanted me dead because I'm evil, wouldn't it make sense that standing this close should enrage you? But you feel yourself shedding that anger, getting calmer. You can think more clearly for yourself now, can't you?"

"You're working some kind of hoodoo on me. That's what the Looker does. It draws you in and then, whammo!"

"Giving you your clear head back isn't an attack. Just like that necklace gave you your clear head back. But it replaced angry voices with angry visions. I'm offering you a completely clear head, free from voices and uncontrollable passions. Freedom, Burt. Free to be your own man, thinking for yourself. How's that sound?"

He frowned and blinked, a lot.

"You are not the first Biter I've cured. And you're certainly not the first person I've quieted their anger. I know what I can do. It only helps. I do not have any powers that can harm you. When you're ready to be free, just let me know. All it takes is a touch. That's how weak the Biter demon is."

"Just a touch?"

She could feel he was fighting to stay mad, but his breathing was slowing. "That's all it takes."

His face contorted as he thought it over. "I don't believe you. Go ahead."

She gently grasped one of his bound hands and held it. She could feel something break in his soul, like a chain snapping. She was pretty sure he felt it too. "Better?"

"My God." He sighed deeply. He blinked many times. "I wanted to kill you. I don't even know you. I'm so ashamed."

"Don't feel shame, it wasn't your fault. The Biter vision is seductive and overwhelming. I'm just glad I had a chance to free you from it."

Burt nodded and winced. "Jesus, my head is throbbing where you hit me."

Nate stepped up and looked at the swollen red mark on the side of his head. It extended far up under his short-cropped hair. "I'll get you some ice." As he stepped past Burt, he looked back at Sarah with a raised eyebrow questioning look.

"Burt, if I cut you free, are you going to jump me again?"

"No way. I don't feel that urge at all now. Like I said, I'm really sorry for threatening you. My mama did not raise a killer."

"Tell you what. I'll cut one arm free so you can hold the bag of ice to your head, and we'll see how it goes from there."

"All right."

Sarah joined Nate behind the kitchen counter. "They've got an army of converts wearing Devourer necklaces. We should cut up Roxie's stone and make our own set of Dreamer necklaces."

"And what, give them to mental patients who can become Dreamer soldiers like you?"

"Well, I guess. Yes. I rather like the irony of having the most shunned people, the mentally ill, come to save humanity."

"I'm sorry, I have a real ethical problem with drawing innocent people into harm's way. You chose to follow the Dreamer's path. You could have walked away with your vision and your mental health and not gotten drawn into this war."

"The meteorites don't take away your free will. They cure schizophrenia. Once they are cured, they can choose to help or not."

Nate gave her a dubious side eye. "You're talking about recruits. You want to cure them so they can join us in this battle."

"It's either that, or we just shoot the Devourer cultists on sight, because they are hellbent on destroying me."

10

"BLOOD IN THE CUT"

K. FLAY

SAMMY BOLLINGER SAT in one of the two rear-facing jump seats in the back of the El Camino as it careened through town, tires squealing and engine revving at each turn. The bite on his shoulder had stopped hurting, but the anger it brewed in him still burned even the next night after Jackson's experiment. He still hadn't figured out what he was so mad about. He wanted to stay at the compound and work on that, but his two fellow bite subjects and their two best friends insisted they needed to go raise some hell. Davis said this was getting ready to kill Lookers when the meteor shower came. How was he supposed to know what a Looker looked like? And what was he supposed to do with all this rage in the meantime?

His fellows seemed pretty happy about it, like it was permission to go wild. Buford, the guy next to him in the other jump seat, hooted and hollered for the merry hell of it. They passed a group of people out for an evening walk and Buford assaulted them with, "You ignorant bastards! You have no idea what's coming! Man, you're all gonna die, and it's gonna be glorious!"

The three in the cockpit joined with their own chorus that Sammy couldn't make out. He really wanted to hurt someone or to destroy something. As obnoxious as Buford was, he couldn't turn his anger on the man next to him. Something about the bites. They were in this together.

The car pulled into a convenience store parking lot, and all five piled out.

"Grab us some snacks!" one of the other men yelled.

"Hell, grab us some payback," another one corrected.

Sammy lagged behind and was the last one into the store. Two of them started grabbing bottles of booze while the others confronted the clerk. There wasn't anyone else in the store. The guy looked Arab — tall, big nose, short hair, wearing a colorful woven cap. Something about him focused and grew Sammy's anger. When one of the men pulled a hunting knife and threatened the clerk, the guy stepped back from the register with his hands up.

"Hey man, I don't want any trouble," he said with some kind of Arab accent. "You can take the money."

"Damn straight we're taking the money!"

The guy with the knife, Sammy thought his name was Don, jumped over the counter. He punched some buttons on the register, but nothing happened. In the moment he turned his back on the clerk, the clerk reached around behind him and pulled out a shotgun and pointed it in Don's face. Don stepped back, but there was very little room behind the counter.

Sammy felt his anger swell to breaking. Moving faster than he thought he could, he dove over the counter and grabbed the gun before the clerk even had a chance to point it at him. He spun the gun around and bashed the clerk across the head with the barrel.

Don and the others let out a hoot at Sammy's move, but Sammy wasn't done. Still aiming the gun at him, he grabbed the clerk by the shirt with his free hand, pulled him up off the floor and threw him face down across the counter.

"Tryin' to be brave, huh? Well, now you're in for a world of hurt." He fleetingly wondered what security cameras might be recording this, but he was too focused on this prey to look up. He grabbed the man's cap off his head. "What the fuck is this for?"

"To respect Allah."

The word sent another surge of adrenaline through Sammy. "You worship a different god. Well, I've seen God. God gave me the strength and speed of ten men." By now his breathing was so ragged he could only speak in bursts. He spotted a pendant hanging by the cash register. It was a blue dot on a white background, like an eye. "Your god is the Devil. The eye of the Devil." In the back of his mind, Sammy knew this wasn't true. "You see with the eye of the Devil!"

The others screamed, "He's a Looker! He's a Looker!"

"No, no!" the man pleaded. "Allah is the same as your Christian God. We are all children of Abraham!"

Sammy could not control himself. With the man still bent over the counter, he grabbed the man's pants and yanked them down.

"Holy shit!" one of the others yelled. "You gonna buttfuck him?"

"Allah grant me protection," the man whimpered.

Sammy knew he would normally have granted the man the mercy he begged for, but he couldn't stop the rage. He watched helplessly as he brought the gun up, jammed it into his anus, and pulled the trigger.

The man's death was quieter and less dramatic than he expected. The blast jerked his body, which then fell limp. No boom, no blood, no scream, no dramatic payoff. There was just one fewer live men in the room. Seconds seem to tick by as he looked at what he had done, disbelieving.

Don was still behind the counter with Sammy, arms stiff at his sides, eyes wide with horror. "We've gotta get the fuck out of here, right now!" He jumped the counter, not bothering with the cash register.

Sammy followed. The pounding of his heart slowed enough for him to squeeze in a thought. He looked at the gun in his hands and thought about fingerprints. So he kept it.

•　　　•　　　•

Jackson Pruitt was paging through mental hospital admission records when the TV on the other side of the room caught his attention. "We have to report another religious hate crime this evening. Five men attacked the Shop-n-Go market on 23rd Street at about eight pm tonight and murdered the owner Salim Chibbari. Police report they have reason to believe the crime was due to Mr. Chibbari being Muslim. They are reviewing security camera footage and will be issuing arrest warrants shortly. This is the fourth crime in the last month aimed at businesses run by non-Christians, but the first one that resulted in murder."

Jackson pulled out his cell phone and dialed Don Headley. "Don, this is Jackson. Hey, did I hear you right that you were going to take the guys from the bite experiment out drinking tonight?"

Jackson could hear Don had to yell over wind and engine noise. "Holy shit, Jackson. You should'a seen it. We went to knock over a liquor store, and Sammy just fucking went off on this Arab dude."

"Sammy Bollinger?"

"Yeah, quiet, keep to hisself Sammy. This dude pulled a gun on me and Sammy just lit up. It was like watching some superhero movie. He flew like lightning, grabbed the gun, and blasted the guy up the ass. Brutal!"

"Up the ass?! Jesus. Did the guy say anything to set him off?

"Oh yeah, he said he prayed to Allah. Sammy thought that made him a Looker. Used his asshole like a silencer!"

Jackson took a moment and closed his eyes to recompose himself. "Where are you now?"

"Headed back. Figured we had enough fun for one night."

"We're you followed?"

"Nah. Clean getaway."

"I know this is going to be a push, but the five of you need to keep this to yourselves. Do not go bragging about this."

"Really?"

"I mean it Don. Keep a lid on this. This could fuck up everything."

"Oh, all right. I'll tell the guys."

Jackson hung up and walked upstairs to Jefferson's quarters. He knocked. "Colonel, it's Jackson."

"Come on in." Davis was lounging on a couch in his living room, sipping a cocktail watching the news.

"Did you see the story about the five men who murdered a convenience store owner tonight?"

"Yes, I heard something about it while I was fixing myself a nightcap. What about it?"

"Those were our men, including the three bite subjects. They told me they were going out drinking. The rage seems to have gotten the better of them."

Davis sat up. "No shit?"

"It gets better. The other men say the killer moved with superhuman speed and killed the man with no hesitation. And here's the best part: the man identified himself as worshipping Allah. It appears the mention of another god blinded our man to think he was a Looker who needed to be dispatched immediately."

"This was one of the bite victims, not one of the necklace wearers?"

"Yes. The rage they feel manifests as xenophobia hunting for Lookers. That will make them very effective once we begin hunting Lookers after the meteor shower. But that's six weeks from now. We should halt any more biting until we're closer to the date. Otherwise we're going to have a bunch of out-of-control killers looking for any sign of any religion except ours."

"You make a good case. What are the chances the police will finger our man?"

"The man who pulled the trigger is normally a quiet, reserved man. He's got no criminal background and very little social media presence. So it's unlikely the police will be able to identify him from the security footage."

"Damn, this wasn't even a violent man to begin with?"

"No, the idea that he might have found a Looker drove him to this."

"I heard the news say this is like the fourth religious hate crime this month, and that's just in Tallahassee. You know, with more crimes against Arabs and Jews, we might just be able to slip under the radar."

Jackson agreed but pressed his point. "I still don't want any more trigger-happy hunters wandering the countryside dragging police back here."

"I agree. I think we can call this experiment a rousing success, and call it quits until we need to launch our army."

•   •   •

Jefferson followed the sounds of grunting exertion to the exercise yard where Hiram Cutler was lifting weights. "Hiram, how are you? We haven't spoken in a few days."

He set down the massive barbell and stood up to his full 6-foot-5 height. "I'm okay."

"Still clear from the old voices?"

"Hell yeah. But the biting vision's getting stronger all the time. What am I supposed to do with that?"

"I want to start you on a training so you can work that vision the same way you work those weights. I've got big things lined up for you."

Hiram snorted and grabbed a towel.

"I hear the assistant I assigned to you took a turn and ended up in a bar fight that put him in the hospital. What do you know about that?"

"Rich was real helpful the first couple of days. Showed me around, got me new clothes that fit, helped me with the equipment here. But then he started to lose his shit. He'd fly off the handle at nothin', started picking fights with everybody."

"With you?"

"Ah, no. He was good with me. He got real edgy, like something was eating him up inside. I wasn't surprised he ended up with a bottle smashed across his face."

Jefferson looked him up and down. "I've got a theory I want to test. Wipe yourself off on the towel, I mean really good, neck, armpits, the works."

He did so, complete with a very suspicious frown. "So?"

Jefferson grabbed another towel and took Hiram's from him using the clean one. He turned and called out to another man in the yard. "Hey! Yeah, you. Come on over here for a sec."

The man clearly recognized their leader. Jefferson did not know the man.

"Let me ask you a question, soldier. Are you feeling good on this fine sunny afternoon?"

"Why, yessir. I feel fine."

"Not mad at anybody?"

"No. I'm not mad at anyone."

"Oh, all right. Do me a favor and take these towels over to the bins." Jefferson pressed the sweaty towel into his outstretched hands while taking care to not touch it himself.

He shrugged at the odd request. "Sure, Colonel. Is that all?"

"That's it. Good lad."

The man turned and walked across the yard toward the laundry bins as requested.

Hiram watched and asked, "What was that all about?"

"Hold up. Two, three," he counted out. There were a couple of other men standing in front of the bins when their messenger arrived. He forcefully shoved them out of the way, threw the towels into a bin with a violent heave, and stormed off swearing at whoever he encountered.

"What got into him?" Hiram asked.

"Your sweat. We have found that your fellow psychosis rescues can imbue a furious anger in those they bite. Yes, bite, as in your vision of biting. As I suspected, you have anger to spare. Apparently you can trigger people just with your touch. That's what drove Rich to pick that bar fight — repeatedly touching you or your sweat over the course of the last few days."

Hiram looked at his hands. "That's some weird shit superpower."

"That's what the new training will be for."

"Does that mean I need to start wearing gloves?"

"No need. Just don't hug anybody you want to keep friendly. Not that you're really the hugging type. Oh, and tell Jackson Pruitt to give you another necklace. I want you to start wearing two of them."

·   ·   ·

Sarah came back up the hall from the back bedroom. "Burt crashed the minute he lied down."

"You know, I'm still not sure we shouldn't call the police," Nate said. "He did come here to kill you."

"He's exhausted and wrung out. Think of it. He's been in and out of mental wards for schizophrenia, he finally gets relief from a band of cultists who replace his voices with a vision of fanged destruction, which I then break. He's free from hateful influences for probably the first time in his life, and his guilt at trying to kill me has left him wondering if he deserves his deliverance. These meteorites are going to leave a trail of bodies that includes the survivors."

The doorbell rang.

"Now what?" Nate said as he opened the front door. "Are you kidding me?"

"Who is it?" Sarah asked.

Nate swung open the door. "Harold fucking Fraily."

Fraily standing there, head down, hands folded, looked tiny and broken. The bravado he had shown during the kidnapping was gone.

"You've got some nerve," she said.

"They killed everyone. I was the only one to get out alive. I had no one else to turn to. I have come to ask for your mercy."

"Who killed whom?" Nate asked.

"The Florida cultists hunted down my band of followers. There was a fire fight, and now everybody's dead. Except for me."

"Florida?" Sarah asked.

"When you exorcized the demon from Daniel, you asked me if the evil charm was from Florida. The men who attacked my house and killed my followers were from Florida. And their leader had one of the evil charms. May I please come in?"

Nate stepped aside and let him by.

"After I left you at Alonzo's place, I heard the police raided it and rescued you. I am still very sorry I decided kidnapping you was justified. It wasn't. I gathered up my immediate followers and we were going to lay low. But a half dozen heavily armed men attacked my house. I didn't know who the hell they were at first. They were after our charms, the good ones, that my followers were wearing."

"Were all of your followers former mental patients?"

"No, and they didn't have any visions. My brother Caleb was like that, and he had God visions. He was how I knew the charms had powers. He was a big guy and he fought like crazy. He got to their leader and the shit really hit the fan. That's when I heard they were from Florida and they all believed in the biting demon that you exorcized from Daniel. Caleb wrestled with the guy and I guess he tried the same exorcism you did, but then the guns all went off and everyone was dead. The carnage was unbelievable. I never saw anything like it, even when I served in Iraq thirty years ago."

Sarah spoke up. "You didn't mention your brother having the Dreamer eye god vision when you had me at the Alonzo house."

"He would never tell me what his vision was, just that it was God. He never said there was an enemy cult. Daniel only told me about the biting demon after you cured him and went to bed. I hadn't connected the dots. I still don't understand why Caleb wanted to get right up to their leader and put himself in that kind of danger. He insisted, like he couldn't help himself."

"That's what the Dreamer vision does to you."

"I was wrong about so many things, and I got my people killed because of it. I no longer believe these charms are Jesus's work. I can't get over that I survived. I came to you because you're the only one who seems to know what's going on."

Nate gave Sarah a very dubious look.

"They did not harm me," she told her brother. "They really only wanted me to cure their afflicted man."

"And I cannot tell you how sorry I am for taking such liberties," Harold threw in.

She waved to the dining table. "Have a seat. I'll give you the short version. First of all, none of this has anything to do with Jesus. It's aliens. Giant, spacefaring alien gods who were at war with one another eons ago, destroyed each other, and their blown apart bodies have started falling to Earth.

"These charms are made from those meteorites. So there's two kinds, one that makes you see the evil biting god, which I call the Devourer. That's probably not its real name, but that's the best I've got. The other kind of stone makes you see the benevolent creator eyeball god, which I called the Dreamer. I only recently figured out its real name is Oum.

"Both visions cure schizophrenia, and they only give visions to the mental patients they cure, but the visions take over your life. They also compel you to either kill Dreamer followers or cure Devourer followers."

Harold's eyes went wide as he wrapped his mind around the story. "My God. It's an invasion, but with our own people."

"Exactly."

Harold frowned trying to make sense of it. "That means you need as many of your, what did you call it, the Dreamer god followers to try to exorcize the Devourer cultists. I collected all the necklaces from my followers after the fire fight. You said you only get the visions if you've had schizophrenia. None of my people had that, or any visions, except for Caleb. But they all got their charms from Alonzo who used the same source stone as the one that cured Caleb."

"What about the bad one Daniel had?"

"He got that from someplace else. We never did figure out where he got it."

Sarah looked over at Nate. "It sounds like all these other necklaces should be Dreamers. How many do you have?"

"Nine."

Nate asked, "Did you take the one off the Florida leader?"

"Yes. I guessed his was the same as the one Daniel had, so I kept it separate. I've got Daniel's with me too. I'll tell you, I'm surprised I even thought to take the necklaces. At the time, I was still trying to figure out why Jesus let all my people get killed."

"I'm really sorry your friends died, including your brother. We've seen people killed over this too."

"Can their necklaces help against these Florida killers? I'd feel a little better if I knew their deaths helped in some way."

Sarah looked to Nate and let him answer. She wasn't sure which way he would go.

"That would be a nice tribute. We'll use them as best we can."

Burt walked out of the back of the house, blinking against the brightly lit room. "Did I hear you guys talking about the Florida cult?"

Sarah realized how badly this could go and she jumped right in. "Harold, this is Burt, who used to be a member of the Florida cult, but he's cured now and completely repentant about his involvement."

Burt looked from her to Fraily. "That's correct. I'm pretty messed up about it. Did they do something awful to you too?"

Harold looked from Burt to Sarah and back to Burt. "Yes, they sent a squad who killed my friends. Just what did you used to do for them?"

"I was a soldier, but I never killed anyone. I had one of those evil necklaces that made it too easy to listen to their hate. Sarah is right: I am repentant. She cured me, and I feel absolutely awful. I'm so sorry they got to your friends."

Harold took a long minute to size up this man. "God teaches us to hate the sin, not the sinner. Are you completely cured, with no more of these crazy visions?"

"Yessir, I am free, thanks to Sarah here. In fact, that's why I couldn't sleep. It was too quiet. All my life I had the voices taunting me, then those were replaced by the biting teeth vision. Now I got nothing. It feels weird. If that necklace cured my brain, will I slip back and lose my mind again?"

Sarah was afraid to venture a guess.

"We don't know what happens next," Nate answered. "We've been trying different things with Sarah and her visions, and we haven't figured out what happens if you take the necklace away."

Harold frowned at Nate. "Why would you want to take away her visions? She's all we have in our fight with these cultists."

Sarah said, "There are negative consequences on my side as well. I won't go into it, but none of this comes free of charge." She turned to Burt. "We will keep an eye on you and, if you start to hear any voices or see anything that's not real, you let us know right away."

"I guess that leaves me space to deal with my regrets."

Harold surprised Sarah with a sudden shift in tone. He looked at Burt and his face somehow softened. "You know, guilt will steal your life faster than a bullet. These charms may be from some forsaken space alien monsters, but here on Earth, God still holds sway. Are you a Christian man?"

"Yessir."

"Are you a Baptist Christian man?"

"Yessir."

"Well then, go back to your Bible for strength. This Devourer is no doubt the Devil here on Earth. And this Dreamer, there is no question he is God made flesh. God forgives all sinners, especially those who have been led astray by the Devil himself. Now, you are a conscientious man, a repentant man, which God recognizes. You will feel guilt for your sins and you will lead a better life to make up for it. But at the end of the day, you must have faith that God has forgiven you. Your path back to righteousness is to accept the bosom of Jesus and God's forgiveness. Do I hear an 'amen'?"

He nodded and said quietly, "Amen."

Sarah and Nate exchanged a look. Harold certainly had a gift.

"Now," Harold resumed, "what can you tell us about this Florida cult that so poisoned your heart?"

"It's led by a guy who calls himself Colonel Jefferson Davis. I'm pretty sure that not his real name. He's got a plantation house compound outside Tallahassee. He's got about two dozen soldiers there at one time. But he's got dozens of guys working for him all over Florida."

Nate asked, "And all of these dozens of men were all former mental patients with necklaces? Where in the world did he get all of them?"

"Oh, hell no. There are only a few of us with the necklaces. Most of them are just hired hands. But just before I left, I did hear about him moving to the next phase of his plan. It seems if one of us with a necklace bites somebody, it infects the victim with a raging hate and a need to go find a Looker and kill them. So when I said he has an army he could send after you, it's mostly these bitten converts."

"They can just bite anyone and convert them?"

"That's what I heard. I didn't bite anybody."

Nate looked over at Sarah and pursed his lips.

She nodded. "You know, this breeding makes sense from the original cosmology. The Devourer divided himself up into hundreds of pieces to surround the Dreamer."

Nate squinted. "These bitten converts don't have a necklace, and they weren't schizophrenic, and they don't have the awful visions. They're just ordinary people, just angry."

"Until they see a Looker, then they go berserk," Burt added. "I heard about a guy who mistook a Muslim for a Looker and he did terrible things to the poor guy."

Nate took a breath. "Hate crimes are rising all across the country, and even in Europe. It's like all the hate folks have been harboring, the racism, the xenophobia, the classism, have all been heated up to boiling. How are we going to distinguish these bitten converts from run-of-the-mill haters?"

"We're not trying to cure society's ills," Sarah said. "We're going to have to assume the bitten ones will get over their rage at some point. The poison has to wear off, right?"

Harold, who had been watching for a while, said, "There was one guy with a necklace in the squad they sent for my people. He might have bitten the others."

Nate added, "The Florida guy we encountered in Arizona was a solo hunter and he had a necklace."

"Me too," said Burt.

"Did Colonel Davis give you direct orders to find us?" Nate asked Burt.

"No. His Lieutenant Jackson Pruitt told me he thought there might be a Looker here in St. Louis, and it would do me well in the organization if I came here and found you." He looked embarrassed all over again. "Like I said, it was really easy to believe whatever they told me. I would like to blame the necklace for that."

"It looks like every hit squad, whether it's one or many, has one necklace-wearing leader," Sarah concluded. "We'll focus on the ones with necklaces. I seem to be able to detect cultists at a distance. That's how we got the drop on you," she said to Burt. "Maybe I can refine that sense to see the necklaces themselves. That way we don't waste time with haters who aren't from this cult. Does that make sense?"

"What do we do if we grab one of the necklace leaders?" Nate asked. "I guess you have to cure them one at a time."

"Well, we can use Burt here as our example of whether my touch is sufficient. I hope taking their necklaces off doesn't send them back into psychosis. We'll have to work it and see." She smiled at Burt. "Nate, you were concerned about us busting up the Arizona meteorite and making Dreamer necklaces. Given these numbers Burt is talking about, I think we need to talk about that some more. I don't know if I can do this alone."

"I don't like the idea of pushing innocent mental patients into the role of warrior," Nate said. "I feel a little better about returning Devourer cultists back into mental patients. At least that doesn't kill anyone. None of these options are really acceptable. It's like you said earlier these meteorites are going to leave a trail of messed up lives, no matter what."

11

"POMPEII"
BASTILLE

"YOU GO ON WITHOUT ME. You know what you're looking for." Sarah knew Nate would take a long time deciding, and that she would not be any help.

"There was the one security camera system they advertised on sale, so it shouldn't take that long," he said.

"I'll catch up to you in Electronics."

"Where will you be?"

"Nate, it's Target. Target has everything," she said with a wide swing of her arms.

As she watched him walk away, she realized she had spent no time thinking about the running of their household, so she had no idea what they might need. *Oh well.* The jewelry counter was seductively close to the entrance. So was a display of cute hats.

After trying on a couple, she got that uncomfortable feeling of someone hating on her from a distance. She casually glanced around and didn't see any of the older men staring at her the way she found nearly every time she went out shopping. There was one really pretty blond woman in her thirties who was looking at Sarah. She had kind of a blank stare. Maybe she was curious how the hats looked on a teenager.

Purses. She had been living out of one of Nate's bookbag backpacks. It was definitely time for her own pretty purse. Long strap, short strap? Lots of pockets, one big pocket? Again, she got the nagging hater signal. Again, she looked around and saw no one who looked like they were hunting her. Maybe Target shoppers just carried around a lot of rage. She decided she could decide on the purses better with an empty bladder. The bathrooms were close by next to the entrance.

She finished her business and was tucking everything back into her tight jeans when the hater feeling suddenly came on like a storm. The only other times she had felt it this strong was when Daniel and Burt had wanted to kill her. Jesus, had she attracted a Devourer cultist here in Target? She listened and heard nothing. She zipped up her jeans and crouched down to look under the stall door. She saw a lone woman standing by the entrance. Just standing there.

"What do you want?" Sarah called out.

The woman didn't respond.

"If you mean to harm me, I can scream really loud in this tile bathroom."

"You wouldn't dare," the woman said arrogantly.

"You wanna try me?"

"If you scream, the whole store's going to find out what you are. You're not going to blow your little secret."

"What the fuck are you talking about, lady?"

"We don't stand for your perverted shit in Middle America. Now come out here and take your punishment like the man you are."

Sarah didn't know what to make of this woman, but at least she wasn't a Devourer cultist. She opened the door and stepped out of the stall, expecting to face her. But the woman, the pretty blonde who had watched her try on hats, dashed right at Sarah and pushed her back into the stall. The woman punched her in the face and clawed at her shirt, pulling it open.

Sarah was so shocked she felt weak and couldn't make her arms push the woman away. She felt betrayed by her own hands while this crazed woman clawed away. The woman's breath was oppressive and her aggression was unrelenting. She managed to tear at Sarah's padded bra like it was some kind of prize.

"Aha! I knew it. You freak!" she yelled in Sarah's face, spittle flying into the girl's gasping mouth.

Sarah couldn't think what to do, and her anger sensitivity was overwhelmed by the woman's rage. She was too shocked to think. She punched the woman in the nose hard enough to make her tear up, hoping to interrupt the attack. The woman was heavier than Sarah, and in heels, so when the woman recoiled from the punch, Sarah slipped under the partition wall into the next stall, letting the woman fall onto the toilet.

"Are you insane? I'm a flat-chested kid. Of course I'm wearing a padded bra!" She ran to the entrance and yelled, "Help! Security! I'm being attacked!"

The woman recovered faster than Sarah expected, and she grabbed her from behind and pulled her onto the bathroom floor. The woman's rage was so intense it blotted out Sarah's thoughts. Looming over her, she launched into a tirade. "Don't lie about your sex. I know a freak when I see one. You don't get to steal womanhood from real women. We work hard to be real women. You and your kind think you can just slip it on like a marabou robe and traipse around pretending. Well, you can take your fake self and your sad squashed little dick and crawl back into whatever hole you came out of."

A crew-cutted male security guard rushed in and pulled the woman back. He didn't even ask what was going on. "You okay, Miss?" he asked Sarah.

"No, I'm not. I want this crazy woman arrested."

The guard led the woman out.

Sarah got to her feet. Shaking, she pulled out her phone and called Nate.

•　　　•　　　•

Nate restrained himself with his arms folded tightly against his chest as he watched the policeman arrest the blonde woman. He listened carefully from fifteen feet back to make sure she didn't talk the officer out of anything.

"I did not do anything that was not my right to do," she insisted.

"I am arresting you for assault and battery. I have a sworn statement from the store security guard. You have the right to remain silent and to have counsel present during questioning."

"Sometimes you just have to stand up for what's right."

Nate's anger flared again in his chest. This bitch's entitlement was bottomless.

"Ma'am, anything you say can and may be used against you in court."

"Well, I'll say it again for the judge. The people have the right to defend themselves." With that she started to take a step towards Sarah who was talking with the store manager.

Nate took a step to intercept her, but the officer blocked her path.

"Ma'am, I suggest you not commit any further offenses, or I will have to restrain you."

She puffed up indignantly. "Restrain me? What, with handcuffs? You know, I pay your salary."

"Come with me," he said stretching out an arm to direct her toward the front doors. "We're done here."

"Where are you taking me?"

"To the station for processing. You are under arrest. Please do not resist."

"But my husband said he was ..."

"Yes, ma'am, I know. He said he would meet you at the station to post your bail."

"Oh, all right, fine!" Nate noticed that for all her bravado, she looked around as the officer escorted her out to see if anyone she knew was watching.

Nate realized he was grinding his teeth as he watched them leave, and he made himself stop. He turned to Sarah just as she was walking up from talking to the store manager. She looked as mad as he was.

"I can't believe that guy!" she spat under her breath.

"The manager?"

"He asked me if I am biologically a girl. I told him that's none of his business."

Nate's teeth clenched down again. "Assault is assault, and nothing justifies it."

"That's what I tried to tell him. It just took me by surprise."

Nate walked past her, straight at the thirty-something guy in a blue shirt and a tan tie. He was talking with some employees. Nate stepped past them too, grabbed the guy by the front of his shirt, and shoved him against the wall behind him. The guy had a few inches on Nate, maybe six-foot, but Nate was not worried about the guy fighting back.

"Are you trying to help my sister's attacker?"

"Hey! What? Let go of me! No. How was I helping her?"

"Asking my sister questions that have nothing to do with her being attacked out of the blue for no reason in your store."

"I was just trying to ..."

"Satisfy your own curiosity? And bring to light things that that bitch can use in her defense. Think this shit through before you stick your nose where it doesn't belong."

The man pushed Nate's hands back. "You should think things through before you get an assault charge against yourself."

Nate leaned forward and looked him in the eye. "You don't scare me. If you're going to be an idiot, at least keep your mouth shut before you do harm to innocent victims."

Nate walked back to Sarah who had both eyebrows up staring at him. "We can go."

"Thank you for not slugging him," she said quietly walking beside him out the front.

"Idiot." Nate took a breath and refocused on Sarah. "Are you going to be okay?"

"I'm still pretty rattled. My God, her anger was too much. It actually started to overload my hater sensitivity. That's what really frightened me. The harder she came at me, the less I could think."

"I hope that's not a problem if we meet up with cultists."

"I'll have to figure out how to cope." She closed her eyes and shook her head. "I don't get it. Why was she so mad? She railed on about me stealing womanhood that I had no right to."

"Oh Christ, she's a TERF. Trans Exclusionary Radical Feminist. There are women who feel all the gains they've made in a male-dominated world shouldn't be available to trans women. They are in fact more dangerous than the lecherous men you've been avoiding. I never would have thought, in a big, open public restroom, no less."

"I've never felt so powerless."

"I am so sorry."

Sarah sighed as they reached their car. Nate wished there was more he could do for her.

"I've got alien-poisoned religious zealots who want to kill me. I've got creepy old men who want to either rape me or kill me. And now there are women who want to kill me for stealing their femininity. Fucking hell. Don't they see I'm trying to save them all from global disaster?"

•　　•　　•

Sitting across the white linen covered table, Jefferson sized up Hiram as a bookie would assess a prize fighter. "How is the new training coming along?"

"Pruitt says I'm up to ten feet now. Hey, thanks for the grub. Real nice and fancy. We celebrating something?"

A waiter walked up the veranda, bringing two plates of steak, grits, and hushpuppies.

Jefferson noticed Hiram's voice was deeper and more resonant than he remembered. The man had also cut his long blonde hair into a military buzz cut. "Yes, we are celebrating your progress. I can admit now that I wasn't entirely sure the visualization technique would work. But you have proven my doubts unfounded." He raised his glass of wine up for Hiram to toast.

It took the big man a second to catch on, but he clinked his glass with his own.

"Being able to inject your anger into men at a distance, you can use this gift tactically in a battle setting, acquiring allies on the fly."

"Sounds cool." Hiram picked up his knife and fork, cleaved off a large chunk of his steak, and popped it into his mouth. When he opened his mouth, Jefferson noticed his lips opened quite further than looked possible. He stifled his alarmed reaction and looked again. Indeed, the man's entire jaw was significantly wider than he remembered. So was Hiram's neck. His gaze dropped to the two charm necklaces he wore.

"I see you've been working out a lot too. I imagine you didn't get enough exercise in the institution. Are you feeling stronger these days?"

"Oh yeah. I'm seeing all kinds of bulk." He held up his bent arm and showed off huge muscles.

"Your jaw is much better defined as well."

"Oh, you mean my new mouth. Yeah, it's a beaut!" he announced and then opened it to inhuman size. His lips spread all the way back into his cheeks and his teeth opened grotesquely far. He looked more alligator than man.

It was all Jefferson could do to keep a straight face. Trying not to clench his own teeth too hard, he said, "A most impressive unexpected benefit."

"I keep hearing about this meteor shower that's supposed to signal the end of the world. I take it that's why you want to put me in the field."

"That's true, more or less. Rumor mills crank out as much chaff as they do wheat. Allow me to fill you in. In the Book of Job, God and the Devil make a bet that this poor sucker Job will buckle and doubt God's love if God makes his life horrible enough. God throws the book at this guy, destroys his life, but Job stays true and never doubts his Lord's love. It's a long hard road, but the Devil loses the bet.

"We are faced with the same situation. God and the Devil have thrown pieces of their magic to Earth, to pit us against our fellow man. You are wearing two of the pieces of God's magic. Our enemies are wearing pieces of the Devil's magic. It is our mission to fight this battle, no matter how long and hard, to ensure our God is victorious."

"How do we know we're the Good Guys?"

Jefferson was surprised. "Your waters run deep, sir. Good question. Throughout the Bible and throughout history, God has instructed his faithful to take up arms against those who would quietly, subversively turn the masses against us. Joan of Arc spread God's glory by force over those who tried to steal land from believers by rule of law. The archangel Michael used force to expel Satan after the Evil One threatened to turn the angels against God. Our enemies, the Lookers, have the power to convince people to put down their arms, to give up their righteous anger. It is subversive, it is the Devil's way. God has given us this vision of taking decisive action. We are Michael's sword."

Hiram took the last enormous chunk of steak in his huge mouth and savored it. "You got this all figured out."

"I think I do."

"Does that make men respect you more?"

Again, an unexpected question. "I like to think so. I've had very few men turn away from my call."

"Men just fear me."

"You are a fearsome figure. But as a leader, you will be inspirational. Being feared and being respected are not so very different."

"You think men will follow me into battle?"

"Absolutely. With your power and my intellect, we will draw men up out of their boring lives to strive for glory."

"Your brains and my brawn, huh?"

"Indeed."

"Let's find out." With no further warning, he reached across the table and seized Jefferson's arm.

"What are you doing?"

Hiram stood up, lifted Jefferson right out of his seat and held him aloft, grabbing a leg with his other hand.

Jefferson felt like a puppet under the giant's unbelievable strength. "Release me at once!"

Hiram opened his gargantuan mouth and dropped Jefferson's body down onto his face. To his horror, Jefferson felt teeth tear through his torso.

Jefferson screamed in agony while beating Hiram on the back of the head with his free fist. Nothing worked. He was so frightened, he couldn't form words. *Can I recover from this?*

The giant swallowed and went in for another bite, this time tearing loose organs which fell all about. It was all he could do to not dwell on the sensation and what it meant. Jefferson tried to pull up his other leg to kick himself free, but his muscles all spasmed and wouldn't respond. His entire body went limp and he lost any remaining hope. Hiram must have torn though the aorta because then came a gushing waterfall of blood. Blood flooded Jefferson's mouth and gagged him, which added to the overwhelming sensation of doom. Jefferson wanted it to end, but he was mercilessly still aware when the next bite came, this one on his throat.

The last sound he made as he felt the teeth close down was to gurgle, "Why?"

He managed to open his eyes through the pain that crushed his entire being, just long enough to see that mouth open around his whole head. He felt and heard his skull shatter like a clay pot in those huge jaws.

The pain finally faded, for which he was hugely grateful. The release of death at last. But the pain was replaced by a sense of ... fullness? Jefferson felt an intense urge to belch. He opened his eyes, which were now over seven feet above the floor, and let out a window rattling croak. He looked down and saw an arm and two legs scattered on the table. He recognized them as his own from the blood-soaked linen suit shreds that clung to the severed limbs. He looked at his hands and, indeed, his entire towering body and everything around him was covered in bright red blood.

A waiter came running at him with a kitchen knife, followed by two other men. Jefferson flashed out his huge hand and, using only his willpower, forced the first man to enrage, then turn around and attack the two followers. He didn't much care to watch the ensuing knife fight.

He was much more taken with what had happened to himself. He was in Hiram's gigantic, muscled body, which seemed to be even bigger. He could feel Hiram's presence, his lust for life, his ever-present back burner anger. But he was still Jefferson. "Your brains and my brawn," Hiram had said. He looked down at the ripped shreds of meat that was what was left of his original body. *I always liked that suit.*

· · ·

Sarah awoke from a nap hearing Nate on the phone. "Yes sir. I understand. Well, he's here now, but I think he's asleep. Sure, I'll call you when he's ready to make a statement."

She walked into the dining room as he was hanging up. "Who was that and who were you talking about?"

"That was the police working on the Target bathroom attack case."

"So why, wait, what? You were talking about me making a statement? I made my statement already. And why were you calling me 'him'?"

"Look, the police are using your biological sex in their report. It doesn't mean they aren't prosecuting the woman who attacked you. She is claiming you attacked her and she was just defending herself."

"What?! When did she say that?"

"When they took her statement, I guess."

"So now they have me as a male who has been accused of assaulting a woman in the Ladies Room? And you didn't tell me about this? What does your lawyer have to say?"

"He says to cooperate with the police investigation."

"And that means going along with me being pegged as a male? That ignores the whole basis of my accusing her! She had no right to question my gender and no right to strike me and tear open my clothes! What could be more obvious?"

"You know, this whole gender thing has just made life so much more complicated. I mean, we're in the middle of defending the Earth from gun-toting crazies, and you get yourself tied up with a TERF."

"Wait, so this is my fault? Are you on drugs? How is this my fault? I didn't invite any of this."

"Well, that's not entirely true. You could have ignored the eye vision and just taken the cure. You could have kept your fascination with being a girl a little more under wraps and not so obvious."

Sarah was speechless. "What? I. You. Hold on. Am I hearing this right? Have you been thinking my gender identity has been my choice all this time? Has your support really just been, what, some kind of appeasement? 'Oh, let's humor the mental kid and let him pretend he's a girl?' Next, you're going to be fucking dead naming me. Nate, tell me this is not true."

"No, that's not how I feel. It's just that, I can't help thinking we could handle things a lot better if we didn't have so many layers of trouble piling up."

"My gender identity is another layer of complication in your life. You are fucking unbelievable. All this time I thought you were on my side. We were a team. But no, it's poor you having to cope with all the shit your sister — no, your brother — keeps throwing on you. What a lying, selfish piece of shit."

"Hey, can we limit the name calling? That doesn't help anything."

"What can possibly help at this point? You've just pulled the rug out from under my whole life!" She felt tears running down her face, tears of both anger and sadness. "I thought you knew who I am, how I survived being crazy for all those years. You were always my anchor — no, my lighthouse in the storm. Tell me you're just punking me. Tell me you don't really feel like this. Please."

"I want to tell you what you want to hear. I don't want to cause you any pain. I just don't know what I really feel at this point."

She fell against the hallway wall and sobbed. "This can't be happening." She staggered back to her bedroom, slammed the door and fell into the pillows. "You know I'm a girl, dammit. This cannot be happening."

Sarah awoke, her face still buried in her pillows. She guessed she had cried herself to sleep after her fight with Nate. Jesus, what a fight. How could he feel that way? How could she have not seen his doubt sooner? He always acted so supportive. Her head hurt from crying. "My God, what am I going to do?"

The battling gods no longer mattered to her. Who was she to save the ungrateful world? A screwed-up sixteen-year-old kid. *Fuck 'em.*

Could she repair her relationship with her brother? Where could she start? So much of what she thought turned out to be wrong.

She needed to talk with him. She was a lot calmer now, and less prone to insulting him.

She rolled over and sat up. Something felt wrong. Something felt very wrong. Was she sick? Was something broken? She clutched her legs and body, but nothing hurt. She shifted her legs to the edge of the bed to get up, and froze. She tried again. "No. What the fuck?" She grabbed her crotch and felt nothing. She spread her legs and felt around. Nothing. She unzipped her pants and yanked them off. Had her penis and balls pulled up into her inguinal canals? She usually pushed her testicles up there when she tucked. But where was her penis? *Where the fuck is my penis!?*

Panicked, she tugged her underpants to the side and faced a vulva. She screamed. "What the hell? How can this be? Jesus, is this a nightmare?" She slapped herself across the face, and it hurt worse than she expected. Her heart was racing with fear. No, she was awake, and that was a vulva. "Oh my God." Her voice shook raggedly. "No, no, no."

She heard Nate come down the hall and she covered herself up. "Are you all right? I thought I heard you scream. Can I come in?"

"Yes, come in. Yes, I screamed."

"Why are you holding your crotch like that? Are you injured?"

"No, worse. Far worse. Oh no, it's the dreams. The goddamn dreams. Nate, did we have a fight just now about my gender?"

"A fight? No. You've been in here napping all afternoon."

"Am I awake now?"

"Yeah. Can you not tell?"

"So, you don't really think my being a girl is attention-seeking bullshit?"

"No, of course not."

"Well, that's something. But this is still worse."

"What are you talking about?"

"I had another reality-altering dream. I dreamt you and I had a big fight about my gender identity. It was really disturbing; scared the hell out of me. It made me doubt everything. And that apparently is where the Dreamer took over. Nate, I am now biologically a girl."

"What? Wait. A dream changed you physically? That's astounding. You haven't been wearing the original necklace that gave you those powers. Oh my God, that's gotta be a huge shock."

It was too much. She curled up and started to cry. "It is."

He sat down next to her and put his arm around her. "Holy smokes, kiddo. That's going to take some getting used to. I guess the Dreamer in you saw you wanted to transition eventually and it moved the calendar up on you."

"No, Nate, that's not how it works at all. This is a disaster. This is a betrayal."

"I get you didn't ask for this. You haven't asked for any of the shit these meteorites have brought us. But they cured your illness. And now they've finished your transition."

She sat up and pulled her pants back on. "That's not the point. I loved my penis. I loved my mismatched body. Yes, I had dysphoria about being a boy. But being trans was who I have been for years. It was who I clung to when the voices screamed that I shouldn't be trans. Sometimes it was all the identity I had to cling to. I liked being a girl, but in my heart I was trans. Trans is who I am. And now I am stuck in a girl's body, with a vagina that I know nothing about. These fucking dreams have yanked away my identity and given me this new shape instead."

"Can we call Dr. Alpaca?"

"Oh, you think? How am I going to explain this?" she said shaking her hands at her body. "I don't think there is much case history of how to deal with magical sex changes."

"I'm sorry I didn't really understand your trans identity. I feel like I should have figured that out before."

She laughed with tears streaming down her face. "My God, are you hearing yourself? Nate, you have nothing to apologize for. I woke up remembering a dream fight where you were doubting who I am. Don't feel bad for missing nuance."

"I still want to know how I can help."

She squeezed his shoulders with her hands. "Thank you. I know what I'm going to do. I'm going to give the Arizona meteorite and all the necklaces to Harold and Burt and send them on their way to go fight the good fight with the Florida crazies."

"Do you mean you're throwing in the towel?"

She sniffled mightily. "Yes. This has all caused too much trouble for someone who has no skin in this game. Harold lost all his friends. Burt has a score to settle with them for making him into a killer. Let them take up the torch from here on. I have taken all the change and all the shit I'm going to take. I am done."

12

"TWILIGHT ZONE"
GOLDEN EARRING

JACKSON PRUITT STOOD STOCK STILL in Davis's bedroom door as the giant walked out of the bathroom, naked and wet from showering.

Davis saw him, stood up straight to face him and laughed out loud. "Pretty impressive, yeah? I especially like the ten-inch flaccid cock. Though it's actually only proportionate to the rest of me now. What do you think: seven foot three?"

Jackson blinked a few times, trying to remember how to form words past his astonishment. "At least. And over four feet across the shoulders. Probably over three hundred and fifty pounds. I heard what happened. Are you actually Jefferson in there?"

"Absolutely."

"Where's Hiram?"

"I hear him in here, rattling around. He'll probably step up if I get mad. That is his specialty. No, he donated his body and I got to keep my mind."

"You are quite a bit bigger and, dare I say, more intimidating than he was."

"This face is quite monstrous, isn't it?" He turned and bent to look in a dresser mirror. He stretched his mouth open and moved his jaw around. "Kind of like a mountain gorilla. Not so sure about Hiram's buzz cut."

More like a hippopotamus, Jackson thought.

"I need the biggest clothing we have on campus. Hiram's pants barely fit my waist, and they're four inches short."

The giant's voice was so deep, yet Jackson recognized his speech pattern as Davis. "I'll see what we've got. Probably sweats. Do you think this was a consequence of the necklace radiation? Should we expect more of the charm wearers to transform like this?"

"I don't think so. I doubled up on Hiram's dosage, and he was special to begin with. His personality was tailor made to fit the Biter vision. Oh, and I see the vision now. I never knew it first-hand. It is glorious. The god has a name too. Gragol. Gragol the Devourer. It sounds Mesopotamian to me. Does that make sense?"

Jackson squinted, trying to keep up. "Sure."

"Speaking of special, I want to test myself on people who know nothing of what we're doing."

"You mean to go out in public looking the way you do?"

"Get me something with a hoodie. I'll pass for a footballer."

"Shall we continue to call you Jefferson Davis?"

"Yes. I thought about adopting a superheroic moniker, but I think I'll keep the brand I've built."

•   •   •

Jefferson parked the restored yellow 1975 Buick LeSabre convertible in front of the Down Low Saloon off Florida Highway 267. He thought he was lucky to have found a good spot at 4:30 on a Wednesday afternoon. The place would fill up soon. He had to pull himself up out of the seat that was rolled back as far as it would go. He always liked this whale of a car, and now especially, since only a convertible could accommodate his torso.

He turned to the door. Now or never. He pulled up the sweatshirt hood and walked into the bar. It took about five seconds for the random chatter to die down as all eyes turned to his hulking form.

He kept his head down and walked straight to the bar. A couple of guys moved aside for him. "Whisky. Make it a double."

"Top shelf?" the bartender asked.

"If you please."

The barman gave him his drink, and he quietly sipped it without turning away from the bar.

When the other patrons saw he was just a very big guy, they returned to their conversations. He waited and listened to hear if anyone around him suddenly became angry. The talk continued as it had.

Jefferson listened in on two guys down the bar talking about college football. It was pleasant banter even though they favored different school's teams. He reached back to his angry Hiram self and pushed that feeling over on the two. A few seconds later, one of the men mentioned a player named Farushdi.

"Farushdi? What the fuck kind of name is that?

"I don't know. Iranian or something. What's your beef?"

"Don't tell me they let a camel jockey play Tight End."

"Really? And you're putting your big mouth money on a Pollock named Krakowski?"

"You can put a cork in it. My best friend in High School was Polish." And with that came the first shove.

Jefferson stopped his prompting and turned to watch.

The pushed fellow started to raise his fist, but hesitated. Instead, he slapped down a fiver on the table and walked out. "We're done, asshole!"

Interesting, Jefferson thought. Of all the things that could have turned, racism was the trigger. Or was it xenophobia? That's what Jackson had said about the liquor store owner. Their man snapped when he saw the guy was Muslim. This wasn't generalized anger, but directed at the 'other.'

He spotted an empty cocktail table across the bar. It was behind a larger table with four women who were just sitting down. This should be interesting. He walked around them, giving them as wide a berth as he could to draw no attention to his hulking self.

"I can't believe he told you to stay late to find the files he lost," said a tanned woman in her early thirties with long, highlighted brown hair.

"Well, I found it right away, which is why I could join you guys," said a younger East Indian woman.

Highlighted hair girl scoffed. "Disgusting what we have to put up with."

A tiny Asian woman commented, "I'm just glad to have a job that isn't in my aunt's nail shop. Talk about disgusting."

"I liked working in my mother's hair salon," added the last one, a tall black woman. "That is until the tax man shut it down."

What luck, four different ethnicities at one table. Now to turn up the heat. Jefferson tapped Hiram's fury just enough to make his heart race and his breathing quicken. Then he imagined it leave him as a cloud of swirling black mist that settled over the women.

"What do you mean your mom lost her salon to the tax man?" the Asian woman asked with a bit of a sneer in her voice.

"She didn't know she needed to pay payroll taxes on her assistants and, by the time they caught up to her, it was enough to break the business."

"If you don't understand money, you shouldn't be hiring people."

"Whoa, hold on a minute! My mama gave a lot of people good jobs."

"Maybe, but you people are no good with money," the Asian muttered, but loud enough for all to hear.

The black woman stood up. "You come over here and say that!"

The East Indian woman meekly offered. "She's got a point."

The black woman was incensed. "What, now I've got the whole Buddhist continent jumpin' on my ass?"

"I'm Hindu," the Indian insisted.

"That gives you even less right to speak up," chimed in the white woman. "She may be a stupid black, but at least she's not a foreigner taking American jobs."

Ah, there it was — the xenophobia. Took it a minute to make it around the table, but at last it appeared. Jefferson was wondering how to test whether he could direct this anger, when a waiter came over to the table to break up the fight. The women had just reached the point of grabbing at each other's clothes.

The waiter was Mexican. Too easy. He turned Hiram on the man, and the women followed right behind.

He got as far as asking them, "Ladies, can you please keep it down, or take it outside? This is a laid-back place for people to relax."

They didn't even speak, and, as one, they threw their drinks at him. Then they got up and started swinging on him.

As other wait staff rushed over to break up the violence, Jefferson pulled back his focus and watched over his shoulder. He was amazed at how easy they were to manipulate. Perfectly reasonable coworkers reduced to senseless animal violence in a matter of seconds. It was as if their anger was already simmering under the surface and he only needed to turn up the heat one last degree to let loose a boil. And the redirection to the waiter was far easier than he imagined. Turning a crowd on a Looker would be child's play.

He got up and stepped past the melee and the broken glass on the floor. Everyone's attention was on the four women and the half dozen waiters in full donnybrook. He slipped out without notice.

He slid his huge body down into the car seat while he listened to the continuing uproar inside the bar. He started the car and considered what he had set in motion. *Fifty feet?* he estimated. He waved a hand as if conducting an orchestra. "Not enough fortissimo."

He reached back and felt Hiram's seething presence. He mentally grabbed it and gave it a good hard squeeze. He felt the rage swell and flare. He flung it forward into the bar, letting it find its own targets.

Within seconds, the yelling increased, followed by screaming. A chair flew out the front window.

Jefferson laughed nervously.

Then came the gunshots.

Jefferson threw the car into reverse and gunned it out of harm's way.

•　　•　　•

"The good thing about tin cans is you can set 'em back a up a few times before they're too ripped up." Harold Fraily set the half dozen cans on the railing of the fence at the back of the Meyer property, beyond which was open farmland. "It's a good thing your house is at the end of this development."

Burt looked around. "Won't your neighbors call the cops on us out here shooting guns?"

Nate pointed to one house. "That place is vacant due to a foreclosure. The bank has let it sit. I don't know what they're waiting for. And on the other side, the guy and his wife are both field sales road warriors. They're gone sometimes for weeks."

Working at the patio table, Burt went back to loading the clips for the two rifles Harold had taken from his car. "I thought Miss Sarah said you and her were done fighting the meteor cultists."

Harold answered as he walked back to the house. "If it was that easy for you and I to find Nate and Sarah, it will not be hard for the cultists to find them too. I want to make sure they can defend themselves. We've seen these bastards are out for blood. You sure as hell can't depend on the police to protect you."

"I appreciate the lesson," Nate said, looking dubiously at the gun in his hands. "But I don't own any assault rifles like this."

"Oh, I'm giving you that one," Harold said flatly. "I've got three more in my trunk." Looking to Burt, he said, "You know what you're doing with that one, right?"

"Well, I've used rifles to hunt before, but nothing like this."

"All right, gentlemen. You have in your hands the semi-automatic, civilian version of the M-4 Carbine, made by Colt Firearms. It has a 16-inch barrel, which gives you accuracy up to a couple hundred yards. It fires a bullet every time you pull the trigger, no matter how fast you pull it. It has a kick, so keep the butt tight against the crook of your shoulder whenever you fire it. These have 30 round clips. The bullets are the equivalent of a 45 round, so one bullet should stop a man."

"Is this the kind of gun you used in Desert Storm?" Nate asked.

"We used M16A2s, which were heavier and longer than these. Those were also fully automatic. Let's get started. Loop the butt strap over your right shoulder. Stand with your left foot slightly ahead of your right, so you catch yourself with your right foot from the recoil, lift the gun up against your shoulder, and look down the barrel. The safeties are on, and we'll get to those in a minute. Now lower the weapon back onto the strap. Then do it again. Stance, set, aim. One more time. Lower it to the strap. Now stance, set, aim. You used to the weight?

"Okay. Now let's talk about the safety. On the left side of the weapon, next to your right thumb, is a lever. It is horizontal. That's how you want it at all times unless and until you have a target in your sights. Bring the guns up. The sequence is: acquire your target, flip the safety down to the firing position, aim, pull the trigger, then flip the safety back on, then lower the weapon. The safety prevents the trigger from being pulled. These are extremely deadly devices. The only time the safety is off is when you are actually shooting.

"So let's try it without actually firing the guns. Acquire, safety off, trigger, safety on, lower the weapon. Let's do that again before we start firing. Stance, raise and set, acquire target, safety off, aim, trigger, safety on, lower. Good. The more you do that, the more natural the motion will get.

"Now for the fun part. Do exactly the same sequence, except this time, aim for a can and actually pull the trigger. Do not be afraid of it. It's going to be loud and it's going to buck you. You do not need to hold the handle so tight out of fear of the recoil. You'll just ruin your aim. Let it kick. Just hold it steady when you squeeze the trigger."

Both guns fired. Neither hit a can.

"All right. Safeties back on. Do you know if you fired high or low? Left or right?"

"I think I was high," Nate said.

"Me too," said Burt.

"Okay. Go again. Remember the sequence." Harold watched their fingers and indeed they were using the safety correctly.

Burt hit his can. "All right!"

Harold heard what sounded like a truck rumbling through the field beyond the fence, but there was no road and no truck visible. "Lower your weapons. What is that?"

"Sounds like hooves," Burt guessed.

Several dark shapes appeared, running through the tall grass straight toward them.

"Shit, those are wild boar!" Nate said. "And they are not slowing down for the fence!"

"Well, you're armed, boys. You've got fifty feet of yard; take 'em out as they come in."

Two boar smashed through the railing with the cans and charged in. Burt and Nate raised their guns and fired. Burt's pig squealed pitifully and tumbled. Nate missed. He fired again and missed again.

Harold stepped up to him and took the gun. "Sorry, son." Harold spun around and coolly dispatched the rushing pig at about fifteen feet.

Three more ran through the breach in the fence. Burt missed the one he fired at. Harold hit one, then another. The third one headed for Nate. He grabbed a lawn chair and smacked it as hard as he could, which diverted its path past him.

"Duck!" Harold ordered, and then shot the pig before it could turn for another charge.

One last pig ran squealing into the yard, and both Burt and Harold shot it dead.

Nate shook his head. "I know southern Missouri is overrun with these pigs, but I didn't think they had made it up to St. Louis."

"Me neither," Harold agreed.

"What the hell happened?" Sarah appeared at the back door, rubbing her eyes, her short hair mussed from lying down.

Harold noticed she had cut her long hair.

"We were target practicing and half a dozen wild pigs attacked us," Nate explained.

Sarah took a step back and blanched. "Pigs?"

"Yeah, we shot them all. We're safe now. Lucky we had guns ready."

Harold did not think she looked comforted by this. In fact, her eyes went wider and she shook her head. "What is it, Sarah?"

"I ... I dreamt them."

"Oh my God, really?" Nate said knowingly.

"Hold on," Harold interrupted. "What do you mean you dreamt them? You heard us out here shooting and you included it in your dream."

Nate took a breath and answered. "That's what we thought too, at first. We've been holding out on you two. There's actually a lot more going on here. The necklace you gave her has given her the ability to alter reality with her dreams. I know, it sounds like fantasy, but we've proved it several times."

Burt and Harold stared at Nate for a long second. "Like a wish?" Harold asked.

"Yes, but it's involuntary. She's got no control over it."

"Is that why you call the eye vision god the Dreamer?"

Sarah nodded, her face still tight with fear. She looked to her brother. "It's like I can't sleep at all anymore without changing something."

Harold did not try to hide the fear in his voice. "Do all the Dreamer necklaces give this ability?"

Nate held up his hand. "Thankfully no. They all give the Dreamer eye vision — the same way all the Devourer necklaces give the biting teeth vision. So far, the one you gave Sarah is the only one that allows dreams to grant wishes."

Sarah lowered her head while still looking at them. "Lucky me."

Harold pursed his lips to one side as he turned this over. "Miracles, on top of being able to calm people with a touch? One thing I have learned in following God is there are only so many things in this world I was meant to understand. I trust God to take care of the rest of it. Healing people of their hate and changing the world when it needs changing, those look an awful lot like what Jesus did. You said these stones came from aliens. I think your answer lies somewhere between the two.

"Y'all come inside. I got something I want to show you." As Harold turned to the backdoor, he noticed Burt was looking rather shell-shocked by all of this. "You too, Burt. I know this is a lot. That's why we're going to need all of us."

They went inside and Harold ran out to his car. He came back with a steel tackle box. "I collected the necklace from the Devourer leader of the gang that killed my people. I also have the necklace we took off Daniel."

Nate said, "Please leave them in there. Burt was wearing one too, and I don't want to re-expose him."

"Oh, absolutely. In fact, my brother Caleb told me he had a vision of how we needed to protect ourselves from evil. He didn't give me any details that could have pointed to the Devourer cult, but he did say we could contain all the evil under a dome. He said it was a pure, smooth white dome. Sounded pretty weird at the time. But I figure it means we need to keep ourselves away from the bad necklace charms. I also collected all the Dreamer ones from Caleb and my people after they were killed. I've got those in the car too."

Nate went to the freezer and pulled out a small foil wrapped object. "This was Burt's."

Harold unlocked the box and Nate added the third necklace. "We can bury this out in the yard where nobody will be affected by them."

"It's getting dark," Nate observed. "We can bury this when we clean up the pig bodies in the morning."

Harold noticed Sarah looking at her brother so dejectedly, he had to comment. "Is there something else I missed?"

"No, Mr. Fraily," she said quietly. "You've been very thorough."

"It's Harold, please."

"I do have a confession to make. This morning Nate and I talked, and I resolved to quit this quest. I figured you and Burt have a stake in seeing it through. I am just so overwhelmed, and my dreaming miracles can be so destructive, I thought maybe it would be better if I handed this over to you. I stopped wearing my necklace a couple of weeks ago, hoping the dreams would stop. But now that I see the dreams are continuing, it's pretty clear that I should stay in the game and see if I can help."

"Well little lady, that's very brave, and I do appreciate it." He interrupted himself. "It is right for me to call you lady, isn't it?" He noted her baggy clothes and short cropped hair hid any sign of gender.

Sarah laughed. She gave her brother a frown and an eye roll that Harold did not understand. "Yes, I identify as female. Thank you."

"So, you're going to stick around for a while, I hope, at least until we can figure out who we're dealing with in Florida."

She nodded. "Sure."

Sarah got some Lucky Charms from a kitchen cabinet and started eating it dry from the box. She sat down at the dining table with the tackle box. Nate, Burt, and Harold moved into the living room and sat down to discuss strategy.

Burt started. "I visited the plantation house once. It's just outside Tallahassee. It's a big spread. They usually have at least a dozen guys there. It's not hard to find. I never met Jefferson Davis, but I did talk to his right-hand man Jackson Pruitt. He was the one who told me to come look for what he calls 'Lookers' in St. Louis."

Harold noticed that Sarah had put her head down on her arms at the table. He leaned over to Nate. "Is she going to be all right? I imagine the pressure must be a lot."

Nate looked up at her and shook his head. "It's actually worse than it appears. Not to tell secrets, but one of her dreams made her hair grow long and another one changed her physically into an actual woman. That came as such a shock, she cut off her beautiful long hair and has gone back to the boyish loose clothes. She's also eating a lot of sweets, and I think I smell cigarette smoke in her room. I'm really worried about her. I wish these dreams would leave her alone. She's really done with this whole fighting with gods thing."

Burt looked dumbfounded. Clearly, he had not realized Sarah was transgender. Harold thought it reflected well on him that he held his tongue and didn't say anything stupid.

Burt did look up at Sarah and blurted out in shock, "What the hell is that?"

He yelled loud enough it woke Sarah and she sat up startled. All four of them looked with amazement and horror at the two-foot diameter solid white dome that sat where the tackle box had been. The men rushed to the table while Sarah pushed herself away from it.

"No, goddamn it, no!" she yelled at the gleaming smooth structure.

Nate was the first to touch it. "It's cold and solid, like stone."

Harold touched it too. "You just dreamed this?"

"I hate this so much!" she growled through clenched teeth. "I can't even tell if I'm still sleeping. My first thought was you guys were punking me. Yes, I imagined what you described about a white dome. I am so tired, I nodded off for just a second, and then bang! This materializes."

Harold rapped on it with his knuckles. "It sounds hollow. I guess the tackle box is under it." He also noticed Burt was not taking this well at all, and had taken a couple of steps back. Harold tried prying up an edge. "It appears fused to the table."

Sarah glowered at it. "You said it would seal away the evil."

Nate frowned at it and asked her, "Can you sense the necklaces? You've been working on being able to sense the Devourers. Do you feel anything under the dome?"

She looked at it hard. "No. Nothing. I guess it works."

"This may have been a shock to have something magically appear like this." Nate commented. "But it's good to know you can create material that blocks the Devourer radiation. I don't know how we'll use it, but it's good to know."

Sarah smirked at Harold. "That's my brother. Always looking for the bright side."

Harold rubbed his jaw while looking at the dome. "Nate, you've been to college studying science, right? Isn't there something that says you can't just create matter or energy out of nothing?"

"Create or destroy. It's a conservation law. Clearly this godlike creature could alter that. And to your unasked question: no, I have no idea how this works."

Sarah squinted at them tentatively. "I kinda do. I was watching a science show on TV and this scientist talked about alternate timelines and universes. He said everything that happens can be a turning point between a universe where an event happens, and the one where the event doesn't happen. I think what Oum could do, and what he's given me the ability to do, is push the march of time down a different path, to choose new things to happen."

Nate frowned. "Then why do we all remember that there was no dome just a minute ago? If you have altered the fabric of time/space, then it would have always been here, and we would remember it always being here."

"No, that's not what she said," Harold held up a hand. "She said there was a turning point. Everything that happened before the turning point still happened. The dome was not here, and we remember correctly that the dome was not here. Then she turned a corner to a world where it is here. And we noticed the change. Do I have that right?" he asked her.

She grimaced and nodded. "Yes, exactly. I've been thinking about that show for weeks now, and I think that works."

"Can you do this when you're awake?" Harold asked.

"No, I've tried. I'm sick of not being able to control it, so I've tried wishing things to happen. It only works in my dreams. The weird thing is, I couldn't dream for years when I was on the drugs. The doctors said I should be able to dream on them, but I don't remember any. They were probably filled with hateful voices and I just forgot them out of self-defense. Or maybe I couldn't sleep soundly enough to actually dream. Now that the voices are gone, I can dream, even though I'm still on the meds. I don't get it.

"Suddenly being able to dream again was like candy. It was a treat and I loved it. I only barely remember what dreaming was like when I was a little kid. Now this has taken over my dreams and I fear them. Nate and I have talked about trying to train me in something called Lucid Dreaming. It's supposed to help you control what happens in a dream, like you're aware that you're dreaming and can steer what happens."

"Yeah, I got you a book on that. It's in your room."

"I'll also look on the Internet. Maybe there's a course online. However I do it, I've got to get a handle on this. Somebody's going to wind up dead. And I can't live with no sleep."

13

"THESE DREAMS"
HEART

SARAH LAY ON HER BED and realized how tired her body was. Her body still felt wrong not having anything between her legs to tuck. Vagina or not, she was exhausted. She tried to let her mind wander and not focus on anything, but it kept rolling back over the last few days: the crazy bitch in Target, the magical white dome, the horrid dream that disappeared her penis, Harold and Burt and the pigs and the guns, and ... Her mind raced and raced with no end. And, at every turn, her memories left her feeling the same: that it was all pointless and there was no way out.

She grabbed her phone and earbuds and pulled up a Spotify playlist called Quiet Club. She tried to let the soothing blues singers carry her away from her troubles, but the somebody-done-somebody-wrong songs brought her back to hopelessness.

Maybe some confident, in-your-face metal? K. Flay's need for noise rang true. This worked for a few songs, but their anger proved they hadn't won against the odds.

As tired as she was, she wasn't any closer to sleepy.

She reached over to her desk and pulled off the book on lucid dreaming. She smiled at the possible irony of falling asleep on a book about sleep. But her mind still raced, and she couldn't manage to concentrate on the words she read.

She noticed her heart was beating fast, too. And her breathing felt tight. *Shit, not an anxiety attack.* Too late. The walls of her room seemed closer, the desk lamp, which was the only light on, seemed too bright. The quiet of the house felt loaded with hidden danger. She put the book down, crossed her arms over her chest, and pounded an alternating rhythm: left hand on right shoulder, right hand on left shoulder. She forced herself to take slow, deep breaths, timed against the drumming, forcing herself to only take and release one breath for each eight beats. She was glad for having learned this at Sandstone over the years. It used to help when the voices got the better of her.

She fleetingly hoped there wasn't anything she needed to pay attention to in the room, which of course distracted her from the exercise. Her heart raced again at the thought of missing something. She had to double down with the breathing and the drumming.

"It will be all right. It will be all right. It will be all right," she repeated quietly, convincing herself this attack would pass like all the others before.

She was so tired, and fighting through the attack was even more exhausting. After several agonizing minutes, she finally felt her heart slowing. She kept up the rhythm and the forced breathing until she felt no more tension or fear in her body. Man, she was hungry.

Walking to the kitchen, she passed the stairs up to the other bedrooms. She had really made Nate's life a hell. In her daymare he had said so. Maybe he didn't feel that way for real, but the facts remained. She had no idea what she had done to deserve all this shit, but Nate had certainly not done anything. She toyed with the idea of telling him how sorry she was, but that train of thought crashed before it left the station.

Turning on only the stove hood light so as to not wake anyone, she was happy to find a bag of chocolate chip cookies on the counter. There was an open bottle of wine on the kitchen island. *Weird.* And there was the white dome, still stuck to the table. She wandered into the living room and experimented with how low she could set the volume on the TV. Surely she could find some cartoons. Nate obviously didn't watch much television. He only had basic cable. Curled up on the couch, one hand working the cookie bag, and the other hand working the remote, she was sure there had to be some cartoons in here somewhere.

Reruns of shows that went off the air before she was born did not interest her. Nor did the infomercial about lawn care products or the home shopping show with the crappiest jewelry she had ever seen.

She was about to flip past a news program when a horrific story caught her attention. "We're just getting this footage in from our affiliate in Tallahassee. What you're seeing is the end of a three-alarm fire that consumed the Down Low Saloon near Florida Highway 267. A fight broke out among bar patrons around five pm this evening. According to eyewitness reports, within minutes the fight led to shots being fired, and a fire breaking out. Over a dozen people were rushed to nearby hospitals with various injuries and our unverified report shows four people dead. The police will have a lot of work figuring out how this all happened, and unfortunately a lot of evidence was destroyed by the fire. We will definitely be keeping you up on this story as more details are released."

"Florida," Sarah repeated quietly. Could this be related to the enemy cult there? A bar fight with gun shots that burns the place down? Why would anyone set off that kind of chaos? The world really was going to hell. She turned it off and went back to her room with the cookies.

On the way, she stopped in the hall bathroom to pee. Having to sit down and wipe with toilet paper every time was just one more annoyance. *Hello vagina I don't want.* It was innocent enough looking, all folded up tidy. This was all just too weird and too soon. She thought of all the proud woman imagery she had seen on television since she got out. She couldn't see how she would ever be proud of having this opening. *I can't wait until you start to bleed on me.* The idea of having sex with it was utterly repulsive. She pulled up her pants and flushed.

Back in her room, she lit a couple of candles on her windowsill and turned off the desk lamp. She lay back and gave sleep another try. Her eyelids felt literally heavy, but her mind would not shut up. She watched the wavering candlelight on the ceiling and the shadows across the room. It was peaceful. It was nice.

She noticed a crystal on the sill. She sat up and held it close to a flame, trying to throw spectra around the room. It didn't work very well, but she was happy with the few spots of color she managed.

The flame was more interesting. Out of boredom, she waved her hand close over it and was surprised that it wasn't that hot. So she moved her hand closer and slower. Ah, that time she felt it.

She reflexively looked to the door, expecting nursing staff to have a clear view of her. Her bedroom door was closed. She blinked as she processed that.

She really was alone. Was this loneliness? Nate said she needed friends. Would a friend stop her from doing something stupid?

Lost in the moment, she considered how it wouldn't be any great loss if she damaged or destroyed this body she hated. She moved her forearm slowly across the flame itself and the burn seized her out of her reverie. That was more of a rush than she expected. Her arm hurt like crazy, but it also felt right. She felt like the fog of despair lifted for a moment. She felt like herself, like she could deal with all the shit that was crushing her.

She remembered seeing all the cuts on girls' arms at Sandstone. She had never felt the urge to cut. The voices wouldn't let her try something so daring. She never really understood why the girls did it. Until now.

She blew out the candle. The clock on her desk glowed 4:06 am. Lying there in the dark, with her arm throbbing, she closed her eyes and they finally felt like they would stay shut. Her brain had one final insult. "You can't even properly hurt yourself." *Fuck you brain.*

•   •   •

Nate tossed and turned in bed until he finally gave up around 1:00 am and walked downstairs to the kitchen. He stopped in the hall and saw a low light on under Sarah's door. He listened and heard nothing. He assumed she had fallen asleep with her desk lamp on.

He knew why he couldn't sleep. It wasn't the danger they faced from the Florida cult. He felt they had some handle on that. And it wasn't all the sudden disruption of their lives. He had learned to live with unwanted change when his parents died and Sarah was institutionalized and he had to grow up all at once when he was sixteen. If he could learn to sleep through that time, he could sleep through anything.

No, this was about Sarah. He had given up any dreams of being a stellar student and finding history-making cures. He had settled for working part-time jobs in labs to make contacts that had not panned out. His dating history had proven he was too angry at the world to make any romantic connections. He had backed away from a lot of things, but the one thing he always thought he could be was a good provider for his sister. Now she was slipping into depression and there didn't seem to be anything he could do about it.

The changes the stones had brought were intense and relentless, more than anyone could be expected to weather — let alone a fragile innocent like Sarah. Her voices had never let her make friends at Sandstone. Now that she was out, she had no social network. Even with all the fights he used to get into, at least he had other kids to relate to. Should he have gotten her into school sooner?

He hadn't taken many classes in clinical treatment. Most of his studies were in neuroscience. He knew he shouldn't jump in telling her to employ the coping skills they taught her at Sandstone. Rubbing her nose in not doing what she had been taught would just make her feel worse. Yet, he couldn't stand by and watch her slip away.

What about Doctor Alpaca? He hadn't set Sarah up with a new psychiatrist outside. Another failure to provide. Sarah scoffed at going to see her about the magical sex change. But what about depression? Would Alpaca see her? How would Sarah get advice if she couldn't share the biggest source of her stress? It would be tricky. Nate could coach Sarah to only answer the questions Alpaca asked, and draw the line at giving away the meteorites. Alpaca had always been open-minded. Nate was still impressed with how she advocated for Sarah's transition when the *de facto* industry standard was to see gender dysphoria as another symptom. Even so, asking anyone to understand these meteorites was too much. Maybe he should try a call anyway. Even with that possibility, he still felt like he had failed her.

He let his hands explore the kitchen shelves while his mind kept tripping over itself and falling down holes. He found a bag of dark chocolate truffles. And a bottle of Cabernet. He didn't even hesitate to reach for the bottle opener.

He noticed all but one of the forks was gone from the drawer. In Sarah's room, no doubt. Oh yeah, most of the glasses and small plates too. At least that was normal enough teenager behavior.

The chocolate tasted of comfort. The wine tasted like deliverance. He raised the glass to toast the dark living room. "Nate, pity party of one."

• • •

Cecilia Bledsoe was walking back from a Portland street farmer's market with a bag of fruit when she noticed she was in front of Grover's Smoke Shop. She looked in the window and waved at Todd the shopkeeper.

He waved back and came out. "Well, look at you. I'm so glad to see you're doing better."

She wasn't sure how to react.

"Thank him for the compliment," prodded her sweet voice.

"Thank you. I am feeling much more myself lately."

"You must be doing something right. I noticed you haven't been out here. I hoped that meant good things."

"Yes, I'm staying at Burnside until I get something more permanent."

"I'm proud of you. Hey, I got some more jewelry in this week, if you want to take a look."

"No, I'm very happy with the necklace I got last month." She touched it under her blouse. "I think that day might have been a turning point for me."

"Sometimes if you do something nice for yourself, you can see that you deserved it."

Cecilia was distracted by a commotion a block down the street. "What's all that down there?"

Todd stepped out onto the sidewalk to see. "Oh, Christ. I heard they might be pulling some shit again this weekend. Looks like they moved it up to today."

"Who's doing what?"

"Rent protesters. Every few months, some eviction case fires them up and they take to the streets. The problem is, once the police show up, things get violent and I have to nail boards to my front window and close up. What a pain."

The sense of anger from the crowd felt overwhelming. It was a sensation she couldn't make sense of, but it was strong and distracting and blotted out her ability to hear Todd. It felt like heat and sound and light all at the same time. She blinked hard and tried to focus. She wished her voice would give her some advice, but it did not.

"I think I'll go check it out."

"I wouldn't go down there if I were you. Those picket signs you see turn into weapons in a flash. And the police have been cracking down on any street protests after all the attempts to set up autonomous zones over the last year."

She didn't know what he meant by that, but his concern was clear. Yet, she felt compelled to go closer. In fact, she really didn't want to go.

"Oh, you needn't warn me about the police. My daddy was killed by a cop for a traffic stop when I was fourteen."

"Oh, Jesus, I'm sorry. I had no idea."

"It's something I live with every day."

So why wouldn't her feet take her away from the crowd? She practically pleaded with her voice to add its warning. Still nothing. And the urge to go, to reach out to all those angry people, to let them know they didn't need to take up arms, was far too compelling.

"I'll be right back," she said as she started walking.

Each step was a struggle between her urge to help and her fear of getting hurt. The closer she got, the stronger both emotions became, with her racing heart caught between. Still, the urge was stronger, and she kept walking.

She didn't know what she could do, and she didn't know why she thought she could do anything. By the time she was a hundred feet away, their anger was tangible, like a furnace on her face. She saw the people waving their signs standing across, blocking the street, and it felt like they were on fire, and somehow she had to put out that fire.

Yells turned to screams on the other side of the crowd. People in the back stepped back and closed the space so she was suddenly in the crowd. She caught a flash of shields and helmets up in front. Her only thought was to flee, but her only feeling was to stay, stay and stop all of this. She stood there paralyzed with fear, confusion, and indecision.

The police pressed forward, and she saw them swinging batons. The crowd backed up further to where she was only a couple of rows back from the front. Terrified by the danger all around her, and the explosive pressure that filled her body, she closed her eyes and prayed.

The eye vision appeared in her mind and her fear evaporated. She knew what to do. She reached out to the people around her and touched them on the shoulders. One by one they stopped yelling and stood back from their confrontation. She saw their fires go quiet.

But then she faced an extremely angry officer. He raised his baton to strike her and she looked into his eyes behind his face shield. She said calmly, "Stop."

He did. He blinked and shook his head. He looked at the truncheon in his raised hand and then lowered it.

Cecilia stood back to look across the line of police and said it again, loudly but with no anger. "Stop. All of you just stop."

The fifteen cops facing her had the same reaction as the first. She also heard the crowd behind her had stopped yelling. She felt their fires all going out too.

The police on either side and behind the affected officers crowded past to advance the attack.

Cecilia raised her hands and yelled, "I said stop!"

Like a wave rolling through the crowd, the police and the protesters all lowered their weapons and signs. The street fell suddenly weirdly silent as everyone stood shocked at what had just happened to them.

Cecilia turned and walked straight back through the protesters and escaped while the crowd blinked and looked at each other in amazement.

14

"LAST WORDS OF A SHOOTING STAR"
MITSKI

MARY ALPACA WATCHED SARAH MEYER refold her legs under herself again in the plush patient chair in the Quiet Talk room. She noted the change in clothes and general demeanor since her last visit a month before. The black and green plaid flannel pajama bottoms, rock t-shirt, black zipper hoodie, and Uggs were pretty typical teenager uniform. The sunken eyes and disheveled hair were new for Sarah.

"Your brother says he suspects you may have picked up some depression since you left us."

"He's not wrong. And you're still my doctor, so here I am."

"Let's start with how your life has been since you went home."

She thought for a moment before answering. "We've been very busy on a big project. My brother and I have been working very closely the whole time, which has been great."

"That's good news. How is the project going?"

"It's turned out to be a lot more difficult than we thought. We've had a lot of setbacks."

"Are you still interested in proceeding?"

Big breath. Recrossed her legs under her in the chair. "I kind of have to. I frankly think it's hopeless, but we're pretty committed."

"You keep calling it a project. Do you want to tell me what it is?

"No. I'm sorry, but it's way too complicated. I know you could probably be more help if I told you all about it, but I just can't."

"All right. Do you find yourself thinking a lot of things are hopeless?"

She thought for a moment. "Pointless, actually. No matter what I do, life just won't have it."

"Have you encountered actual resistance?"

"Oh, yeah. I was attacked in a Target bathroom by a TERF. It was ugly, police and everything."

"Oh goodness. I'm so sorry. Were you hurt?"

"Not really. Shook up more than anything."

"I wish you and Nate had called me right after. You shouldn't just dismiss that kind of trauma. Has that affected your willingness to go out?"

"No, I know she was just a freak. It has made me more aware of people's reactions to me."

"Did the incident trigger any dysphoria?

She rolled her eyes behind half-closed lids. "No. I still know I'm a girl.

"All right. I see you dyed your hair, The red looks nice."

"Yeah, I had it long at one point, but that didn't work for me."

Mary mentally noted the incongruity. Sarah had only been home for six weeks. "Have you been eating well? You don't look like you've lost or gained any weight."

"I am snacking a lot. I think I'm too tempted by having a whole kitchen at my fingertips."

"That might take some adjustment."

"Yeah, frankly it took me a while to learn to get up and do things. Everything was precisely timed out for me here. Having that structure suddenly gone was weird."

"What do you do during the day, besides this big project with your brother? Have you started any studies for school?

"No, not yet. Nate and I have talked about it, but we haven't signed me up.

"What do I do all day? I listen to music on my phone. I've tried reading, but I can't focus long enough for the words to sink in. I find myself re-reading the same page four times, so I give up. And I spend a lot of time crying."

"Every day?"

"Yeah. Usually in the bathroom."

"Why the bathroom?"

"I'll check my look and it'll just hit me."

"Can you describe that feeling?"

"Overwhelmed. Hopeless, like I said."

"How about your sleep?"

Multiple eye blinks. "Sleep has been a big problem. I am dreaming a lot more than I remember from when I was here. But it's a lot of nightmares. I'm actually afraid of going to sleep."

"Do the voices come to you in your sleep?"

"No, the voices are completely gone, thank God. These are just scary and disturbing. I don't get enough sleep, so I nap a lot during the day. A lot of times I can't tell when I'm awake or when I'm still asleep. It's not good."

"Have you tried antihistamines or sleep aids? I can prescribe a good one."

"No, I probably should try that."

"You almost never remembered your dreams while you were with us. Do you remember them now when you awake?"

"Sadly, yes."

"Do you dream about abstract things, or about things from your real life?"

"I used to only dream about things that weren't real. I always assumed that was because my real life in here wasn't worth dreaming about. Now they're almost always about real stuff, which I kind of hate."

"Do you care about what happens in your dreams, while they are happening?"

"Oh yeah. I am fully invested."

"That's actually a good sign. I'm sorry you're having nightmares, but caring about the content of your dreams while you're having them is a sign of brain health."

Sarah stifled a smirk at that comment.

"Are you still taking the Clozipine?"

"Yes."

"Have you had any anxiety?"

She grinned weakly. "Good guess, Doctor. Yes, more and more. I have an attack pretty much every night when I try to go to sleep. Which means I don't go under until really late, like four am."

"Do your coping skills help?"

"Yeah, some. It would be worse without them."

"Is it your fear of sleep that sets them off?"

"Not really. It's mostly the hopelessness of our big project."

"Which you can't tell me about."

"Right."

"Have you had any other traumas or big negative experiences, other than the bathroom attack?"

Another round of eyeblinks. "Yeah, I've been a witness to several ugly, um, accidents where people have been hurt badly."

"Several? How many?"

"Three."

"You've witnessed three major accidents? That can be overwhelming. We're you in any of them?"

"Well, yes, I was involved in one."

"Were you physically hurt?"

"No, miraculously."

"So, in six weeks, you were attacked in a bathroom, you were in an accident, and you witnessed two other accidents where others were hurt. Sarah, you have been through far too much for someone trying to get back on their feet. Your cortisol level must be sky high. I'm not surprised you're giving up on things and can't sleep. I wish Nate had told me you've been through all of this. Is there anything you can do to get away from all this trauma?

"The big project is coming to a close in two weeks."

"That's something. If the project is a success, will it be something you can feel good about?"

"Yes, absolutely."

"It is part of my job to draw out details from patients who either don't recognize bad things are happening to them, or who are straight up reluctant to tell me. Neither you nor your brother told me you had been exposed to so much stress. You can't brush that off, not after you've just regained your perception of life. I will be prescribing medications and therapies to help you with this. If this project of yours is one of the things that has impacted your outlook, I really need you to tell me about it so I can do right for you. Do you understand?"

"Yes, I do. I know you could do a better job if I opened up about it. Truth be told, all I want to do right now is get up and walk out. Just talking about it is stressing me out. I do trust you, Doctor Alpaca. That I am staying here and talking to you proves that. I'm really sorry. You're going to have to do the best you can with what I can talk about."

"All right. We need to get you help so you can cope, to knock down the depression and you can get back to recovery."

"Nate said something about re-regulating my Default something Network."

This time, Mary rolled her eyes. "I will have to chat with Nate about the damage a little knowledge can do. He should not be sharing psychological theories with you. It only adds to suppositions and errors. Yes, the centers of the brain that regulate our inherent negativity bias are useful in both stopping schizophrenic delusions and depression."

"Oh, I remember negativity bias. That's why we run from lions instead of petting them."

"Yes, that's probably the explanation we gave you when you were nine," she said with a smile. "I was hoping whatever higher brain function finally re-activated to quell your voices would also keep depression at bay. For a long time, we had you diagnosed with schizoaffective disorder, which has depression as a component. All this trauma has beaten back your defenses. It is really important that you keep taking your meds to keep your dopamine levels under control and make sure this depression is the only imbalance that shows up.

"All right, so we're looking at post-trauma depression and anxiety. Let me start over. Have you had any suicidal ideation?"

"No. I don't think my death would be a good idea."

"What about self-harm?"

She looked away.

"Cutting?"

She pulled up her sweatshirt sleeve to reveal three painful looking red lines across her forearm. "Burning."

"That happens at the top of the anxiety, right?"

A nod.

"Your brother says he smelled cigarettes in your room. You don't smell of them now. Did you try smoking?"

"Yes, but they tasted like death. I also looked them up. Did you know nicotine addiction is harder to break than heroin?"

"Yes. Yes, it is. Have you tried anything stronger for your anxiety, like marijuana?"

"No. Nate would kill me."

"Okay, we need to get you re-centered. My initial thought is to jump start you with something to bring down the anxiety, like Lexipro. Only thing is, I really want to get you refocused to bring you out of the depression, and Lexipro can lead to flat affect. Effexor might be a better choice. It takes longer to take effect, but it doesn't grey you out. If the anxiety gets bad enough that you can't pull out of an attack, we can get you Clonazepam, but that's only for extreme cases.

"The good news is, coupled with the right medication, this kind of post-traumatic depression and anxiety is highly treatable. It's a lot of work, and it takes a commitment from you, which is tough because you're depressed."

"What kind of work?"

"Mindfulness practice. Do you remember a few years back we tried you on Dialectic Behavior Therapy?"

"Yeah, DBT. It was a lot of paying attention to my breath and my guts. It didn't do anything with the voices criticizing my every move. Same thing happened with CBT."

"That's true. We tried to use Cognitive Behavioral Therapy to teach you to tell what was real and what was not. But the voices are gone now, and DBT is really good at teaching you to focus. The more you focus, the easier it gets. It's like exercising a muscle. It's that higher brain focus that drives out the depression. You retrain your brain to act as you want it to, and not wander down into depression."

"Not that I don't want to do it, because I do. How much work are we talking about?"

"Some practice every day, if possible. Expect to be doing this for a while, at least a few months. It has to become part of your nature. There are workbooks you go through. It's all laid out."

"I actually did some research online before I came today," she said with a crooked grin. "I know you warned about having just a little knowledge. I saw that DBT is supposed to be good for depression. I also saw that mindfulness originally came from Buddhist practices. I saw a lot of reference to accepting things as not permanent. That struck a chord with me."

Not permanent. "Are you having trouble accepting change?"

Sarah's eyebrows shot up and she looked away to hide her reaction. "That's the understatement of the year. I am quite sure it's the changes that have set me off."

"Change can be challenging, and people can react badly to change they don't want. The Buddhists cope by accepting that life is full of change. They even preach that hanging on to things you don't want to change, that insistence on permanence, is the source of all suffering. I don't know if that's true, but they're right that we make things harder for ourselves if we don't roll with the changes life throws at us. Are you not adjusting to life outside of Sandstone? I thought you were handling that fine."

"Oh, no, the move home has been great. I taught myself how to cook, how to do makeup, how to go shopping. It's not being out that has messed with me."

"Are you afraid the schizophrenia might come back?"

"No, thank God. That's like the only thing I'm not worried about."

"Has the change come from this mysterious project you won't tell me about?"

She looked at the floor and sighed. "Yes, the project has brought a lot of change to me personally. You could say it's another trauma. Let's treat it like another trauma."

Mary pushed ahead while planning how she could learn enough to be helpful. "All right. The dialectic therapy teaches acceptance of things that look like opposites. Validate your feelings as legitimate but at the same time realize they might not be helpful and change them. Accept unwanted change if you must, but also see opportunities that come out of change. Part of the therapy is to build up your defenses against future stressors, what we call Distress Tolerance. So yes, while you're reducing your depression, you'll also be training yourself to cope with life events going forward."

"That sounds amazing. This is all in workbooks?"

"We try to make it easy to stay on the program. The books come with online sessions where you check in with a coach."

"No lie, I could use help learning to cope with change. I am overloaded with change lately. While I have you, can I change the subject a little? What do you know about lucid dreaming?"

Mary wasn't sure if this change of subject was due to her depressive distractedness, but she decided to play along. "I teach it to my patients with PTSD. There are a couple of techniques, but one of them I do not recommend for patients with depression. Lucid dreaming is being aware of your consciousness while you are sleeping. If you get good at it, then you can use the skills to be more aware of what your thoughts are doing while you're awake."

"Isn't that what DBT does?"

"In a way, yes. Lucid dreaming helps with that distress tolerance we talked about. Did someone suggest lucid dreaming for your anxiety?"

"Sort of, yeah. Nate got me a book about it."

"It can help. If you try lucid dreaming, stick to Reality Testing and Mnemonic Induction of Lucid Dreams, or MILD techniques. Stay away from the Wake Back to Bed technique. That involves waking yourself up in the middle of the night, and you don't want to do that."

"Does it really teach you how to change the content of your dreams?"

"Yes, and it is good for nightmares. If you are aware that you are sleeping, you can make decisions that change the course of the dream.

"I will level with you. You're looking at a lot of stressors. You've got trauma from the accidents, you say you're struggling with a lot of changes beyond just being out in the world, and nightmares leading to sleeplessness. And then there's this big project you find you're trapped in, but you feel it's not going to succeed. Are you sure you can't tell me about it?"

"I wish I could, but no."

"Is your brother testing out some theory he has about how you were cured?"

"No, he wouldn't do that."

"You've asked about dreams. You've said you are tied to it. And you've said you think it's doomed to fail. If this has anything to do with your mental health, you have to tell me. You know anything said in these walls is strictly confidential."

"I promise Nate is not experimenting on my brain. I promise to tell you all about it in two weeks when the project is over. In fact, I think you'll be the perfect person to tell about it."

"All right. Working with what you have told me, I see a few positives and a path forward. You've kept your grasp of your own identity. That's important."

Sarah blinked and looked away when she mentioned identity.

Mary opted to let that reaction pass. "You're able to describe what's going on clearly. That means you're staying aware, even if you don't think you're in control. Also huge. Give yourself credit for those.

"Going forward, I'm going to prescribe Propranolol to help you sleep. I'm going to prescribe a low starter dose of Effexor to help with the depression. And I'm going to enroll you in a beginning DBT course so you can start that practice.

"In fact, I want you to really dig into the DBT course. A few weeks in, there is a concept that I think will really help you. With all the changes pushing in on you, you want to learn Radical Acceptance."

"I think I've heard of that, but I never knew what it meant."

"A big part of coping with things you can't change is to accept some things as inevitable, stop fighting them, and to build your life around them instead of letting them stop your life. You want to get to a place where you can see unwanted changes as challenges you can face, not the universe personally trying to defeat you. It's a tough concept. It takes a lot of practice, but it's worth it. I am really glad you came in today."

"Me too. I have to say, I wasn't sure what we were going to talk about. Everything has just descended on me lately. You've always been in my corner. I should have realized you could help."

"I understand your reluctance to come talk to me. I am sorry we weren't able to resolve your schizophrenia for so long. Yours was one of the most intractable cases I have ever encountered. Now that you are on the other side of that, there are lots of things we can do to help."

15

"THE LAST IN LINE"
DIO

NATE SIGHED AND TURNED AWAY from his living room computer desk while Harold and Burt were finishing cleaning the guns on the coffee table.

"I swear, the world is going to hell in a handbasket. Hate crimes and riots are up all over, Europe, Asia, South America. I thought it was just here."

"There is a backlash resentment against the liberal movements of the last twenty years." Nate was taken by Harold's confidence on politics and the news. "The South wants to rise again here, and the entrenched rich all over the world have had enough of equal rights and equal access. They are funding all these hate groups, make no mistake."

Burt did not look convinced. "You think the rich are behind all these riots? How would the rich benefit from people being afraid of change? Half these people are fighting to keep the poor from taking what they worked for, and the other half are the poor who are fighting for what they think is their fair share."

"I completely agree with you on who is rioting and why they have taken up arms. Let me ask you this. Who benefits from having the middle class go to war with the lower class?"

Nate recognized the preacher rhetoric taking over Harold's tone.

"Who needs the vast majority busy fighting amongst themselves, while the vast majority of the wealth is being quietly stolen from everybody who actually earned it?"

"The rich own the businesses that employ the people. They've got all the money they can use. Why would they want civil unrest?"

"Burt, you are a thorough thinking man after all. Why indeed? What if the people who, as you said, make all the wealth, suddenly realized they aren't able to reap the rewards of their labors? What if they realized that no matter how hard they work, or how smart they are with their money, they are only ever going to have the scraps the rich have deigned to leave them? The tax laws have all been changed, the labor laws have all been changed, the marketplaces have all been changed, so that people like us cannot win."

Harold emptied a box of bullets on the table, then portioned them into three piles: one with most of the rounds, one with a few, and one with only a couple. He pushed the smallest stack toward Nate, and the most to himself.

He pointed to the middle stack. "Those are yours," he said to Burt. "Now you've got a bunch of bullets. You'd probably be happy with your bullets unless you happen to look over here and see that I've got almost all of them."

"But you're the rich guy that owns the business I work for. I don't mind you being rich if you can keep me employed."

"That's your choice to be satisfied. And that's fair, unless you notice that for every ten bullets of wealth you make, I get nine and you only get one. Then you'll cry foul. So what can I do to make sure you never do the math?"

Burt frowned.

"Let's say Nate is a black man, or an immigrant, or even a poor white guy. He's got next to nothing. Now, what if I lean over and whisper in your ear, 'Hey, that poor guy wants some of your bullets.' Right?"

Burt's frown only deepened.

Nate was fascinated that Harold was so liberally minded. He had to check his assumption that an evangelical preacher would be staunchly conservative. He was a conspiracy believer, which fit. Then again, Harold preached to poor people. He saw their struggles.

"Who makes a stink when the government starts giving out aid to the poor? Senators who work for the rich. Who comes to you, the workers, with a raised fist of indignation when the government starts giving out health care to the poor? They need you mad at Nate, so you won't take up arms against me. And while you're busy letting the police beat Nate to death in the streets, I'm robbing you of more and more of the pie every year. Did your grandmother work outside the home?"

"Me? No. My grandad supported my parents and my aunts and uncles with no problem."

"Was he a rich man? Did he have two jobs? Did he have a fancy degree?"

"No, he had a factory job."

"How many of your friends can support their family on one factory job today? None. How did the wealth creation pie get redivided, leaving us less and less?"

Nate spoke up. "So, we have a world full of angry people ready to tear out each other's throats. Whether that's because of some multigenerational conspiracy of the rich or not, it's a powder keg waiting for a spark. When this meteor shower hits in two weeks, the Devourer stones are going to create a whole race of people with violent visions and no regard for the law. How are we going to sort them out from all the normal, run of the mill mass shooters and window smashers? They could double the wave of violence and people are going to think it's just things heating up. Against the daily violence in the headlines, we aren't going to be able to convince the authorities there is a cosmic danger erupting."

"Were you thinking we could get help from the police?" Harold barely contained his cynicism.

Nate spotted Sarah standing by the hall. He glanced at his watch which said 11 am. It was warming up, so her shorts seemed right. But the heavy sweatshirt made him wonder if she was hiding her arms. Had she moved to cutting? He decided not to mention it to her.

"It would be just as helpful to know where Dreamer stones landed," she said. "Or better yet, where the other Dreamers like me are already."

Harold asked her, "Do your abilities include sensing other Dreamers?"

"No, but I can sense Devourers that are after me. That's how come we were ready for Burt, here. Hi, Burt. Oh, Harold, do you still have your brother's Dreamer necklace?"

"Yes, in my car, along with the others my friends wore."

"Could you go get it? We should give it to Burt. He's been walking around for a week with no necklace. We never figured out if taking one off lets the schizophrenic voices back in." She looked at Burt. "I figure all the Devourer influence should be gone by now. You'll get the Dreamer vision from the new one, but it will keep you sane."

"Will it give me the dream wishes thing?"

"No, that necklace didn't give Harold's brother any special abilities."

Nate connected a dot. "Hold on. The Kansas Devourer meteorite gave me a vision of the whole cloud of them out in space. It was like the stone was still connected to the original mass. When Sarah held the Arizona Dreamer stone, she saw the Dreamer god trying to create a planet. I wonder if the Arizona stone would show me where the other Dreamer stones are, here on Earth." He didn't wait for any response, but walked right to the hall closet to pull it out.

Burt couldn't contain his surprise. "Jesus, you've got a whole meteorite?"

Nate set the box on the dining table and pulled out the stone. "Yes. Sarah inherited it from another Dreamer who died fighting a Florida cultist."

Nate noticed Burt and Harold trade a glance. "Will the radiation have any other effect on you?" Harold asked.

"The Kansas stone only gave me the vision. As far as I have been able to figure, these stones have no ill effects on folks who are mentally healthy."

Sarah said, "Hang on a minute," and went back into her room. A moment later she came back and unfolded a large map of the United States on the table. "I remember this was folded up in the back cover of an atlas I had as a kid. Nate was kind enough to put what's left of my old things in my room."

"How should we do this?" Nate asked her.

"Well, maybe stand here next to the table. Hold the stone and close your eyes. If you see anything that looks like a location, call it out or point to it and I'll mark the map." She shrugged her shoulders. "I'm guessing."

Nate stepped up and stood with his feet apart. "The other stone made me feel weightless. It was kind of frightening."

"Me too," Sarah said.

Harold and Burt took up positions on either side of him if he needed steadying. He smiled at them, then closed his eyes. "Here goes."

As he recalled, there was nothing at first. Then it felt like the floor dropped away. Then he saw scattered starlight across the black of space. "So far so good," he said. "Now let's see what this one shows me." He looked around and didn't see anything in particular.

"I found that if I wanted to turn then I would turn," Sarah said.

"Oh, okay." She was right. He looked purposefully to the right and his view seemed to rotate that way. "Oh, I see the meteor cloud." He turned some more and saw the Earth. "It looks like it's not very far away from the Earth."

"You said two weeks," Burt said.

"See if you can move closer to the Earth and spot stones," Sarah suggested.

"Right, the map." He imagined himself flying in closer, and his view changed. "Whoa, I feel like if I get too close I'm going to fall to Earth."

"You're standing in the dining room," Sarah reminded him.

"Right, of course. Okay, I'm flying around to above the U.S. There are clouds over a bunch of places. Hey, does that mean I am looking down on us right now?"

"I guess so," Sarah said. "My visions have been what the Dreamer wanted to show me, which included things that happened a long time ago. We're hoping your visions are from the stones all being connected to one another right now."

"I am hovering just high enough to still see both coasts with the curvature of the planet. I guess that's what, a few hundred miles up? All I see is geography."

"When I feel a Devourer, it's just a feeling, not a visual thing. But it is directional."

"I don't know if it means anything, but my attention is definitely being drawn to a few spots. It's weird. It's like I think I'm going to uncover something if I focus there."

"Here's a pen," Harold said from alongside him.

"I am getting draw from the Portland area. And there's another one around the Great Lakes — I guess Wisconsin. Oh yeah, there we are. I am definitely seeing us. There might be one in like Vermont or Maine. Oh, and there's one in Mexico south of Texas. That's all I got."

Nate opened his eyes. "I did not see anything in Kansas or Florida, so this stone did not connect to the Devourer stones."

Harold was smiling broadly. "That's four other Dreamer champions."

"Maybe. That's four other meteorites of the right kind. They might still be in the ground where they fell. They might also be actively engaged with a champion like Sarah."

Burt spoke up. "It would be great to know we aren't alone"

Sarah said quietly, "We've got Harold's collection of other necklaces, but no one to put them on."

Nate shook his head. "This does look like good news. I hate to be a downer, but we also don't know how many enemy cells there are around the county."

Harold bit his lip. "We should focus on the Florida cell. We know who they are, and they know who we are."

Sarah did not look like she was taking this well. "I gotta get some air," she said as she headed out the back door.

Harold pointed to Florida on the map and asked Burt, "How long did it take for you to drive here from there?"

"It's about eight hundred miles. It took me twelve hours driving straight through."

"We would arrive exhausted, or we could stop in Montgomery and get a fresh start the next day."

Nate noticed Burt bristled and fired back, "Are you planning on attacking them there?"

"Better than waiting for them to come blow us up in this suburban tract house," Harold said with a flourish. "No offense, Nate, you have a lovely home. But it's not the fortress we will need if he they show up in numbers."

Nate spotted Sarah walking around the backyard. He turned back to the map. "Harold has a point. These guys are used to being the attackers. They sent a guy to Arizona. They sent guys to Harold's brother's house. They sent you here. We might get the drop on them if we go there. We can't just run in there with guns blazing. We'll have to do recon and really plan it. Go there and spend time in the area to learn about them."

He was interrupted by a commotion out front and he looked up. One of the front windows shattered with a gunshot.

"Get down! There's three trucks full of guys with guns!"

Harold grabbed a rifle and a couple of clips and headed out the side door to the trash cans alongside the house. "Somebody get upstairs for high advantage. The other take the front window. Do not let them get to the house!"

Burt grabbed a gun and ran upstairs. Nate returned fire through the front window. He doubted he would hit anything, so he just unloaded a fury of bullets to keep them at bay. The gun was unbelievably loud inside the living room and the smell of gunpowder filled the room. The phrase 'going down in a blaze of glory' popped unwanted into his head.

What looked like maybe fifteen men ducked behind their three large pickup trucks. A gunshot from alongside the house caught one of them when he stuck his head up. *Thank God for Harold.* Nate heard a couple of shots from his bedroom window upstairs.

After only a moment, the men all popped up aiming across the truck beds and opened fire on the house with a hail of bullets that ripped through the living room, shattering walls and furniture. Lying on the floor, Nate wasn't sure the front wall would stop the bullets. Lying on his stomach, he pulled the overstuffed arm chair up to the window for cover. He heard more shots from beside and above. As long as he kept hearing those, he knew nobody was hit.

Harold hit another man, leaving what Nate counted as twelve or thirteen. This was going be a while. Nate assumed Sarah had taken cover in the backyard.

Nate struggled between fear and anger. His anger wanted to blast away while his fear wanted him to stay as low as possible. He peeked around the chair, gun aimed, hoping to spot a body part. Who was he kidding? He couldn't hit a damn thing — which made him even madder. He had to let Harold and Burt pick them off. Okay, his job was to hold them back. He started firing one shot after another to keep them down. Then he stopped, hoping to sucker them into popping up for Harold.

It worked, another man stuck his head up, a shot rang out from the side of the building and the man went down. Nate heard the men swearing as they figured out what happened. Which meant they weren't going to be so gullible again. Still, it was the only plan Nate had.

He changed clips and started another series, when something moved in the front lawn. At first he thought it was a trick of the light, but in a few seconds a large mound pushed its way up, lifting the lawn. One of the men noticed it too and peeked around the back of a truck. It was the last thing he ever saw thanks to Harold's shot.

The men swung their guns around together and unleashed another hail on the front of the house. They were definitely focused on Harold's position at the corner. A couple of them ran out around the back of the truck farthest from Harold and advanced on the house. Nate risked getting caught, but he had to stop them. Letting his anger overtake his fear, he opened fire at them as best he could. His heart raced so fast he could feel it shaking his arms.

They ducked down behind a hedge. This surprised Nate since there was no hedge on that side of the property. He looked across the lawn, and there were hedges on both corners that did not belong there. And the front yard was deeper too, with the house farther back from the street. Was he so anxious he was hallucinating?

"What the hell is happening to your lawn, Nate?" Burt yelled out the front window down to him.

"I dunno man! But it gives us more room to hit them if they come running."

The mound in the center of the lawn continued to grow and was now a five-foot tall column of dirt splitting up out of the grass.

"Oh, Jesus," Nate muttered. "Sarah's dreaming."

Nate's head started pounding from the pressure of his racing heart. He blinked and almost missed the two guys make a dash from the hedge. The others popped up and fired on Nate and Harold to cover for their friends. Harold fired on the guys that popped up. Maybe Harold couldn't see the two on rushers. Nate took a breath and swung his rifle into the window frame and fired on them as they ran. To his amazement, he hit them both. They crumbled to the ground moaning.

"Nice shooting!" Burt yelled down.

The group acted as one again and plastered the house with bullets. Nate had to duck back, and assumed the barrage was to recover their fallen. He expected to hear Harold picking them off, but he did not. Had Harold been hit? They were screwed if they lost Harold.

The last thing Nate expected to hear was the piercing whinny that came from Harold's corner of the house. This was followed by galloping hooves headed to the back. He looked out the back kitchen window as best he could from the front of the living room.

A white unicorn raced away across the back yard.

"Jesus, Sarah!"

Burt came running down the stairs. "Where's Harold?"

"I think he's gone. Watch yourself in front of this window."

Nate's warning came a second too late as a bullet ripped through Burt's shoulder. Nate glanced back out front and the remaining ten men were all running for the house. Nate took aim with as little time as he dared for each shot. Even with the weirdly elongated lawn, he had maybe three seconds before they were inside. Each bullet hit, but that wasn't the most surprising part. Each wound exploded as if ripping open a bag of blood. The gore was astonishing. It was all Nate could to do not to gasp and keep on firing.

The running men didn't seem to notice what was happening to their comrades. Nate gritted his teeth and just kept shooting them and watching them explode.

His gun stopped firing. He was out of bullets. He had no more clips.

The last two men busted in the front door. Nate dove across the room and snatched up Burt's dropped rifle. He kept rolling behind the kitchen counter. Burt scrambled into the hallway for cover. The men opened fire on the kitchen, shattering the cabinet doors, sending fragments of dishes raining down on him.

Nate had had enough of these assholes. He ducked out around the other side of the island and shot one of them in the chest. His torso erupted in a waterfall of blood as his head flew back and his arms dropped off his body. Nate pulled the trigger on the last man, but he was out of bullets.

The last man made it into the living room and spotted Burt on the floor around the corner.

Burt recognized him. "Sammy?"

He hesitated and didn't shoot. "Burt, what the fuck, man? You're one of us. We tracked you here with your phone."

"Hey, man, you've got it all wrong. These aren't the bad guys. You've been brainwashed. I know you, you're a reasonable man. Think before you just throw your life away."

Sammy shook his head, raised his gun at Burt, and said, "Bullshit."

He didn't get to pull the trigger. Nate blasted him in the back with the shotgun he grabbed from the kitchen broom closet.

Burt was covered in splashed blood, but his astonishment was still clear on his face. "What the mother fucking hell?"

"Sarah came to our rescue in a dream," he said as he ran for the back door.

He didn't need to, as Sarah was coming in. Her terrified wide eyes made it clear she had seen the whole thing, even if in a dream.

"Are you all right?" she asked her brother.

"Yeah, miraculously I am okay. Burt here is in bad shape. That blood all over him is not his, but he took a round in the left shoulder."

"I'm really sorry about Harold. I couldn't stop it."

"Yeah, shit happens. At least you gave me good aim and exploding bullets."

Burt struggled to his feet. "What happened to Harold?"

Nate glanced at Sarah. "He got swept up in the dream. He's gone. It's what we have feared all along."

"Gone? You mean he just ceased to exist? You can do that?"

"In my dream, he turned into a goddamn unicorn and ran off. I can't aim it at someone on purpose." She turned back to Nate and her eyes did not relax. "Am I still dreaming? I can't tell anymore."

Nate put his arm around her. "No, you're awake. The crazy changes have stopped."

"I wanted to reach out to the men to stop their anger in the dream. I mean I really needed to reach out to them, like as strong as I have ever had that urge. But I couldn't go to them in the dream. I tried. Then I saw they were going to hurt you, so I let the dream act against them. The dream had no reservation about killing them. I guess the Dreamer was resigned to killing the Devourer after all."

She looked past him out the blasted front window. Something caught her attention and she walked over the gore-strewn living room and out the unhinged door.

Nate followed. The dirt pillar had taken a final shape. Standing over seven feet tall, it was now a hardened clay statue of a hugely muscled man with upstretched, threatening arms. His face was inhumanly large, with a monstrous jaw opened as if screaming. Nate blinked several times trying to understand what he was seeing, the creature was so intimidating. The visage was all the more terrifying covered in splashed blood.

"Was this in your dream?"

"This is our enemy."

Burt had managed to get to the front window. "Jefferson Davis is our enemy," he yelled out. "He's just a man, not even a very big guy."

Sarah turned her haunted gaze back to Nate and pointed at the statue. "That's what he has become."

16

"HIGHWAY TO HELL"
AC/DC

JEFFERSON DAVIS TAPPED his size-fourteen combat boot impatiently on the passenger side floorboards of the step van. "What are we waiting for again?"

Jackson restrained his own impatience in his reply. "That is Southern Ohio Correction Facility, otherwise known as the Lucasville maximum security prison. They do not have adequate facility to treat their floridly psychotic prisoners. They have contracted with Allen-Oakwood Correctional Facility which is a medium security prison 180 miles north of here in Lima, Ohio. Oakwood has an entire mental hospital at their campus. They cycle insane prisoners they can't control here up to Oakwood for treatment until they are manageable, then they bring them back here. We are going to take the next batch of prisoners to be transported from here to there."

"Right, I got it. Because it's a lot easier to knock over a bus than the actual prison. So what's taking the bus so long? You said they were supposed to leave at ten am on the dot. It's 10:23."

"I don't know." Jackson sized up Jefferson's outfit for the first time. The six bulletproof tactical vests strapped around his enormous body and the helmet he wore made him look like some kaiju version of a mutant ninja turtle. It should have been funnier.

"How many guys are we getting?"

"Six. At least five of them are known to be wildly schizophrenic. So much so that we may have to sedate them to get them into the van."

"We only have two weeks till touchdown, and it takes about two weeks of exposure for the necklaces to take full effect. This will probably be our last raid like this."

"That's why I wanted to get as many men as possible in one trip."

"This will certainly be more exciting than our usual raids on civilian mental hospitals. Kidnapping people that no one cares about," he scoffed. "This will be a big honking deal. You've done well. Now if the damn bus would leave, we can get this soiree started."

The outer gate started to roll open and Jackson could see white vehicles moving inside.

"What the hell?" Jefferson squinted. "That's not a bus. That's three separate vans!"

One of them turned to their right while the other two went left. Jackson started to radio the other step van with instructions, but it raced past them following the two leftward ones.

"Shit, we're going to have to do this here or we're going to get separated," Jackson said through gritted teeth as he accelerated toward the rightward van.

Out of the corner of his eye, Jackson caught Jefferson's face contort into something even less human — an almost demonic scowl. The van in front of them veered for a moment, nearly careening off the road. Jackson swung their truck around and rammed the right rear tire, spinning the van in the street. Jackson floored it and pushed his target around until it stopped. Jefferson jumped out and scowled at the cab again. Jackson could only assume this was him driving anger and confusion into the guards inside.

Machine gun fire peppered the street around Jefferson and a few bullets hit him. His body armor absorbed them without slowing him down.

The main gate rolled open again and Jackson saw guards run out. He grabbed his own assault rifle and opened fire on them through his window. They ducked for cover.

Jefferson scowled at the tower. The guards at the gate were caught unawares as the tower rained gunfire down on them.

Jackson looked down the street and saw the other truck had plowed into the other two white vans and stopped them. There was quite the firefight underway.

Jefferson saw this too. He waved at Jackson to take care of their stopped van. Jackson banged his fist on the bulkhead behind him and their half dozen soldiers piled out the back to attack the captive van.

Jefferson reached into the cab and retrieved the six-foot steel concrete-breaking spike he had brought as a hand weapon. He spun its eighteen-pound weight around under his arm and ran down the street.

Jackson grabbed his backpack full of explosives and accompanied his men to advance carefully on the van. Their caution was unwarranted as the two guards in the cab were busy inside fighting each other and not even looking out the windows. Realizing he had seconds before more reinforcements came from the prison, he pulled out one of the bombs, looped it on the back door handles and triggered a five-second timer. He and the men took cover behind their own vehicle until the blast.

He started to run around to the back when one of the guards in the cab started firing at them through a portal in the driver's door. One of the men was hit in the body, but they were all wearing flak jackets so he only staggered. Jackson signaled his men to get the prisoners out of the back. He circled their truck and ran at the captive van head on where the guards had no way to shoot him. He slapped a bomb on the windshield and set a two-second fuse. He barely made it back behind his truck before the explosion shattered the windshield and flooded the cab with fire and glass daggers.

The two prisoners inside were screaming and holding their ears from the blast that set them free. This made them easy to hustle into the step van. As soon as the last of his men were on board, Jackson climbed back in and drove to assist Jefferson and the other team.

What he saw gave him pause even after the violence he had just inflicted. The guards in the vans were firing at their men through portals. Jefferson had just arrived running down the street. From fifty feet away, he flashed his hand out and growled like an animal. Two more shots fired, but inside the van's cab, then silence.

The other van's guards were still shooting and keeping their men pinned down. Jackson steered his truck at the driver's door and floored it.

"Hang on back there!" he yelled to his passengers.

The impact caved in the door and deformed the cab into a trap that Jackson hoped would at least keep the guards from being a threat.

He pulled his truck back, got out, and watched Jefferson step up to the intact van.

"Shit and tarnation!" he yelled as he realized the back doors were still sealed.

Before Jackson could suggest explosives, Jefferson hoisted his spike like a javelin and rammed it into the gap. The metal screeched as it gave way. It screamed again when Jefferson pulled with all his might to one side and broke the locks.

As their men rushed in to retrieve the two prisoners, gunshots went off and two of their men were hit: one in the back of his bulletproof tactical vest and the other man's head exploded. The remaining guard from the crushed cab had escaped and circled behind them. Even with him lying on his belly on the street, three of their men opened fire on him with their assault rifles and ripped him apart. Jackson ran around to the open door of the other van and, reaching past the carnage that was the dead driver, found the latch handle to open the back doors.

The two prisoners in the last van were fighting mad when the doors opened. Even in handcuffs, they came out swinging and yelling and biting. One of their men had a taser and a syringe of sedatives ready, He shocked the nearest prisoner until he jerked stiff, then jabbed him in the neck. Two other men had to wrestle the last prisoner to the ground, beat him into submission, and drag him to the truck. "Just don't bash them in the head," Jefferson advised. "We need their brains intact."

They had just gotten the last of the prisoners into their trucks when Jackson noticed the tower was no longer firing on the front gate. "We gotta go!" he told Jefferson. They ran to the cab and climbed in.

Jefferson still held his spike. "I guess they took out that tower guard."

"It was too good to last," Jackson agreed.

He assumed they would be pursued, so he let the other truck get in front so Jefferson could use his magic on those that followed. He checked the rear view and, right on cue, four police cars sped out of the front gate, sirens blaring.

The cars were much faster than the trucks and soon caught up. Jefferson stood up and leaned out his open window to get a clear view.

"Jesus, don't let them shoot you," Jackson warned.

"They'll be too busy shooting each other," he joked before letting out that inhuman growl.

Jackson looked in the mirror, and a moment later the lead car turned suddenly and slammed into parked cars on the street.

Jefferson sat back down, grinning. It was not pretty. "Like shooting fish in a barrel. Hey, don't we have a sharpshooter in the back?"

"Don Turner. He was decorated in Afghanistan. I think you called him Dewey when we had him bitten."

Jefferson hollered back through the hatch. "Hey, Dewey! Time to go Afghanistan on the next driver. Have someone hold the door so it doesn't swing open and expose the lot of you."

By now, the next car was only a hundred feet behind them and gaining. One of the men opened the door a crack while Turner slid onto his stomach and aimed out the back. The cops in the car reached out their open windows and fired on the truck with pistols. One bullet made it in the door and slammed into a wall without hitting anyone. Turner opened fire with his assault rifle, punching a hole in the windshield with multiple rounds and killing the driver. The man at the door quickly closed it. Jefferson let out a hoot.

"The last two cars are right on us," Jackson warned. "That trick isn't going to work again."

One of the cars pulled up alongside Jefferson and the driver shot at him through his window. Jefferson glared at him, and the man fired again, hitting him in the shoulder, which was protected.

"Shit, he's alone, and now I've got him fighting mad." He unbuckled himself and opened the door. "Hero time!" he yelled as he leapt onto the car roof with the giant steel spike in one hand.

Jackson didn't know what he could do to help, so he just kept driving straight. He saw Jefferson land a handhold on the car's light array. He then swung the bar around and down through the roof and into the driver. The car veered into parked cars and tumbled to a crashing stop. Jefferson was flung free and rolled bouncing over a parked car.

Jackson slammed the brakes and the last pursuit car turned and passed him. He started to get out to see if Jefferson was all right, when the giant rolled onto his feet and jogged back the truck.

The sound of a helicopter distracted them both. They looked up to see if it had joined the chase, and were met with a hail of bullets as the chopper opened fire on them.

"This right here is some bullshit," Jefferson cursed before he growled up at the attackers.

The helicopter dipped its nose and flew down right at them, as if the pilot meant to ram them. The back doors of the truck popped open and four of their men jumped out and unleased their own storm of firepower as it approached. Jackson figured the men could get themselves out of harm's way, but he needed to move the truck. He jumped in and drove it away as fast as it would go. The road was two lanes in each direction, so he should have room to avoid a crash. But he couldn't see the path of the falling helicopter from inside the truck. So he just punched it.

He heard the crunching, scraping metal before he saw it in his rearview mirrors. It was behind him, but skidding faster than he could go. Once he saw it, he turned into another lane and let it slide past him. He braked, and the mass of flaming, twisted metal spun to a stop a hundred feet ahead.

He looked down the street and the other truck and the police car that chased it were long gone. He pulled out his phone and called one of that team's members. "This is Jackson Pruitt. Are you still being pursued by prison guards?"

"No, we killed them, but we picked up a city cop on our way back to you. He's a really good driver and we haven't been able to shake him or hit him."

"Are you coming back down this same street?"

"Yessir."

"Okay, just keep him coming."

Jackson jumped out and called back to Jefferson and their men. "The other truck is headed back, but they're being followed by a lone squad car they can't shake."

Jefferson snarled as he ran past Jackson. "I've had just about enough of this nonsense."

He ran around the flaming helicopter wreckage and down the street another hundred feet. He then planted himself in the middle of the street.

One of the men came up alongside Jackson and asked, "What's he doing?"

"Taking back control. Get in the truck. We're leaving as soon as he's done."

A moment later, the other truck came racing into view, with the police car close behind. Jackson heard Jefferson's growl echo off the nearby buildings. The truck steered around Jefferson and the wreckage, but the police car sped up straight at the giant. Jackson wasn't sure he wanted to witness this, but he could not look away. At the last possible instant, Jefferson leapt straight up five feet in the air as the car flew under him and straight into the crashed chopper. The impact flung flaming debris all across and down the street.

Jefferson walked back, looking pretty pleased with himself. He smiled his hideous smile at Jackson as he passed. "Jerry Bruckheimer, baby."

As planned, the two teams wasted no time driving to a downtown parking garage where they had three nondescript minivans waiting. They transferred the six very upset and disoriented prisoners and drove away.

They took three different routes out of Ohio and across the South back to Florida. All the while, Jackson listened to police radio bands to follow any pursuit. Once the police found the two step vans, they ran out of options to follow further. It was a long, tense drive, but they arrived without incident.

It gave Jackson a lot of time to think about what Jefferson had become, and how cavalier he was taking all those lives. He really did see himself as a superhero. His fervor in their mission had always worried Jackson. Now that the man seemed invincible, there did not seem to be any moral limit to his crusade.

17

"HEROES"

DAVID BOWIE

S T. LOUIS POLICE DETECTIVE MARK JOHANSSON stepped out of his car and looked across the street, past the line of squad cars that crowded the front of the two-story suburban tract house. Even from there, he could see the front of the house was riddled with bullets.

"Nathaniel Meyer, what have you gotten yourself into?" he asked of no one. He pulled his badge lanyard out of his inside blazer pocket so it hung out as he walked across the street. The dozen policemen at the front of the property let him pass with a nod. He saw the police cars were actually in the street, corralling three half-ton pickup trucks at the curb. The bodies of five men lay on the ground with various weapons as if they had been hiding behind the trucks attacking the house. They all had been shot in the head. *Mickey Spillane would be proud.*

The front yard was even more interesting. A seven-foot tall clay statue of a man with a giant deformed mouth and upstretched arms was planted in the lawn. Several gallons of what looked and smelled like blood covered the lawn, littered with body parts of what he tallied was probably another eight men. Explosive charges? He let the photographers to do their job. The front of the house was even worse close up. There he saw at least a hundred bullet holes.

Inside the living room, more blood was scattered with parts of another man, plus one who had been shotgunned in the back. Bullet casings covered the entire living room floor like confetti after a party.

Some party.

He imagined how loud the gun fire must have been. It always struck him how quiet a room sounded when you could see the aftermath of bullet holes and shell casings.

An officer called to him from the back door. "Detective! You'll want to see this."

He stepped out to the back yard patio and the officer pointed to six dead wild pigs stacked up against the back of the house. They had been shot, but their wounds were dry and looked at least a day old. The human blood all around the front of the house was still wet. "Anything else out here?" he asked.

"We found some tin cans with bullet holes out by the busted fence. It looks like they were target practicing when the boar attacked."

Johansson held up a hand and his bushy eyebrows. "Never assume anything. Just record and report."

The officer smiled and nodded.

Johansson returned to the house and noticed a two-foot diameter, smooth, white glass dome glued to the dining room table. He examined the bond and found no glue residue, yet it was clearly fused.

That's when he noticed the box sitting on the table: a cubical cardboard box eight inches on a side. He called out to another officer who was measuring things in the living room. "Has anyone touched anything here on this table?"

"No sir. We're just taking it all down. We haven't started collecting anything yet."

"Good. Thanks."

He bent down and looked all around the box without touching it. It was completely covered in clear packing tape. One side had been cut open. The shape of the newspaper padding wadded up inside it suggested that it had held something spherical.

A mailing label covered one untorn side: Jake Goldblatt, West Winslow, Arizona.

Ah, now for a bit of Sherlock Holmes.

Johansson pulled out his phone and took a picture of it.

•   •   •

Jackson Pruitt rolled over and saw that his clock said 8:47. *Shit.* He was so tired after getting the prisoners settled in after driving for two days, he forgot to set his alarm. He had things to do. This place did not run itself. He hastily threw on some clothes and headed downstairs.

The place was empty. Even the technicians who were never away from their computer screens in the main salon were gone. He heard men's voices and motorized equipment noises outside. He went out back and saw what looked like the entire company of the camp all working on clearing a patch of land at the center of the back of the compound. They had a backhoe and a skip loader scraping out a large square, while other men used forklifts to move pallets of cinderblocks off of a flatbed truck. In the middle of it all stood Jefferson with what looked like drawings, directing the whole affair.

He walked out and raised his hands questioningly.

"I had a vision. I am building the temple of Gragol the Devourer."

"Did the god demand this tribute?"

"No, but he showed me how to construct a proper home for his vessel."

"You mean the main meteorite?"

"Precisely. It will sit atop a ziggurat, overlooking the entire countryside. From there it can spread his influence like the rays of the sun," he said gesturing sweepingly with his enormous arms and hands.

"You'll be able to enflame everyone's anger for miles around?"

"Indeed. We will need this when the Lookers descend upon us like locusts."

"Did he show you such an invasion?"

"He didn't have to. We needed our new recruits into necklaces as soon as possible, but our attack in Ohio gave our enemy over a week to move against us before the shower. We need to be prepared."

Jackson watched the men scurrying about with the construction. He nodded and said, "I'm glad to see Gragol thinks strategically."

•   •   •

Sarah was walking back to her and Nate's room on the upper exterior walkway of the Super 8 motel when she realized she did not recall how she got there. She remembered Nate and Burt hustling her out of the shot-up house. They didn't want to be there when the police arrived. She got in the back of the car with all the stuff the men had grabbed, and then her memories ran out.

Maybe she was dreaming this. The lucid dreaming book said to check your surroundings and the continuity of your memories. If you suddenly show up somewhere, and you don't recall how you got there, then you might be dreaming. Oh, okay. She could handle this. How cool to see she was dreaming during a dream.

She glanced over the railing and saw their car. That made sense, and it explained a lot. Maybe not a dream after all.

Burt came out of the room next to hers. He was smiling and nodded to her as she walked by. "Oh, Sarah. I want you to meet our neighbors. I was looking for the ice machine and they showed me."

A middle-aged man and woman stepped out of his room. Sarah thought it was a bit odd that he would have invited strangers into his room. Then again, she didn't know Burt, and maybe he really was the friendly, Southern gentleman he appeared to be, especially now that he was no longer driven to anger by the Florida necklace.

"Sarah, this is Leonard and Elizabeth."

They looked vaguely familiar. The woman stepped forward and reached to shake Sarah's hand. "Call me Betsy."

Sarah froze. They were her parents. She looked at them deeply to make sure. Her father was wearing the green polo shirt she always remembered him wearing. She caught herself staring and she shook her mother's hand politely while her mind reeled. They didn't recognize her. Sarah hoped with all her might this was just a dream. She wanted to say something, but her brain was too busy to operate her mouth.

Her mother smiled and stepped back. "Oh, you're shy. Sorry, I come on strong sometimes."

"No, I'm sorry," she finally found her voice. "You just remind me of someone that I thought I would never see again. The resemblance is quite striking."

"They said they were here looking for their two sons," Burt supplied. "I told them we'd only been here a few hours, but I hadn't seen two boys around the place."

Her father spoke up. "They're nine and sixteen. Nathaniel and Timothy."

"That's funny," Burt said. "We're here with her ..."

Sarah reached over and gave his arm a squeeze to cut him off. "Burt, we shouldn't keep these nice people from looking for their children." Turning to them, she said, "It was very nice meeting you." Keeping her grip on his arm, she said, "Burt, will you come with me please?"

"It was nice meeting you too," Betsy said, and they walked to their room a few doors down.

Sarah hustled Burt into her room. "Please do not tell them anything about Nate and me."

"What's got into you? You look like you saw a ghost."

Her racing heart made it hard to think. "I don't know what I saw. I think I recognize them. But until I can talk to Nate and figure this out, please do not tell them about us."

"Are they trouble?"

"No. They're from our past. It's complicated. Just let me talk to Nate."

"All right," he said. He turned and left, but paused at the open door. "Here comes Nate, now."

Burt and Nate traded places. "What's up?" her brother asked.

"Close the door. The couple in the unit two down from Burt are our parents."

"Excuse me?"

"I must have dreamed them, but I don't remember any such dream. They're here looking for their two sons, Nathaniel and Timothy, aged sixteen and nine."

"That's how old we were when they ..."

"Died. Correct. I must have been dreaming about them as I remember them, and *blam*, they're here."

"Don't you usually remember the dreams that change things? You remembered the attack on the house as if you had been awake."

"Yes, normally I do. Maybe the dreams have moved to a new phase of changing shit while I'm not even aware. Do you understand how dangerous that is?"

"That really is *Forbidden Planet*," he said looking randomly at the floor.

"You mentioned that before. Is that a movie?"

"Yeah. A guy's subconscious links up with a machine that can create realities. Only thing is, Doctor Morbius is a terrible example. He ends up having to kill himself."

"That's fucking great. So what are we supposed to do with Mom and Dad in #5? They're looking for kids from seven years ago. Can we tell them they skipped all that time? They're going to see the date at some point."

"Are you sure it's them?"

"Yes, I shook Mom's hand. She didn't recognize me, for obvious reasons. But they're going to recognize you. We can't just walk away from them. I brought them back."

"And I really miss them."

Nate surprised her with that touching reaction.

She thought about it, and had to agree. "I do too."

"I guess we should go meet them."

Sarah's head swirled with the possibilities. She had to sit down on a bed. "Wow. This is the last thing I ever would have imagined."

"At least consciously," Nate added.

She took a deep breath, raised her eyebrows as high as they would go, and blinked several times. "Apparently. If we're going to meet our parents, I want to take a shower. I am covered in nervous flop sweat from the gun battle dream."

"You go ahead, I already did when we first got here."

She frowned. "I don't remember you showering, or us arriving."

"You were really out of it. I'm pretty sure you were half asleep and you passed out as soon as we got you to the bed."

"That must have been when I dreamt of Mom and Dad. Nate, I'm sorry I just keep making this more complicated."

"This is not your fault. Please do not beat yourself up over the content of your dreams."

"I'll try." With that, she went into the shower.

The hot water wasn't just comforting, it felt familiar, normal, expected. Having something feel just as it should was a surprising additional relief.

When she got out, Nate was not in the room. He wouldn't have gone to meet them without her. He must be doing something else.

She propped up the pillows and sat back against them to gather her thoughts. What would she say? How would she explain the missing seven years? How would she explain her sex change? She didn't even know where to start.

Sarah awoke propped up on the pillows, wrapped in a wet towel from just having showered. "Jesus, I nodded off. I can't let myself nap like that," she complained to herself. "I can't trust my dreams for a second."

She got up and started dressing. Where was Nate? She found her cell phone and called him. "Hey, where did you go?"

"Oh, you're up."

"Yes, I'm up. I showered, but I'm done now. I need you up here."

"Oh, all right. I'm just down here in the lobby. I'll be right up."

She finished getting dressed. She was glad Nate had made her stop and stuff a bag of clothes on their way out. She looked at herself in the mirror on the back of the bathroom door. It wasn't exactly coordinated, but she didn't look like a homeless person. It would have to do.

What was taking Nate so long? She decided to meet him in front of #5.

He came up the stairs at the end of the walkway and met her there. "What's in here?"

"Your sense of humor, sometimes," she scoffed as she knocked on the door.

Leonard Meyer answered it. "May I help you?"

Nate turned white and looked like he was going to pass out. Sarah did not understand.

"Whoa, young man," their father stepped out and took Nate's arm to steady him. "Are you all right?"

Nate just looked at the man wide-eyed for a long second. Then he shifted his astonished gaze to Sarah.

"Oh my God," Sarah mumbled. "You didn't know."

Now it was her turn for her head to reel. This was the first Nate had heard about them.

Nate held the balcony rail and smiled at Leonard. "Thank you. I don't know what came over me. How embarrassing," he chuckled weakly. He frowned at Sarah. "It's like I was suddenly *dreaming*. For a second there I thought you were my father."

Leonard sized him up. "Come to mention it, my son would be about your age if he had lived. And he looked a lot like you."

Sarah stepped up. "I'm sorry, did you say you lost your son? I'm so sorry for you."

"Yeah, lost both my boys in an accident, seven years ago. Biggest tragedy of my life. But time moves on, right?"

Nate stared at Sarah fearfully and slowly shook his head.

Elizabeth came to the door. "Who is it, dear?"

"These two young people knocked. Actually, why did you knock?"

"Wrong door," Sarah said with a smile. "We're looking for our friend, Burt. I guess I got the number wrong. I'm so sorry."

Their mother stepped past her husband to face Sarah. "Have we met? You look really familiar."

Sarah found it almost impossible to keep up the façade. Her heart beat so hard it hurt in her chest. She could barely keep her thoughts straight, there were so many of them crowding in at once. She needed to break this off and regroup with Nate.

"I get that a lot. I guess I have one of those faces that everyone thinks they remember. Brother, we should let these nice folks go back to their day." Sarah held out her hand and her mother shook it. "It was very nice to meet you."

"You too, child. What good manners your mother raised you with."

The handshake had been hard enough. That last comment was too much. Sarah smiled as best she could, then walked briskly to their room, tears breaking free and streaming down her cheeks. She could hear Nate make his goodbyes and follow.

She threw herself face down on the bed.

"What the fuck just happened?" Nate fumed.

"I dreamed Burt had discovered them and introduced me. Then I told you all about it and we agreed to go meet them. Now I see that was the dream where I created them." She turned over and sat up. "Which left you finding out about them for the first time when I knocked on their door. I am so sorry I put you through that. I honestly thought you and I had talked about it at length first."

"You've said it a few times, but is this what you mean when you say you can't tell when you're sleeping and when you're awake."

Sarah wiped her tears on her cuffs. "Yes. I am constantly terrified that I can't tell which is which. This is worse than my schizophrenia ever was."

"So, now you've dreamed our parents back into existence. Do they have a seven-year gap?"

"No, they don't. That's the worst part. Their timeline has us dying seven years ago. They've been alive this whole time, grieving our deaths."

"Wait, wait, hold on. How can they remember us dying and then living all this time, when we know they died and have been dead all this time?"

"It's like the stupid dome on the dining table. It wasn't there, and we all know it wasn't there. And then it appeared, as if it had always been there, but we know it wasn't."

"Do we need to worry our timeline is going to unravel? Them being alive with history for that time, doesn't that cancel us out?"

"No, my dreams don't care about continuity or logic. Shit just is. We don't vanish just because they remember us dying. We remember them dying, yet here they are."

"The memories mean time was spent."

"Yeah, that would be some turn. They didn't die, which means I didn't lose my mind, which means I never got the damn necklace, and never made them reappear. There is no path where our reality and their reality fit together. When I just dreamed them into being, I gave them the memories of seven years of life that did not happen in our real world. They were on one of Tyson's alternate timelines, and now they are in ours."

Nate sat down on the other bed. "Clever of you to not use my name in front of them. God, I hardly ever think about them anymore, but I really miss them."

Sarah started to cry again. "You just said that in my dream. I miss them too. I just want to go down there and throw my arms around Mom and tell her how much I've missed her and love her.

And I can't! Them being here is impossible. Trying to explain who we are would be even more impossible."

"We can't just ignore them, can we?"

"I keep wanting to ignore all the changes. I used to try ignoring my voices. I'm not worried about our timeline unraveling, but I am worried all of this is just in my head. What if I'm still dreaming right now? I thought Burt introducing them to me was reality. I think this is reality. My brain is used to making shit up. It wasn't just the voices. I used to see things that weren't there, people that weren't there. I had conversations with people I later found out did not exist. What if all of this is just one giant, layered psychotic illusion? I can't trust anything I see at this point. That includes you sitting here talking to me."

Nate looked around the room thinking. "What if this isn't *Forbidden Planet*, but *Nightmare on Elm Street*?"

"Yes! That! Finally a movie reference I know. And that's exactly what I'm scared of."

"I used to wonder if being a science fiction fan would prepare me for an alien invasion. Here we are. Wait a minute. I've been making movie references to films you've never seen, like *Close Encounters* and *Forbidden Planet*. How could you be hallucinating me making references to things in the real world that you don't know?"

She thought about that for a second. "Are you suggesting that whenever you make a stupid movie reference, that's when I can trust that I'm awake and you're not a figment of a dream?"

"If that's a handle you can hold onto. I mean, Jesus, any port in the storm, right?"

"That's actually not so far off from the stuff they suggest in the lucid dreaming book."

"So, back to our parent problem. Would it be entirely selfish to put them through the trauma of realizing we are alive, that they spent seven years grieving us by mistake, just to spend time with them because we miss them?"

Sarah fought back a tear. "I feel like their appearance is a gift. Yeah, it comes with strings attached, but we get our parents back. The Dreamer has been giving us gifts all along. He gave you exploding bullets when you needed them. For fuck's sake, he gave us a unicorn."

"I only needed the exploding bullets because he turned Harold into a unicorn."

"Nonetheless. Maybe this has all been so stressful because I keep treating these changes like problems. Maybe I should be looking at them as gifts."

"That's very DBT of you."

"All right, Mr. Psych Degree, maybe it is. My ability to sense haters was something I needed when I was trans. I still haven't figured out how being turned into a female is a gift, but I'll work on that. What if our parents appearing is something we should embrace?"

"They're going to think we're frauds. I would. Two people show up, the right age, but one of them the wrong gender, claiming some cosmic accident has moved two separate timelines together so now they get to have their children back? The only reason you and I believe that is because we lived it for the last two months. And I still have a hard time believing it."

"Could we …? I want to … I feel like we should be able to comfort them somehow, to let them know their kids are okay. That they can stop being sorry they lost us."

"I agree, except their kids did not turn out okay. Not to put too fine a point on it, but you tumbled after their deaths, I spent my youth being mad at the world, and even now we are faced with horrors day after day. Maybe it's better for them if they just find peace thinking we died."

"We can't decide that for them," she countered.

"What are you suggesting? Should we invite them to have lunch with us across the street at the Howard Johnson's and make small talk about how kids grow up to be fine like us, if they don't die in a car crash? Or what a comfort it is knowing that in some theoretical alternate universe, their kids survived, and everyone lived happily ever after? I want to comfort them too. We went through the nightmare of losing them. In their universe it must have been the same for them. I'm sorry, but you were right when you said it is impossible to explain how we and they are in the same place at the same time."

"We used to live in a suburb of Chicago when we were kids right?"

"Yeah, a little town called Naperville."

"And now they're in St. Louis."

"What are you driving at?"

"If they go back to Chicago, in this world, they're going to find records that they died seven years ago and that we survived instead."

"Maybe. We don't know what your dream changed. The merging of the two timelines could have changed everything so records all make sense somehow."

"Does this motel have Wi-Fi?"

"Yes." Nate thought for a moment. "You want to look up whether they still show as having died in this world?"

"Correct. The white bowl appearing did not change our memory records that it did not exist a moment before. They're appearing now doesn't go back and change our memories of them dying, and it shouldn't change the public records that they died."

"Do you want to show them that public records show they died as a way to convince them of the cosmic accident that allows us to all be together?" Nate frowned at the floor for a moment. "I grabbed my laptop, and I saw the front office has a printer for guests to use. Are you sure about this?"

"Aren't you just as desperate as me to reconnect with them?"

"Yes. Yes, I am. It's going to be one helluva lunch conversation. But if we can convince them, then yeah, we get our parents back."

"You go do the research and make the printouts. I'll go next door and invite them, just on the pretense of apologizing for the weird rudeness earlier."

"Okay. Let's stay in touch by text."

•   •   •

Nate stood by the door of the Howard Johnson's diner and checked the Google calendar invitation Sarah had sent him for 1:00 pm. It was 1:10. He considered texting her to make sure everything was still moving to plan, when he saw her walking across the parking lot to him. There was still no sign of their parents. When she got close, he saw she was crying. In fact, she was bawling so hard she was having difficulty walking straight. He ran to her. "What happened?"

She threw her arms around his ribs and buried her face in his shoulder. She never did this. "They're gone," she managed between sobs.

"All right, I'll wait until you can explain."

She shook her head slowly against him. "This is all too much. I was wrong. This isn't a gift, it's a curse."

"Do you think you're still dreaming? Because I think we're both awake right now."

She took a big sighing breath to compose herself and stepped back. "No, I am positive I am awake. This much torture could only happen in reality. I invited Mom. She was very gracious."

"I figured that part worked when you sent me the invitation."

"Then I went back to our room and cried some more. I was just overwhelmed by it all. Then I cleaned myself up and started to come over here. When I passed their room, they were coming out with their luggage. I asked them what about lunch. Dad said they had to go right away, that they had received bad news. He said they needed to go talk to the police about the death of their boys."

"But that was seven years ago, even in their timeline."

"That threw me too. Then I realized I was dreaming. I had fallen asleep while I was crying back in our room. I was dreaming of them leaving, and I realized that meant my dream was reorganizing reality again, so they would be gone in the real world. Nate, it was horrible. I was standing there watching them walk away, knowing I was pushing them out of this timeline, and there was nothing I could do about it."

"My God. I can only imagine."

Sarah sniffed to clear her head, and looked him in the eye. "So I called out to Mom, trying to stop her, and I used the word 'Mom.' She turned and smiled, and said 'Goodbye, darling Timmy.' I was dumbstruck. I wanted the dream to end before it did any more damage, so I ran back to the room and threw cold water on my face to wake myself up.

"When I walked back to their room, it was open and the cleaning lady was bringing in new towels and stuff. I looked in and ..." She broke off and cringed to stifle another crying jag. "I looked in, and the room looked like no one had been there at all. I asked the lady and she said the room had been vacant all week, and she was just checking to make sure it was ready for the next guest."

Nate felt like a piece of his chest had been ripped out. He was just getting his hopes up that they might be able to keep their parents. He was frustrated and angry and sorry and all the things he had buried so deeply when they died the first time. He had spent years getting over that feeling, and in the space of less than an hour it had all come roaring back. He didn't know whether to scream or cry. If he blew up, Sarah would take the blame for sending them away. No, the one thing, the only thing he needed to be right now was a good brother.

He stepped up and wrapped his arms around her. "Oh, sweet Sarah. I am so sorry."

"No, I'm sorry. We had it all worked out. We were going to get them back. And then I wished them away. Gone." She gave him a little squeeze of a hug to break off, then looked up at him. "Nate, I can't do this anymore."

He led her back across the parking lot. He noticed a car pulled in and parked at the motel. "That car looks kind of familiar," he said. Then he recognized the man in a blue suit who got out. "Oh, shit. That's Detective Johansson." He steered Sarah away, heading down the street.

The detective called out to him. "Nate, don't run. Right now you're a victim. If you run, then you'll be a suspect."

Nate stopped and rolled his eyes. "I guess we should go up to our room?"

"That would make it a lot easier."

When they got to him, Sarah smiled in spite of her tear-streaked face. "Hello, Detective. Are you here to rescue me again?"

Nate saw him frown at her tears.

"Possibly." Johansson spoke as they walked together. "We found Harold Fraily's car at your house. Another group of men from Florida had attacked his house and killed a bunch of his followers. It looks pretty clear he was with you to fight against the Florida cult. Do you know where Fraily is now?"

"No, he ran off after the firefight," Nate said. "I honestly don't know where he is. And yes, he found us to come help us against the Florida cult."

"Did you know about this Florida cult when Fraily kidnapped Sarah?"

"Yes, we knew about them, but they had not targeted us yet."

They got to the room and Nate let them in.

"What changed that made them turn on you?"

Nate had to tread lightly here. "They are the enemies of a benign cult we learned about, and they came to think we are aligned with that group."

"You were at the God Seeker ranch in Winslow when a Florida cultist killed Roxanne McClenahan. And Jake Goldblatt mailed you their religious icon meteorite."

"Jesus, Detective, you've got this all figured out. Why question us?"

He smiled with a crooked dimple in one cheek. "I had to do a little Agatha Christie homework. When Sarah was kidnapped, she had what I am assuming — and I do not like assuming — was a vision of you receiving a phone number while you were in Kansas." He bounced his thick eyebrows as he worked through the details as if he were checking off a list. "That number was for the house where she was being held captive. Is that how that fit together?"

Sarah spoke up. "Yes."

"Fraily kidnapped you because he thought you could rid one of his followers of an evil spirit. Is that right?"

"Yes."

"Would it be fair to say you are a sort of medium?"

"Yes. Empath actually."

"Do you think this is why the Florida cult is after you?"

"Yes. Jake mailed me their meteorite because he hoped I could use it to stop the Florida cult."

"What else do you know about the Florida cult?"

"They have their own meteorite icons. They are at a plantation outside of Tallahassee. They are led by a man who calls himself Jefferson Davis."

"Yes, we actually know all that. I need to know about their religion, what is driving this Davis leader. He kidnapped six mental patients from a prison in Ohio. He killed eleven officers in the process. He is wanted for murder, and half a dozen other crimes, and across state borders. That means Ohio and Missouri law enforcement and the FBI are all ready to move against him. I need to know what makes him tick. He and his men have been suspected of crimes for a long time, but now he is acting with impunity. It's like he doesn't even care about the law now. What changed?"

"He thinks the apocalypse is coming in two weeks with the arrival of a meteor shower full of stones like these religious icons."

Johansson looked away and shook his head. "Another apocalypse cult."

"Not just any cult. This one has actual powers." Sarah looked over at Nate and shrugged. "These meteorites give mentally unstable people visions, and with those visions come abilities, weird, almost supernatural, abilities."

Johansson raised his eyebrows as if he had made a connection.

Sarah wasn't sure what connection. She pressed on. "There are two kinds. One is peaceful and empathic, with a calming touch like me. The other one is violent, like them. We think they may have figured out how to spread hatred into other people by biting them."

"Biting people, with their teeth? That explains the teeth tattoos."

"Your men have to be careful not to let these guys bite you. If they do, then you become one of them."

"You said these stones work on mental patients, which would explain the prison attack. Do they only work on mental patients?"

"That's what we think. I was one, as was Roxie. Harold's friend that I cured was one too, He had one of the bad necklaces." She looked over at Nate and mouthed the word, "Burt."

Nate spoke up. "Sarah also cured the first Florida man to find us. His name is Burt Cowell. He was a mental patient as well. We took his bad necklace away and gave him one of the good ones. He is on our side now and we do not want to press charges."

"Was he with you at the house?"

"Yes, he fought alongside us. And, he is staying next door."

"Does he know details of the cult property?"

"Yes, he's been there."

"Good." He paused to collect his thoughts. "Before I forget, why were there six dead wild hogs stacked up against the back of your house?"

"We were practicing with Harold's rifles on beer cans in the backyard when the pigs charged us. We were lucky to have been armed at the time."

"Fortunate coincidence. What was that giant clay statue on your lawn?"

"We believe Jefferson Davis has transformed himself into some kind of monster. That statue may or may not be what he looks like now."

He turned to Sarah. "Did you make that guess based on your empathic abilities?"

"Yes, I did."

"You say this is all about the necklaces. Are they charms carved from the meteorites?"

"Yes," Sarah said. She went to her bag and pulled out a small metal box and handed it to him. "This was mine. I stopped wearing it because it started to make me sick."

Johansson opened the box and his eyebrows slowly climbed on his high forehead.

"Detective, if I might make an observation of my own," Nate started. "You are handling this news of visions, empathic powers and monsters with remarkable calm. Do you have many cases like this one?"

He looked at Nate and a small smile tugged at the corner of his mouth. "Since you have been so forthcoming, and since it appears we will be continuing to work together on this, I think it safe to share a little something about myself.

"My grandmother was an empath. She could calm down even the most out of control child or even the angriest man by just laying her hands on them. My mother made passing reference to how Grandma had been mentally ill when she was younger, and how she had been cured by a faith healer who gave her the gift of her touch. I never really believed that story. Until today. My grandmother wore a necklace that looked just like this one."

18

"BLACK HOLE SUN"
SOUNDGARDEN

MARK JOHANSSON CLOSED HIS NOTEBOOK and put his pen back in his shirt pocket.

"Thank you for all the information you've given us. We knew there was a lot we didn't understand about the cult, and you've answered all my questions. We're ready. The sun will be up in half an hour and we will make our move at first light. Sorry to keep you up all night. You can get some sleep now."

Nate stood up when he did and shook his hand. "Good luck."

Sarah and Burt did the same.

As he stepped out the door, Johansson looked back at Burt and his left arm in a sling from being shot. "I hope that heals up all right."

Nate appreciated that the detective had their safety in mind, so he played along as he left their Tallahassee motel room. He watched at the window as Johansson drove away to join the army of FBI, Florida State Trooper, and SWAT teams waiting to raid Davis's plantation estate.

Nate heard Burt behind him ask Sarah, "I assume we are following right behind him?"

"Yes. This fight is between Oum and the Devourer. I can't say how all those police are going to fare, but I am sure Oum will not let me stay here."

"Don't dreams work wherever your thoughts take them?"

Nate wondered if Burt was curious about the dreams in case he started having them.

"That would be nice, but these dreams work with what's going on around me. I could only communicate that phone number to Nate because I was in the house and saw the number while I was awake. I could only give Nate's gun exploding bullets because I knew we were being attacked at the house." She looked to Nate. "Remember when I said I never used to dream about things in real life? I've been experimenting, and when I dream about made up stuff, nothing in the real world changes. The reality-altering stuff only happens when I'm dreaming about real stuff going on around me."

Nate finished the thought. "Which means, if we want Oum to use his magic against his ages-old enemy, we have to take you there."

She shrugged. "'fraid so."

Nate asked Burt, "Are the guns and ammo still in the car?"

"Yeah. I kept the car out of sight while Johansson was here so he wouldn't think to confiscate them."

Nate grabbed a couple rolls of duct tape and handed them out. "Grab pillowcases and tape them around your forearms. Use lots of tape. When they come at you, stuff your arm in their mouth so you can go in for the hug. I told Johansson to have the cops armor up the same. We don't want any converts to the other side in the middle of the fight. Sarah, can you help Burt with his arm?"

Nate kept up his brave face and tried to not think about the terror he had felt in the gunfight at the house. His heart sped up anyway. He knew they were scared too. This was inevitable. They had to give it their best shot if they were ever going to end this nightmare. He made a point of smiling at either of them when they looked his way. He wondered if he looked stupid, or if they could tell he was covering.

While they wrapped themselves, Sarah told Burt, "You may not have the calming touch yet, since you've only been wearing the Oum necklace for a few days."

Burt perked up. "The vision started. I see him when I close my eyes and just wait for it. It was really freaky at first, but then I started feeling his calm."

"That's great. The vision will get stronger with time. He will become something of a companion."

"Sure beats the voices I used to have."

"Tell me about it! Oh, one other thing. I can sense a cult member wearing one of their stones. You might have picked up some of that too. It is also possible they will be able to sense you at a distance because of this stone. So be careful."

Nate finished his own arms. "Are we ready? Burt, are you sure you can aim a gun?"

"Yeah, I do all the work with my right. I just need to bend my left hand up to steady the barrel."

"All right. Let's do this."

•   •   •

Burt sat next to Nate in the front seat humming a tune as they approached the plantation.

"What's that song? I almost recognize it."

"Oh, that's 'Bad Moon Rising' by John Fogerty. I've had it my head all day. Kind of fits, doncha think?"

"I guess. Are you sure coming in the main gate is the best plan?" Nate asked.

"They've got twenty-foot fences with barbed wire on top hidden in the trees all around the back. There's a gate back there, but they heavily guard it. Until we know the cops have breached that gate, the only way in is right up the front."

"I hear hurricanes a-blowing
I know the end is coming soon
I fear rivers overflowing
I hear the voice of rage and ruin"

Sarah recited tunelessly from the backseat.

Nate turned around and she pointed to her headphones plugged into her phone.

"'Bad Moon Rising'. That's a pretty cool song. Found it on Spotify."

He frowned at her nonchalance.

"Hey, I'm going straight into anxiety back here. I gotta listen to music or something."

Burt said, "All right, here's the driveway."

Nate turned in. "And there's the cop cars. Jeez, that's a lot."

He pulled over a hundred feet back from the twenty cars and trucks parked along the sides of the drive. Nate could see the main gate was another hundred feet beyond the cars. There were no cops with the cars, and he could hear rapid gunfire inside the compound.

"We're here."

Nate turned around to Sarah in the back seat. "Do you feel anything yet?"

She was staring wide-eyed at the line of cop cars. "Oh, yeah. My senses are lit."

"Do you want to come with us, or work from here?"

"I can feel where they all are. I'm pretty sure I can navigate in the dream from here. Do you mind if I stay?"

"Not at all. I'd rather you stay safe. As long as you can know enough from here to make changes."

"I think so."

Nate and Burt got out and got the guns from the trunk.

As they divided up the ammo, Burt smacked Nate on the shoulder. "Let's see if that deadeye aim she gave you last time stayed with you."

"That would be awesome. Are we ready for this?"

"Hell yes!" Burt barked without yelling out loud. "I've got a score to settle for them turning me into a mindless killer. Hey, what's in the backpack?"

"Secret weapon." Nate waved at Sarah as he passed.

Burt waved too. "Sweet dreams!" he laughed.

They walked through the weeds on the side of the drive, in front of the cars to not be seen by any police in the SWAT trucks that had stayed behind as support.

"What the hell are you doing in the bushes?" came a commanding voice from behind them.

Nate turned around, but not without noticing Burt was dressed as a SWAT officer. So was he.

The police captain did not wait for an answer. "Get your asses up there on the line. I know it's turned ugly, which is why we need every man we've got."

"Yessir!" Nate said as he waved Burt to join him running up the drive.

Burt kept looking at their clothes as they ran.

"She's getting good at this."

The gun fire died down, but there was a lot of yelling coming from inside the open ornate iron gate. Nate saw police up in the trees and hiding behind bushes on either side. He and Burt ran up the right side, staying ducked down. He was not prepared for what they saw inside.

Two dozen policemen were swinging away on each other with batons. Other cops tried to pull them apart, while others aimed their guns into the camp to fend off any cultists who would take advantage of the pandemonium. The outbreak had diverted the attack on the camp, with most of the cops not even onto the main grounds in front of the plantation house.

"What the fuck?" Burt whispered to Nate.

"I don't know." He looked deeper into the property while he talked. "They act like they've all been bitten mad, but I don't see any cultists over here."

Nate looked back and Burt waded into the fight. He grasped them on the shoulder from the back, and one by one they disengaged, shook their heads, and joined the cops trying to pull apart the combatants. *Burt's got the touch!*

Nate wondered why the cultists didn't attack in the midst of the mayhem. They fired a few shots, and the non-possessed cops returned fire. But the massive retaliation Nate expected with the cops so occupied did not come.

The driveway opened into a large gravel area with several parked cars. Beyond that, an expansive lawn stretched up to the main plantation house and back past a couple of smaller houses and a barn.

After a couple of minutes, Burt had broken the spell on all of the cops and they took up positions to advance again.

Then Nate spotted him. On the far side of the lawn, two hundred yards away, a giant man, over seven feet tall, wearing body armor head to foot, walked out from behind a pyramid-like stone tower. He threw his hands up in what looked like exasperation, and started to march forward. The police on the ground in front of Nate fired on the man, but missed. Nate leaned up against a tree, took careful aim, and hit him square in the chest. Nate smiled at not having lost his aim. The man was unharmed, but further infuriated. He waved to someone out of view and gun fire erupted from all around the property at the police who were still regrouping. The cops dove for cover.

Burt hustled over to Nate's side. "They say that giant guy yelled at them from across the yard and they all lost their shit and had to beat up whoever was closest. I guess he's Davis. I heard about the biting, but this guy can launch it."

"Sarah said he'd become a monster."

A commotion of gunshots and yelling broke out in the trees behind the main house. It seemed a SWAT team had broken through a fence. The cultist fire on the main gate halted for an instant as they looked to the side, and the cops pressed their advantage, swarming onto the property and fanning out behind buildings and vehicles.

The giant was not happy. He raised his arms and yelled what sounded like a lion's roar. The cops all froze where they were as they were overcome with uncontrollable rage. Nate felt it too, and it was all he could do to not attack Burt next to him. Burt didn't look like he was affected.

"Burt," he squeezed through clenched teeth. "You're immune. Shoot him."

"I don't know if I can hit him from here."

"Just fucking unload on him!"

Burt obliged, but after four rounds he didn't hit him. The man was visibly shocked anyone had weathered his attack. He waved behind him again, and a dozen cultists jumped out from cover and ran across the yard toward the immobilized cops.

Burt fired on them and hit a couple, but several reached their targets. They fired at close range, and the cops fired back, turning their anger on their attackers. Burt was saddened to see the cops in tight groups attacked each other again. The whole field was a chaos of shouting, blood, gunfire, and bodies being thrown down.

Burt started to jump up to calm the cops who were fighting each other again, but Nate grabbed his arm.

"I know you need to help them." Burt saw Nate was gasping for breath like his chest was too tight. "But you're the only one left. Go set the house on fire."

Burt lit up at the thought and ran off around the edge of the yard.

One of the cultists hiding on the front porch saw him coming and shot at him. Burt tried to weave his steps to make himself a harder target. He hoped the police flak jacket Sarah gave him would stop a bullet if he got hit. The man fired again, and this time Burt felt an impact, but it was light, like a paint ball hit. He jumped up on the porch and fired on the man from only a few feet away, but the man didn't go down. The man looked at his own gun to see what was wrong and Burt took advantage. He leapt forward and bashed the man in the face with the butt of his rifle.

Slick move, Sarah.

He ran into the house, pumped for whoever he met. There wasn't anyone. The entry hall opened up into a grand salon with desks along one side with computers. A grand staircase led up off one side. Burt listened for any movement in the other downstairs rooms and heard nothing over the ruckus outside. He ran up the stairs as quietly as he could.

He heard someone in a bedroom at the end of the hall. Burt pushed the door open slowly and saw a bald man rummaging through papers with his back to the door. Burt pointed the rifle as if it would work.

The man heard him and turned. "Shit!" he muttered and started to run into another room, but he stopped and looked closer at the cop facing him. "Burt Cowell? What's with the get-up?"

"Stole it. Lets me get around. What are you doing there, Jackson?"

"Getting ready if we have to bug out. Are you still wearing your necklace?"

Burt felt his anger growing, and it wasn't because of any magical mumbo jumbo. "Oh, yeah, I wouldn't go anywhere without it." He crossed the room to face him. "You know. I never thanked you proper for curing my voices."

Jackson looked nervous that Burt got so close. Burt saw his left hand slide around behind him on the desk. "Oh, sure. My pleasure."

"Or how you turned me into a mindless murder machine," he spat as he reached for Jackson's throat.

Jackson swung his hand around with a letter opener knife, but Burt saw it coming. He sidestepped the swing and brought his good right hand down to grab Jackson's wrist. He stepped back and brought the blade up under the man's rib cage, piercing his heart.

Burt looked him in the eye as Jackson died. "Never abuse a Southern man's good nature."

He let the body drop. Burt took a deep breath to regain himself. Then he remembered he came here to create a fire to distract Davis out on the yard. He grabbed the box of papers Jackson had been going through, opened the French doors, and poured them out on the veranda. He used his Zippo to set them on fire.

Burt made it down the stairs when he saw a man in a suit sneaking around. "Detective Johansson?"

"Burt Cowell? What in hell are you doing here?"

"I couldn't let you guys have all the fun. How come you're not overcome with Davis's hate spell?"

"I was inside the house and didn't hear it. What's upstairs?"

"Nobody."

"Do I smell smoke?"

"I don't smell anything."

Johansson started running up the stairs. "Did you set the house on fire?"

Burt left.

•   •   •

Nate looked around the yard and saw cops and cultists alike realize their bullets were no longer lethal. Several cultists ran from their hiding places and attacked the struggling cops with their fists. A few came at them with their teeth. The cops weren't able to think and use their training effectively, but they were able to turn their rage on their attackers. The cultists who didn't kill on the first blow were beaten to death by the out-of-control officers. Nate couldn't tell if the cops who attacked cops were bitten or enraged by the Davis attack.

A nearby car that a couple of cops hid behind suddenly disappeared. They looked terrified and attacked each other with their bare hands.

Nate prayed that at some point Sarah would find some combination that would help.

Nate looked across the yard and saw the giant was doing something with the weird Mayan-looking stone tower. It was a tall, thin ziggurat, forty feet wide with stairs up the front to the top fifty feet high. Whatever he was doing, it was distracting him from directing his troops.

The cops were hindered by their fury, but they had body armor and training that evened their odds. The fight was raging all across the property, with people dying on both sides, and no one winning.

What a shit show.

Nate started walking. If the bullets were harmless, and the cultists were all busy in combat, what was to stop him from just walking back there?

He got halfway across and the giant spotted him. At this range, Nate could see he was a deformed monstrosity with a mouth like a hippopotamus. *So that's Jefferson Davis.*

The giant roared at him, and he felt it hit him like a shot of adrenaline. His heart raced and his head pounded, his skin heated up, and sweat broke out over his whole body. His muscles strained against one another so it took deliberate effort to move. But he kept walking.

"All right, superman," Davis quipped. "You aren't a Looker, but that doesn't matter. My attack is but a shadow of my god's." He finished whatever he was doing and picked up a switchbox that was connected to the tower by a thick cable. "The laser inside this tower will superheat the meteor cradled at the top. My god will radiate his vision of destruction across all the land. No one will be able to resist."

Nate kept walking.

"Have it your way." He pushed the button and a loud humming came from inside the stone pyramid. "Behold the majesty that is Gragol the Devourer!"

Nate looked up and saw the top of the tower glowing. The glow spread, reaching out like a fountain shower of light, blue, green, and purple. No, it wasn't light, it was darkness that only looked like colors against the sky.

He wouldn't have thought it possible to get any angrier, but, when the wave hit him, he felt like his very arteries were going to rip out of his limbs and strangle him. He started to climb the stairs.

The giant ran around to the front and yelled up. "The stone cannot be moved and the laser cannot be shut off. You will simply burst under the pressure of your anger."

Nate stopped just long enough to look back at him. "I've spent the last seven years learning to keep moving through crippling anger. This is nothing."

Davis started to scramble up the steps to follow Nate. Out on the front of the structure, he made himself a target. A few officers managed to focus long enough and opened fire on him, knocking him down on the stairs.

Nate reached the top. The glowing stone was roughly round and the size of a volleyball, with metal straps holding it on an altar. The darkness that radiated out of it penetrated him and he felt like his brain swelled against the inside of his skull. The pounding of his heart accelerated to where it felt like his whole chest strained to explode. He couldn't even catch a breath.

He looked at his hands and forced them to move, to reach into the backpack. He found the Arizona meteorite and let the bag drop off. The round stone felt cold and solid and reassuring. He pushed his stiffened face into a triumphant grin. With the only breath he had left he said, "Oum, kill your enemy," as he smashed the stone down on its counterpart.

Being numb from the tension in his body, he wasn't sure what he felt as the explosion flung him back and he landed unconscious.

•   •   •

Sarah walked through the mayhem, knowing she could move freely in the dream. But could she change what she needed to? She was sad to see so many people dying, so much pain fueled by anger and fear.

She felt a presence, a calming influence that took her by surprise. It was by the gate. She shifted her attention to a black woman who was walking in, holding her hands up in front of her. She looked unafraid, despite all the violence around her. She was calming them. All of them, for yards around in front of her. Sarah thought she recognized her. She concentrated, and a name came forward: Cecilia. In a flash, Sarah realized Oum had seen this woman, through Nate, when he saw her on the map in ... Portland. This amazing woman had come, and she could throw calm the same as Davis could throw hate.

As the police recovered, they rejoined the battle in the yard.

Sarah followed and again was shocked by the destruction. Both sides had taken enormous losses and neither looked ready to stand down. And there, at the back of the yard, on his failed temple, lay Davis the monster. Sarah moved her attention to him and tried to erupt the ground to grab his legs. Nothing happened. She tried to congeal the air about him so he couldn't breathe. No effect.

Cecilia did not stop at reviving the cops. She marched across the yard toward Davis. What was she thinking?

He roared at her and Sarah was amazed when Cecilia blinked it off.

She raised her hands and yelled, "Stop!"

Davis leaned back and bellowed with laughter. "Is that all you got?"

Cecilia's proud stance shrank and she stepped back.

He ran three giant strides and closed on her. "I may not be able to affect you, but I can still destroy you!"

He grabbed her by the waist with one enormous hand and yanked her off the ground. When he grabbed her legs with his other hand, it looked like he meant to pull her apart.

But he dropped her when he was impaled in his side by a lunging unicorn. Its horn cleanly pierced between the plates of his body armor. He howled in pain and swung on the beast. It was too fast and ducked the blow. It reared up and whinnied triumphantly before running off to attack other cultists. Cecilia scrambled to safety.

Sarah wondered if her abilities could affect Davis. He was immune to Oum's calming power. She couldn't make anything change to slow him down. She had to resort to pulling poor Harold out of space-time to save Cecilia. What if her ability to change the world wasn't enough?

Cecilia could project the power. Sarah assumed she had achieved full communion with Oum and could do everything possible with his power. Could Cecilia have found yet another of the god's body parts? What if all the Dreamer stones were the same, and the powers manifested differently depending on how mentally ill the person was to begin with? What if Sarah could do so much because she was more fucked up than Roxie or Burt? Maybe Cecilia was really fucked up too.

Maybe I've been looking at this all wrong.

Sarah woke up with a start and got out of the car. She started to march into the camp, but had to stop and lean on the cop cars every few steps, she was so weak. She made it to the gate and stopped at what she saw. She had seen the carnage in the dream, but seeing it in person was much more horrifying. Bodies and blood lay strewn everywhere. The fighting continued across the yard. Everyone had stopped using guns with the bullets nullified. She sidestepped fist fights and kept moving as best she could. Her limbs hurt, and she couldn't take a full breath. She felt feverishly hot and cold at the same time, and on the edge of nausea. She had to swallow purposefully every few steps.

Davis spotted her and walked forward. She had to clench her teeth at the full horrific sight of him standing over her. His hatred and anger felt like standing in front of an open furnace.

"So here you are, the queen at last. Not much to look at, are you?"

Davis's attention was pulled away by a burst of flames coming from an upstairs window of the main house.

"Fuck," he said quietly before returning to Sarah. "First things first. You think you can just walk in here and destroy everything I've built?

"You haven't built anything. You're just like your god. You only steal what treasures others have made."

"Oh, you mean your god Oof."

"Oum."

"Well, I am here to show you what real power looks like. I am going to devour you entirely, head to toe, just like Gragol devoured Oum so many eons ago. And there isn't a goddamn thing you can do about it."

"Gragol died trying to do that. What makes you think you'll survive?"

"If I recall correctly, both Gragol and Oum died in that match up. Now look at us. I am four, maybe five, times as big as you. I think I'll take my chances."

Sarah knew she had done all she could, but in that moment the terror of this finality took hold. *Could I have done more?*

He snatched her up with one hand and lifted her up to his gigantic open mouth. She stuffed her left arm in and twisted it to try to fill as much of the huge tooth-filled chasm as she could.

He saw what she was doing, shrugged, and bit off her arm.

The pain was much worse than she had expected. She was so weak to start with, the sensation of her arm cleaving away overwhelmed her.

Davis swallowed, then blinked and shook his head. "What the fuck was that?"

A ray of white light erupted from the palm of his free hand and shot out across the field. "What's that?!"

Another shot from his chest, under Sarah's aloft body. "What have you done?"

More rays erupted from his body, from his thighs, his shoulders, and his feet. The rays hit a couple of his men who were grappling with cops nearby. They crumpled to the ground when the light hit them, the fight gone out of them.

He looked back at Sarah. "I'm just gonna have to finish eating you." He raised her up again, but was interrupted when scores of light rays broke through his skin and shone out across the yard.

"This can't be happening!" He yelled at her. "I am the Sword of God!"

She managed the best smile she could, pathetic though it was. "You are now."

He dropped her to the ground as his body disintegrated into a million white light shafts that flashed out and blanketed the property, lancing every one of his followers, and extinguishing all the hate he had bred in them.

Sarah smiled, if only to herself. So much pain had made her numb. She was sure she would die now — whether from bleeding out her shoulder, from her back that she was sure was broken from the fall, or from the magical poison she had filled her body with as her final solution. She didn't mind. Death was natural. More natural than anything she had experienced in many, many years.

She felt herself being lifted by strong hands, not the giant crushing hands she just felt, but comforting, supporting hands. She felt pressure on her shoulder which made her wince, and heard voices reassuring her. She wanted to tell them not to make a fuss. She had done what she set out to do, and that was enough.

She opened her eyes when she felt the jostle of being put on a stretcher. Two policemen carried her, and she saw Nate and Burt had joined them. Detective Johansson was there too. She figured they knew what they were doing, so she let them. She was taken by how detached she was from the mortal danger she was in. Maybe it was shock setting in.

They loaded her into an ambulance and Nate climbed in.

He talked while the paramedic put in an IV. "He fucking bit your arm off."

"Better than my head."

"Jesus fuck, isn't that why we left you in the car?"

"The dream couldn't stop him."

"Really? I guess you figured out something. I woke up on the pyramid just in time to see what you did to Davis."

"I saw what you did to their meteorite. Oum must have been pleased."

Nate laughed. "I hope so. What on Earth did you do to him?"

"Nothing. I couldn't change him. I tried. Cecilia showed me Davis was immune to Oum's calming power. He was the full embodiment of Gragol the Devourer."

"Cecilia? Was that the black lady who confronted him first? Who is she?"

"She's the Dreamer you saw on the map in Portland."

"I don't get it. All those rays of light. They canceled out his influence. What do you mean you didn't change him?"

"I changed myself. I've been fighting all the changes Oum put me through. I freaked out about how I couldn't control the changes my dreams made on the world. The answer was to accept the change. I had to change. I could change me. I know how to face making changes to myself.

"I knew he was going to try to eat me. That's what the Devourer does."

"So you made yourself into a trap. Didn't Oum do that originally?"

She closed her eyes and relaxed. "Yes."

19

"ANGEL"

SARAH MCLACHLAN

"YOU WERE ADMITTED with orders to check for toxins in your blood." The Physician's Assistant looked up and down Sarah's chart while she talked. The thirtyish woman's fit physique and calm tone gave Sarah comfort that she was in good hands. "We ran a preliminary panel when you first came in, and found nothing. So we ran a more complete panel and still, nothing. Your blood has all the usual activity we would expect from you losing a limb, but you are free from toxins. How are you feeling?"

"Really tired. Pretty dopey. But not poisoned like I felt yesterday."

The PA checked the bag hanging off the bed rail. "You're draining well. The nurse will be around later to check your dressing."

Nate came back from getting himself lunch. "What did I miss?"

"I'm toxin free."

"Great!" He turned to the PA. "When will the doctor who stitched her up be back to check her arm?"

"The surgeon will come tomorrow. He won't be able to see anything until everything is clotted and the swelling starts to go down."

"Has anyone said how much of her arm could be saved?

"The file notes show the first aid applied at the scene prevented additional damage, and it was a clean break. Your shoulder joint is intact, and you have just over four inches of the humerus. Barring complications, and after rehabilitation, you should have full use of your shoulder. The surgeon can talk to you about prosthetic options."

"Thank you."

"Sarah, I'll be back to see you tomorrow."

When she left, Nate smiled at his sister. "Toxin free? Your poison converted Davis into pure energy, and you're clean one day later?"

"The demand I made of the dream was to wipe the slate clean. The poison left me when it entered him. I didn't know that would happen. I was willing to do it anyway. But you know, I think we need to talk about that clean slate."

"Johansson said the cultists were stripped of all their hate and anger, including the bitten ones and the ones wearing necklaces. That light erased Davis's entire influence."

"It might have erased Oum's influence too. I didn't have time to specify. And I wasn't exactly in a position to watch where all that light went. I am quite sure I gave up the ability to change anything with my dreams. I wanted to be free of that almost as much as I wanted to stop Davis. Sadly, that means I can't dream my arm back."

"Do you still see Oum when you close your eyes?"

"I have to be in contact with a stone to see him like that. The vision stopped when I took off the necklace, and I only saw him again when I handled the Arizona stone. I guess we could ask Burt. He's still got the one I gave him."

"Yeah, well, that's a different story. Burt took his revenge on the guy who gave him the bad necklace, and the cops are after him for that. Burt is in the wind. We probably won't see him again."

"Oh, no. He's such a great guy. I sure wish him well. Wow, consequences, huh?" She went silent when she heard herself say that.

"What's worrying you?"

"If my clean slate wiped out Oum's influence, I could go back to being schizophrenic. Burt too."

"Roxie locked away her stone for years after it stopped converting people. Her voices didn't return. Maybe once cured, you stay cured."

"You know, back when we started trying to figure out this stuff, I commented that you say 'maybe' a lot."

He smiled. "You got me. Professor Franco called me on my brainstorming, too. It is testable. We've got other stones, and we can certainly keep an eye on you.

"Oh, speaking of Franco, I've got fantastic news," he interrupted himself. "I should have started with this. I just got an email from him. He said the meteor cloud with all the pieces of the two gods, it's no longer going to hit the Earth after all. The moon moved right into the path and they're probably all going to get pulled down onto the back side of the moon later this week."

"No more doomsday meteor shower? That's amazing! I know I had nothing to do with that."

"We finally got a lucky break."

Sarah took a breath and refocused. "I still want to level with Dr. Alpaca too. Especially if I might develop symptoms again."

"Do you have a plan for how you're going to tell her about all the changes you've gone through?"

"I'll have to work that out. She warned me about how all this trauma was going to drive me further into anxiety and depression. Now I've gone and lost my frickin' arm. You know, you should probably get some help as well. You've been through it too."

"Oh, wait a minute. What about all the mental patients Davis hung necklaces on? They are definitely going to revert. Poor bastards. Plucked from hospitals, made sane but turned into killers, and now headed back to insanity. Yikes."

Nate shook his head. "We'll have to tell Johansson to expect that."

A knock came at the door. "Hello. Can I come in?" A forty-something black woman came in with a *Get Well* balloon. "I hope I'm not interrupting."

"Cecilia!" Sarah called out. "Come in!"

The woman was visibly surprised to be recognized.

Sarah explained. "I'm sorry. Up until yesterday I had a gift for seeing things in my dreams. I saw you and figured out who you were on the battlefield. Thank you so much for coming all the way from Portland."

"Hi. I'm Nate, Sarah's brother."

She shook his hand. "Oh, I know who you are. I saw what you did with those meteor stones on that tower."

"How did you know we needed your help, and how to find us?" he asked.

"I have a spirit guide who told me you were looking for me last week. She told me to drop everything and get on a bus. I don't usually do such drastic things, but she insisted."

Sarah held up her hand. "May I ask you a very personal question?"

"Honey, we brought down the Devil together. Ask away."

"Are you wearing a grayish-green stone necklace?"

Cecilia took it out and showed it proudly. "Yes, I am."

Sarah looked to Nate. "When you used the Arizona stone to look at the map, the other stones saw you looking.

"And did you used to suffer from schizophrenia, which went away when you started wearing that?"

"You've almost got it right. My bad voice went away. My kind voice is what I call my spirit guide."

"You still have that voice?"

"Oh, yes. She gives me good advice, like to come help you."

Nate chimed in. "A lot of schizophrenia patients never get rid of their voices completely. The drugs quiet the bad ones so they can function."

Cecilia pointed to Nate. "What he said."

Sarah looked at Nate. "Maybe I could learn to live with a low level of symptoms like Cecilia here."

"Call me CeCe. Are you saying you think you're going to lose your mind?"

"Sarah suspects that her spell that killed Davis might have undone the healing the stones gave her. Wiping the slate clean, as it were."

CeCe took Sarah's hand, even with the IV stuck in the back of it. "Oh, Honey, do you have any more stones? They work wonders."

Sarah smiled and squeezed her hand back. "We will try that. CeCe, when you close your eyes, do you still see the eyeball vision?"

She stood up straight and closed her eyes. "Yep, he's right there." She blinked. "I guess I have two guardian angels. I'm double blessed."

Sarah and Nate exchanged a hopeful look.

Another knock at the door interrupted them. "Hello. It's Mark Johansson, may I come in?"

"Of course, Detective," Nate greeted him,

Sarah noticed he was wearing a polo shirt and jeans, not his usual dark suit. "I'm here on my own time today. So today, it's just Mark. How are you feeling, Sarah?"

"Tired, drugged, but happy to have all this company."

Mark turned to CeCe. "I'm Mark Johansson from St. Louis. Nice to meet you."

"Cecilia Bledsoe from Portland. Likewise."

"Thank you for your work yesterday. You were very helpful in getting our men back on their feet after the tower went off."

CeCe looked uncomfortable talking about her powers.

Sarah helped out. "Detective … um, Mark here, his grandmother had a stone and was a medium too."

CeCe lit up. "Oh, I see. Yes, I was just glad I could help."

Mark turned to Nate. "Speaking of the tower, Nate. How did you keep climbing those stairs when he set off the stone? The rest of us were paralyzed with rage."

Nate smiled and looked at the floor before looking back up and answering. "I guess that's my superpower. Sarah could change things with her dreams, Cecilia can calm down a whole street full of people with a word. Me, I'm always angry. All Davis did was feed my determination to beat him.

"I'm curious, though," Nate continued. "How are you going to explain all the bizarre things that happened on that battlefield, or how Davis made himself into such a monster?"

Now it was Mark's turn to smile shyly. Sarah thought it was a charming look on him.

"You mean the rubber bullets and flash of light? I'm not. No one is asking me for explanations. Nate, you're a science fiction fan, right? Well, me, I'm a mystery and detective fiction fan. I'm going to borrow a page from Ellery Queen, stick my hands in my pockets and walk away. I know you had something to do with it, but that doesn't matter now. We've got our suspect survivors in custody, and I'm done."

Nate held up a hand. "About those suspects. Any of them wearing the necklaces, they were mental patients with schizophrenia, and their symptoms are going to come back."

Mark squinted as he pieced together the logic of what Nate said. He looked to Sarah. "Right, because you canceled them. I'll tell the various jails.

"Now I have a question for both of you," Mark continued. "You were not the only confrontation that went down yesterday. Four other battles were fought all over the world, just like ours. Well, not exactly the same, but clearly the same meteorites driving the same conflict. I was hoping you could explain how the weirdest battle in police history was not unique, but also carried out in places like Buenos Aires and Moscow."

Nate leaned in. "Did the good guys win?"

"Yes, thankfully, the folks with the peaceful stones prevailed in all the fights. What's really going on?"

Sarah and Nate looked at each other. "They're all still linked," he said.

Sarah pursed her lips and rolled her eyes toward Mark.

Nate held his hand out for her to answer.

"There is no way I can explain this without sounding completely nuts, so you're going to have to just take my word for it. My brother keeps reaching for science fiction movie references to try to make sense of it. These meteorites are the shattered bodies of two ancient godlike creatures who killed each other out in space millions of years ago. The radiation they emit creates the effects you've seen in people with schizophrenia, and apparently in no one else.

"The spirits of these creatures are still alive in the stones, and they are still trying to kill each other. That's where the visions and the powers come from. These fights all happened at the same time because all the stones were working together.

"That's not all. We also know that the bulk of these fragments are in a cloud that the Earth was going to pass through later this week. It would have been an epic disaster. Davis was counting on it. Luckily, the moon got in the way, and the stones are all going to strike the back side instead. Astronauts won't have mental health issues, but if they bring any of those stones back, it could be a real problem. We need to tell NASA or whoever that the back side of the moon is off limits."

Mark pushed his thick eyebrows together and said nothing for a long moment. He reached over and picked up the remote that was attached to Sarah's bed and turned on the TV. After some fumbling and surfing, he found a local news station.

The view was of an oceanfront expanse with banners flying over a crowd of people on a beach in the foreground. There were buildings on a far beach around a bay, but it was hard to make out what they were. A newscaster was reporting with that same forced enthusiasm usually reserved for sporting events.

"And here we are in the final countdown. It has been decades since mankind has set foot on another celestial body, and you can tell from the excitement of this crowd that they appreciate how rare and wondrous this will be. The return of manned visits to other worlds."

Sarah, Nate, and Cecilia traded worried looks.

"And here we go! You can hear Mission Control count it down. Ten, nine, eight, seven, six, five, four, three, two, one, liftoff! We have liftoff. You probably can't see it through the television filters, but the light from those engines, even at this distance of three miles away, is as bright as looking into the sun. How magnificent. And off they go. Two men and two women, the first humans to explore the dark side of the moon. Previous missions have only been on the side that is locked facing the Earth so as to maintain radio contact. We heard earlier from Bill Nye about gravitational tidal locking. This crew will use satellites to relay signals around the moon as they explore the back side."

Sarah could not contain her disappointment. "You've got to be fucking kidding me."

ABOUT THE AUTHOR

Jay Hartlove is the award-winning author of the urban fantasy "Goddess Rising" trilogy (*Goddess Chosen, Goddess Daughter,* and *Goddess Rising*) and the fantasy romance *Mermaid Steel*. He is also the playwright, director and producer of *The Mirror's Revenge*, the musical sequel to the "Snow White" fable, which had its theatrical run in the San Francisco Bay Area in August 2018 to rave reviews.

His stories are filled with conspiracies and the supernatural, gods, dreams, angels, and hidden connections. His creative motto is "Dark Secrets Revealed". He loves to take stories where the reader does not expect, with sympathetic villains, heroes with very dark pasts, and lots of plot twists. He turns victims into heroes. He was selected as one of the "50 Authors You Should Be Reading" by *The Authors Show*.

Jay is a former competitive costumer, having won Best in Show at both San Diego ComicCon and WorldCon. You can read more about Jay's creative adventures, including much of the research he put into his books, at *jaywrites.com*.

ALSO BY JAY HARTLOVE

GODDESS CHOSEN

BOOK ONE OF THE "GODDESS RISING" SERIES

The man who would beat the devil isn't a hero, but a ruthless madman.

GODDESS DAUGHTER

BOOK TWO OF THE "GODDESS RISING" SERIES

How far can you genetically alter someone before she becomes someone else ... before she loses her soul?

GODDESS RISING

BOOK THREE OF THE "GODDESS RISING" SERIES

Saved by a goddess ... but only as a tool for revenge?

MERMAID STEEL

The power of love over hate.

A grand adventure, a hero with a dark past, a powerful goddess, and a message of hope for us all.

Available from Water Dragon Publishing in hardcover, trade paperback, digital, and audio editions
waterdragonpublishing.com